AMORA

by
Grant J. Hallstrom

Amora
Copyright © 2020, Grant J. Hallstrom

CLEARSTONE
PUBLISHING

15615 Alton Parkway, Suite 175
Irvine, CA 92618
www.clearstonepublishing.net

ISBN 978-0-9821503-3-7 (Paperback)

1. Fiction - Historical
2. Fiction - Christian - Historical

Acknowledgment

I would like to thank my wife, Jean, and the many other individuals who spent countless hours editing various drafts of this novel to help turn it into the engaging story that it has become. Thank you.

Dedication

I dedicate this book to my murdered younger brother, Calvin, who was killed by his youngest son because he blamed his father for his sibling's suicide. Calvin suffered from much heartache in his life, yet he never became bitter. Even though most people did not see past his mental disability, he was a great man! His example of forgiveness is one worth emulating and helped inspire the message of this book.

Foreword

Grant Hallstrom has written a powerful story based on an event in history which is well depicted and detailed. The novel is inclusive of historic figures and gives a fascinating insight into the Roman society of that period. Most of all, it brings much needed illumination as to how God turns tragedy into triumph.

Saul, the man commissioned to destroy the church, was converted by the forgiveness of God and then became the greatest evangelist in history. Each of us has a journey in life, but as the book portrays, there are challenges for everyone, no matter their station, reputation or social standing. The book shows that it's not what happens, but how you handle what happens. Today, people in Western civilization do not contend with the same opposition and punishment that the early Christians did. We don't risk death for going to church or risk torture due to our religious persuasion. The deep conviction that Amora demonstrated after her conversion, her unwavering faith and her willing sacrifice, and most of all, her God-given ability to forgive, are lessons in submission for all of us. Grant's brother, Calvin, suffered unimaginable anguish in his life, but always chose to forgive, to love. This is the way Christ lived and died. It is the core of the Christian message.

Amora is a great read. It has so much spiritual truth. For me personally, I connected with a clear illustration in the story that I am sure many will understand–the terrible mistake of not forgiving yourself. Even knowing that self-forgiveness is essential, knowing the solution is provided for through Christ, and having quoted every scripture in the Bible dealing with this issue, there is still a tendency to want to fix everything yourself and right the wrongs you've committed without God's help. The book shines a light on this problem and the damaging side effects that come as a result.

Grant is a dear friend and a man I admire and respect primarily for his humility and his sincerity. Both always have been and always will be rare commodities. He understands the importance of Justin Martyr's role in history, our need for an eternal plan, and displays an uncanny sensitivity to the subject matter. Most of all, he sees the need to recognize that forgiveness is the essence of God's love.

Terence Rose
Past International President of FGBMFI
Full Gospel Business Men's Fellowship International

This book is beautifully written. *Amora* illustrates the power of forgiveness in such a deep and substantial way. You could not have written these deep and profound chapters unless you had walked that road before. God clearly expects us to be obedient in the face of pain and anguish. As illustrated in this book, the beauty that comes with obedience is deep, right and freeing. Grant Hallstrom most definitely has captured the principle of love in his novel, *Amora*.

Brenda Shakarian Rose

Preface

My distinguished friends Terence Rose and his wife, Brenda Shakarian, convinced me, with great resistance on my part, of the need to share the backstory of my decision to write this novel. I hope that you accept it in the spirit that it is shared and respect the tenderness of this account for all those involved.

Every family has tragedies. This is the story of one of our family's tragedies. Despite some mental and emotional disabilities, my younger brother, Calvin, married and had three children. He worked hard and held down three low-paying jobs to support his family and purchased a small home. However, he was difficult to live with, so when he traveled to California to attend our sister's wedding, his wife changed the locks on the house and filed for divorce.

The divorce was hard on everyone—Calvin, his ex-wife, and their children. Their oldest son moved out on his own shortly after high school. When around twenty years old, the middle child came out as transgender. The youngest boy developed social anxiety and basically did not work or go to school after high school. Instead, he spent most of his time playing video games in their basement.

Sadly, a few years after coming out as transgender, the middle child committed suicide. Calvin's ex-wife excluded my brother and our side of the family from the funeral and even refused to let us know where Calvin's child was buried. Throughout this ordeal, Calvin refused to let anyone say anything negative about his ex-wife in his presence.

The youngest boy blamed his father for the loss of his sibling and only confidant, so six months later, he contacted my brother under the guise of reconciliation. Calvin was ecstatic. He told our mother, "My counselor was right! She said I needed to let my boys go but keep the door open, and someday they would come back to me." Calvin drove over to take his boy to dinner, and after they met and embraced, his son stabbed him to death.

As soon as I received the news, I booked a flight to be with my mom, who had lived with Calvin. While driving from the airport to her home, I got the distinct impression that Calvin was with me, that he still loved the son who had just murdered him, and that he wanted me to tell everyone that we need to forgive one another. This experience made it easier for me to embrace his ex-wife when she contacted me, sobbing, expressing her grief for our loss and her sorrow for excluding us from the funeral six months earlier. It was just something that she could not deal with at the time. We shared tears as I felt her pain from the double loss she had suffered.

So, in addition to my comments at Calvin's funeral (YouTube: Calvin Hallstrom Funeral or https://youtu.be/zo8zzVfoMTQ) and my testimony at my nephew's sentencing, I wrote this book in an effort to honor this charge from my deceased brother to tell everyone that we need to forgive one another so that we can find the love and healing that we all desperately seek. I hope that my effort in some small way helps you along the difficult path of forgiveness so that you, too, can enjoy the peace, comfort, and security that forgiving and being forgiven brings. May God bless you in this endeavor is my humble prayer.

Sincerely,
Grant J. Hallstrom

Table of Contents

AMORA

A historical novel based on the true story of the noblewoman who inspired Justin Martyr's petition to the Roman Senate.

Chapter 1

The Decision

Light at the end of the arched tunnel. Blood on the stone wall. Rust on the cell's bars. The glance of a gladiator sitting in his cell. The soldier's sandals stepping in front of her. Amora grasped every detail as her world moved in slow motion, drawing her closer to her fate. The stench of death permeated the suffocating darkness, making a mockery of the heightened vitality within her. Time began to transition to match the sound of the soldier's steps. Her chains rattled, gears ground, animals roared, and people cheered. She gave them no heed.

Amora, in an elegant white gown, moved with natural grace in front of a cell of prisoners. Her sixteen-year-old chained slave, Maria, followed behind wearing a simple tunic; a second soldier brought up the rear. One of the prisoners, an old man, stood up and walked to the cell's gate. He grabbed the bars and looked intently at Amora and Maria as they walked by. Amora maintained her focus on the light ahead. Maria glanced over and offered him a hint of a smile. He nodded.

Amora stepped out of the dark tunnel into the entrance corridor between the raised seating on both sides. The blinding light and ruthless roar of the crowd welcomed her. She ignored the garbage thrown by the heckling horde above. A ripe tomato hit Amora and splattered. Unfazed, she continued. An apple core bounced off Maria. She looked up toward the spectator who threw it and spotted Antonio among the mob, waving his arms and calling down to her.

"Maria! Maria!"

"Antonio!" she yelled as she slowed down and tried to raise her chained hands to motion to him. The soldier behind Maria shoved her, nearly knocking her over. Enraged, Antonio tried to jump into the passageway but was restrained on the edge of the Colosseum by two soldiers.

"Oh God! Help him," Maria prayed.

The guards marched the prisoners to the front of the raised imperial box above the arena. Amora looked up at Emperor Marcus Aurelius. Various officials accompanied him while several soldiers stood guard. Amora stood erect in front of Caesar, awaiting her fate, unafraid, while Maria glanced around at the jeering crowd. Marcus gazed at Amora staring at him and turned aside. He rose to the roar of the crowd and raised both hands high to acknowledge their adulation.

The soldiers unchained their prisoners and exited the arena. Amora noticed her husband, Leo, sitting close by the imperial box. Tears welled up in her eyes as they met his gaze. She sensed Leo's loneliness and desired to share the peace, vitality, and freedom she had discovered in her Lord. She offered Leo a quivering smile as tears streamed down her cheeks. Leo's stone face melted as he watched Amora enunciating her words clearly so that he could read her lips.

"I love you," she said.

Tears began to form involuntarily in Leo's eyes. As they flowed down his cheeks, they began to dissolve the icy walls of his heart's prison, allowing emotions to invade his private world. His eyes darted from side to side as he struggled to make sense of the renaissance of long-forgotten feelings and the scene in front of him.

After basking in his subjects' praise, Caesar motioned to the crowd for silence. Once the thunder of the horde subsided, he stretched out his arm with his thumb sideways. The mob began to chant, "Death. Death. Death."

The gravity of Leo's actions pressed heavily upon his conscience. He grimaced, slightly shook his head, and jumped up, determined to gain Caesar's attention. Waving his arms wildly, he yelled, "Mercy! Mercy! Mercy!"

Leo caught the emperor's eye.

"For the sake of Jupiter, Caesar, show her mercy!" Leo bellowed.

Marcus stared at his friend for a few moments, analyzing his options before he again surveyed the crowd, which was chanting "Death" more loudly. Caesar glanced over at Senator Quintus and Prefect Rusticus, who were sitting next to him, and then back at Leo pleading for mercy. Marcus turned to face the crowd beyond his outstretched arm, waiting, as a hush began to fall over the Colosseum. All eyes were glued to Caesar.

EIGHTEEN YEARS EARLIER

Chapter 2

Daughter of Rome

The large atrium of Amora's parents' ornate villa was decorated with flowers and tapestries for the wedding ceremony. The atrium opened to a manicured courtyard garden containing a flowing fountain and marble statues surrounded by porticos.

Leo stood erect on the right side of the altar at the end of the atrium across from Amora's parents, Amado and Livia. A sudden hush fell over the throng as the *Salii priest* and the matron of honor stepped in front of the altar. Leo was pleased that he had ascended so far that he was able to marry into such an influential family. He was proud that his strategy to wait and not settle for a less prestigious alliance earlier in his career was now paying off. Most of his peers had sought to benefit from the connections created through marriage when they were in their early twenties, but Leo was glad he had chosen the long game, giving himself time to prove his competence and build influential friendships so he could marry at the highest level of society.

The assembly turned to watch the arched doorways on either side of the foyer. Everyone stared in anticipatory silence when two bridesmaids burst the tension as they simultaneously entered the hall through the two facing doors, followed by a stream of bridesmaids entering from each side. The bridesmaids formed two rows facing one another with a walkway between them leading to the main entrance. The company, transfixed, waited while the intensity of their vigilance grew.

Suddenly the front double doors flew open, flooding the *vestibulum* with sunlight. Several of the guests caught their breath at the sight of Amora radiating this celestial light as it shone through her traditional bright-orange veil, which flowed over her white tunic. The flower garland that crowned her head proclaimed her royalty. Amora's bright veil parted at her forehead to reveal a glimpse of her fine features and her dark reddish-brown hair arranged in the *tutulus style* with tendrils framing her exquisite face. Amora beamed. She shone like the sun breaching the crimson dawn of a new day as she approached the commencement of marital life. Leo smiled approvingly. "How beautiful! And what staging," he thought.

The assembly parted, opening an aisle to the altar as Amora floated gracefully between the bridesmaids, who fell in line two by two behind her. Amora paused a few feet from the altar, glanced over at Leo and grinned. Turning toward her parents, she removed the *bulla* from around her neck and handed her childhood locket to her father. Tears formed in Amado's eyes as he looked at his daughter's glowing face. He grasped her hands, pressing them tightly. Amora smiled reassuringly, her eyes reflecting confidence in her future. He reluctantly released her. Amora turned to face Leo and smiled. He could not have been more pleased. He was more confident than ever that this marriage would provide him with more than just a powerful strategic alliance. His wife was already making him look good. "Yes, I can go far with this young woman as my wife," he said to himself. "I am glad I was wise enough to choose her."

The matron of honor stepped between the couple. She

took each of their hands, joined them together in front of her, raised them high for the crowd to see, and then retreated. Amora grinned again as she faced Leo and declared the bride's traditional wedding vow: "Wherever you go, there will I be."

Leo parted Amora's veil and ardently kissed his bride while the crowd hooted and hollered their approval. Still holding hands, they turned to face the altar and knelt in front of the priest, who raised a small loaf of bread high above his head.

"I offer this cake to the great god Jupiter so that he will bless those who partake of it with strength and fertility."

The priest dutifully broke the loaf in half, placed one portion on the altar, and offered the rest to Amora, who broke off a piece and delicately fed it to Leo. Leo tenderly repeated the ritual. Once the morsel was in her mouth, Amora grabbed the rest of the loaf from Leo and jumped up. She proceeded to break off pieces of the bread and throw them into the crowd as she twirled and laughed. The guests cheered. The bridesmaids and other women leaped and scrambled for the pieces of broken bread as Leo rose and embraced his bride. Leo adored her vivaciousness.

"Come, everyone!" Amado shouted out with joy, inviting his guests to join him in the *peristyle* for the wedding banquet. "We have a great feast planned for you. Come!"

Leo could tell Amora was thrilled that her father had spared no expense for her wedding feast. It truly was a banquet fit for a princess, but she relished even more all the attention she received. Her father allowed her and her mother to sit at the head table in the *triclinium*, which was traditionally reserved for the host, the groom, and the most important male guests. These notable figures of society seemed to enjoy vying for her attention, and she loved it. She didn't even object when they tried to see who would be the first one to make her blush.

It all started innocently enough when a slave brought a stuffed peacock on a platter adorned with its vibrant feathers, and Marcus Aurelius mentioned how pretty the bird looked. Leo then said it seemed a shame to eat such a beautiful creature, but he would venture. Senator Quintus immediately chimed in that Amora was even more beautiful as he glanced over at Leo and winked, drawing chuckles from the men. Noting that Amora smiled, the men then began a series of crude jokes that climaxed when a slave brought a roasted sow's udder stuffed with cheese and sausage to the table. Amora seemed to enjoy the vulgar wit of their guests, possibly because it made her feel more grown up. Leo sensed that she was excited to enter the adult world and run her own household. He was sure she looked forward to participating in the adult activities of theater, dinner parties, and other social gatherings where she would be admired as a beautiful sophisticated woman instead of a precocious child. Yes, she was ready to represent him well and share with him the full benefits of privilege that she was born to enjoy. Leo was pleasantly surprised at how much he actually enjoyed Amora's company and looked forward to sharing all these events with her. He had never counted on this political alliance being so personally satisfying.

Leo glanced over at their guests, who were reclined on couches surrounding low tables set on the peristyle's broad porticos. They gorged themselves on the endless stream of exotic foods and especially seemed to enjoy the dormice sautéed in a sauce of figs, nuts, and honey, a delicacy that was technically forbidden, which may have enhanced its appeal. Slaves attended to the guests' every need, bringing food, drink, basins of water, towels, and even an occasional song when requested.

A continual stream of beautiful dancers, musicians, acrobats, and contortionists performed for the crowd's admiration in the center of the courtyard by the fountain and then flowed around the peristyle, entertaining guests at their individual tables as new entertainers took their place on center stage. Amora leaned over to Leo and observed that she had never seen such adroit acrobats before, then jumped with a start when a large black leopard raced past them and leaped up on top of the fountain in the center of the peristyle's manicured garden. The guests were thrilled as the beast obediently responded to its trainer's every command.

Suddenly, without warning, the ferocious beast stopped, turned, and glared at the wedding party sitting in the triclinium halfway down the side of the peristyle. The frozen assembly gasped and watched breathlessly as the fierce hunter moved stealthily stalking its prey—its body, low to the ground, its tail outstretched and twitching near the tip. The beast slowly placed one paw in front of the other, approaching the hosts. Amora's heart raced as her mother scrambled behind Amado. The cat sprang, Amora's heart stopped and the crowd screamed as the creature landed in front of Amora, where it rolled over on its back. Amora sighed in relief, reached down and rubbed the feline's belly. The assembly broke into laughter and cheered as the cat's trainer took a bow. Leo smiled proudly at Amora and nodded in adoration.

The visitors relished these demonstrations of man's dominion over nature, whether they displayed human talent or control over the ferocity of wild beasts. Even the symmetry of the peristyle, with its garden and art pieces, reflected their aspiration for order and control over the environment. Man's rational mind was the source of civilization and was its highest achievement as well. The elite especially delighted in witnessing evidence of human superiority, with its implication of their own enhanced, elevated status in the world.

People were enjoying the wedding banquet so much that they hardly noticed when the sun set, and the lamps and chandeliers were lit. Leo saw Amora scanning the gathering. Even though the sumptuous feast showed no signs of tapering off, the novelty of the entertainment had begun to wane as the company settled into the routine of an ordinary dinner party. The bones and scraps that littered the floor around each table were piling up, and some guests were exiting to relieve themselves or vomit to make room for more sumptuous cuisine. Amora rose and began to circulate among her guests. She was the perfect hostess, knowing instinctively that the festivities needed an injection of zest to liven up the evening. Her timing was impeccable. Each group she visited came alive with laughter. Leo could not have been more pleased. His new wife was the life of her own party.

The festivities illuminated Amado's estate as darkness enveloped the countryside. Even though the stuffed revelers had abandoned their tables, they still filled the air with boisterous chatter as they congregated in small groups and continued to consume the ever-present wine offered by the slaves circulating among the guests. The intoxicating conversation and drink seemed to insulate them from the bite of the crisp night air, except for a few older women sitting in the corner with their shawls wrapped tightly around them as they quietly shared juicy gossip.

Leo and Marcus stood conversing with Gaius, Titus, and Quintus when Rusticus, Marcus's philosophy tutor, approached and introduced Crescens to the group.

"Marcus, I'd like to introduce you to Crescens. He's a

young man studying philosophy."

"Excellent. What school of thought appeals to you?" Marcus asked.

"I'm more of a hedonistic skeptic," he answered. "I don't believe anyone can prove that metaphysical ideas are true."

"You don't?"

"No. They are too abstract," he said as he lifted a cup of wine. "I believe Dionysus is right. This is real. Drink and enjoy life. That's what it's all about."

"Well, Rusticus." Marcus laughed. "I see that you may have an even harder time turning him into a Stoic than you did me."

Amado approached and politely said, "Leo, it is about time for the procession to leave." Turning to Marcus, Amado said, "Caesar, I was hoping that you would say a few words."

Marcus smiled, glanced at the young philosophy student, and said, "Well, Crescens, it's time for you to grab some walnuts."

The guests were gathering around Leo, Amora, and her mother near the atrium as Marcus and Amado approached the newlyweds.

"I understand that the newlyweds are anxious to leave," Marcus declared loudly. "I certainly can understand Leo's eagerness, considering how long he has waited for this night. When I first met this surly old warrior, I joked that he had more wounds from unrequited love than battle scars," he continued to the laughter of the crowd. "But now I see the wisdom of age has its benefits. Leo has waited to marry the most beautiful, gracious, and charming young woman I have ever met." The throng nodded in agreement. Marcus raised his cup and proclaimed, "We all wish this new couple a long life of love and happiness." The guests cheered their approval of this benediction. Leo was pleased to realize that his feelings for Amora rivaled the temporal benefits this planned marriage offered him.

Silence fell over the congregation as the crowd spread out around the newlywed couple and the bride's parents. On cue, in an unspoken tradition, Amora stepped close to her mother, who embraced her daughter in a pretended protective grip. Leo approached and extended his hand, inviting Amora to join him. Amora's mother retreated with her daughter in a staged ritualistic show of protection. Leo advanced, grabbed Amora's hand, and in a pretended show of force, ripped Amora from her mother's arms. Amora embraced Leo as they spun around laughing and ran and skipped to the villa's entrance underneath a shower of walnuts. The guests followed closely in a light-hearted procession with flutes playing and people singing, laughing, and dancing. Leo could not recall a time he was happier.

Chapter 3

Saturnalia

Amora picked up the gold sun ornament and stared at her reflection framed by its shape. She reminisced how much she had enjoyed Saturnalia as a child. Sure, it was everyone's favorite holiday, she surmised, but for children it was magical. Everything was turned upside down for a whole week, where all of the rules evaporated. Everyone partied and children could stay up as late as they wanted. They even got to give orders like adults. She enjoyed the sumptuous evening meal where slaves joined their masters and ate together, all waiting with anxious anticipation to discover who would find the hidden coin in the cake and become the household mock king for the celebration and the mischief he would cause. She loved seeing all of the decorations throughout their villa and going outside after the evening meal and seeing their fir tree sparkling with the light of candles and ornaments reflecting the moonlight as they danced in the breeze. She chuckled to herself as she remembered the annual race with her brother to the tree to find treats hidden in its branches. But, most of all, she enjoyed the feeling of excitement and anticipation while doing what she was doing now, decorating their tree with her family in preparation for the festivities.

She smiled and hung the sun on a high bough where all could see it shine to welcome the resurrection of the sun this winter solstice. However, things were different this year as the matron of her own house with all the accompanying responsibilities. Yet, she still felt that childhood anticipation and sense of familial unity. She glanced over at Leo hanging a silver moon on a lower branch and took a deep breath, filling her breast with love. Many masters of the house would not waste their time performing such menial tasks, so she was happy to see her mate share this experience with her. As they continued to adorn their tree with other symbols of fertility—stars, infants, and young stock animals—she wondered what the new year would bring. Maybe next year they would have their own infant to share this special time with. They grinned at each other as Amora placed the last ornament—an image of Janus—in the center of the tree while Leo strategically placed an unlit candle next to it. They stepped back and admired their work—silver and gold ornaments reflecting sunlight surrounded by numerous candles to be lit later that evening to invite the sun to return to its full glory. Leo leaned over and kissed his bride before he excused himself to join his associates at the forum in preparation of the public sacrifice and feast.

This holiday celebrated Saturn temporarily taking back his rule of earth from his son Jupiter. It ushered in a week of festivities reminiscent of the golden age when Saturn ruled humans who lived in total equality with no social restraints, where all property was held in common and everyone was free to eat, drink and frolic without inhibition. The festivities mimicked this mythical time by encouraging everyone to forsake social norms, their class distinctions and to party with abandon. Both men and women often donned the cap worn by freemen and the simple colorful *synthesis* Saturnalia tunic that allowed both arms to move more freely than the traditional toga and *stola*. Role reversal—men and women, slave and master, death and conception—was the order of the day in recognition of the impending reversals of nature associated with the winter solstices and the approaching new year. This carnival atmosphere would all begin at noon with the public ceremony at Saturn's temple near the foot of Capitation Hill. It was an event one didn't want to miss.

Amora busily directed her slaves in placing arrangements of holly throughout the house and in hanging the evergreen wreaths adorned with red ribbons above the doors of her home while she excitedly waited for her friend Julia to accompany her to the celebration. Amora smiled down at Lupita, a four-year-old slave, helping her tie ribbons on the wreaths. "Now, hold your finger right here...That's good...It's ready." Lupita giggled as Amora handed the wreath to Lupita, who carried it skipping to her mother standing by the door.

Another slave's little girl ran through the door past Lupita and announced that Julia was at the door. Amora rushed to greet her friend, whose jaw dropped when she saw Amora.

"You're not going to wear that, are you?" she asked.

"I was planning to."

"Oh, Amora. You can't wear a stola to a party like this."

"Some women wear stolas."

"Where is your season spirit? Now, where is your synthesis?"

"It's on my bed. I tried it on, but I felt like I was wearing my tunica intima in public, so I took it off."

"You need to loosen up. Come, I will help you change."

* * *

Amora and Julia saw the imposing temple with its twenty-meter-high columns from quite a distance. They could see that the forum was filled with citizens awaiting the festivities and banquet. As they rushed forward, the large statue of Saturn, holding a scythe and its feet bound by wool cords, came into focus. Each year this god of agriculture and fertility was filled with olive oil in petition of a fertile season and bounteous harvest. They could sense the increasing excitement of the crowd as they drew near.

Julia was the first of the two to spot the Arval Brother priest, wearing a bright white tunic, approach the front of the temple above the crowd as a hush fell over the assembly. The priest stepped next to the statue of Saturn and poured incense on the altar next to it. The fumes dissipated as they rose towards Saturn's four-meter-tall head. Amora and Julia made their way down the hill towards the Forum while two more priests approached the one standing by the altar. A priest carried a squealing suckling pig in the air by its hind legs and the other held a knife out in front of him with both outstretched hands. The one with the knife stepped forward and handed it to the first priest, then turned, grabbed the suckling's front feet and together with his companion raised the pig high above their heads, invoking a loud cheer from the multitude.

Amora and Julia arrived at the Forum just in time to see two additional priests carry the deceased gladiator from the morning's games onto the stage and lay him on a sofa in the center of the platform. The two priests took their position on each side of the sofa and stepped back as two female priestesses entered and stood between the priests and the sofa. The priests and priestesses performed their fertility ritual as the sound of drums increased in tempo and intensity. At the climax, the priests held the suckling pig over the altar while the first priest slit its throat. Blood gushed down on the searing hot coals as the priest placed the pig on the altar to the approving roar of the mob of people below.

The priests stepped to one side of the altar, turned and welcomed the elected King of the Saturnalia. The mock king entered bowing repeatedly to his audience as he stepped forward to the loud cheers and applause of the horde. The king stood next to the priests, took one last bow, and then faced the priests, who handed him their knife. The king waved the knife high in the air as the assembly cheered. He then raised his other hand, signaling to the crowd to quiet down. Once silence was obtained, he stepped over to the statue of Saturn, knelt down and cut the cords of social restraint around its feet. He jumped up, waving the cords and knife high above his head, and shouted, "Lo Saturnalia!" The assembly echoed a boisterous, "Lo Saturnalia!"

The week-long revelry had begun.

* * *

Amora looked around at everyone in her household, slave and master alike, eating the evening meal together, and smiled. It was actually fun to openly interact with her staff on such intimate terms, and listen to their banter. She really wasn't hungry. She had gorged herself at the banquet all afternoon and felt a bit light-headed from the amount of wine she had consumed. But she still made a valiant effort to sample the food that had been prepared, and even took her turn serving it to others. Lupita and her young companion giggled with delight when their mistress served them a helping of roasted duck stuffed with pomegranates, a delicacy they had never encountered. Amora enjoyed participating in their fantasy of being little princesses as they were served a royal meal.

She had a great time earlier that day at her maiden adult Saturnalia festival. At first, she was taken aback by the wanton debauchery, but she soon joined in the fun—singing, dancing, joking, and consuming an insane amount of wine and exotic cuisine. She had never experienced such unbridled passion before. She looked forward to exploring the

17

sensations that the next day's upside-down activities would bring. She turned to Leo and said, "I would like to see the female gladiators fight in the Colosseum tomorrow."

Leo laughed. "It's quite a sight. I hear that the final duel will be to the death."

"Oh, I've got to see it."

"It won't be until the afternoon."

"Julia said that it is unlike anything I have ever seen. The women fight even more viciously than men!"

"It is surprising sometimes."

Their conversation was interrupted when several of the slaves brought in the traditional individual cakes for dessert. The anticipation was intense as everyone waited until the last cake was placed on the table. A couple of the male slaves took advantage of the holiday's relaxed morals for slaves and made bets on who would be the mock king. It didn't take long before Leo's chief assistant, Cato, bit into the hidden coin. Everyone cheered and laughed as Leo rose and bowed down before him and asked, "What is your first order, my lord?"

"Bring me my crown and robe," he said as laughter filled the room.

"Yes, your majesty," Leo replied as he bowed once more.

While Leo was retrieving the ordered paraphernalia, the others finished their cakes and gathered their gifts to exchange. Leo returned and placed a robe on the new king and crowned him with a wreath of holly, to the amusement of the household. He then asked, "What is your next wish, my lord?"

"Clear my place so we will have room for the gifts," he ordered.

Leo laughed, made another exaggerated bow, and replied, "Your wish is my command." He then grabbed his slave's plate and goblet and tossed them across the room to the enjoyment of all except some of the younger slaves, who watched nervously as the dish and cup banged against the wall and crashed to the floor.

"The king mentioned gifts," Leo said. "Where are they?" He then grabbed his bag full of coins and tossed them into the air as the slaves scrambled to gather the money as they laughed and squealed in delight.

Once the ruckus had settled down, the slaves exchanged small gifts, typically small figures carved in wax. Everyone was pleased with these tokens of love and appreciation. When the last gift was distributed, Leo looked around the room and observed, "I believe we forgot the mistress of the house. Shall I go see what I can find?" Everyone nodded with approval.

Leo left the room and soon returned carrying a large container covered by a sheet of fabric. He set it down in front of Amora. All eyes in the room were glued with anxious anticipation on the large present. "Let's hope this doesn't fly away," Leo said as he ripped the sheet off with a jerk, allowing it to float down to the floor while the household cheered. Inside the exquisite cage stood a large exotic parrot staring at Amora. The bird's brilliant plumage consisted of a bright red body with splashes of green next to the baby-blue wings and red and blue tail. Its white face was a clean canvas for its deep dark eyes and bright yellow beak. Silence filled the room as everyone stared in awe at this exquisite creature. The bird looked around the room and then back at Amora, cocked its head and squawked. Everyone burst out laughing, followed by applause.

Chapter 4

Natalie

The following year was a wonderful year for Leo and Amora. He formed a company with his associates that was successful in securing the *publicani* office in Egypt, which turned out to be even more lucrative than their highest hopes. Leo's esteem among his compatriots rose exponentially, which was even more important to him than the wealth that the venture generated. Amora relished all of the luxury and finery that wealth and status could provide.

Married life also suited Leo and Amora well. They adeptly played the roles of patrician and dutiful wife as expected. Leo continued to make shrewd political and business decisions, and Amora was the perfect hostess. Despite her youth, she efficiently ran an orderly household with over two dozen slaves. But most important, their union was blessed with a beautiful daughter, Natalie. Unlike some of Leo's colleagues, who had such a diminished view of the female gender that they abandoned their newborn daughters to die from exposure, Natalie was the center of Leo's and Amora's world. Life was good.

Amora's first hint that something was amiss with her privileged existence came on a lovely spring morning when Natalie was five years old and while she was pregnant with their second child.

When Amora awoke, the singing larks confirmed that

spring had arrived. She arose and looked out her window at their garden and took a deep breath. The bouquet of cherry blossoms and jasmine filled the air. Euphoric, Amora closed her eyes and inhaled. A whiff of frying bacon stirred her sense of hunger. She wondered if her daughter had already eaten her breakfast. Normally, Natalie would have already joined Amora in her bed, telling Amora about her dreams and dragging her out of bed for their morning meal. She wondered why Natalie had broken their routine.

Amora peeked into Natalie's empty room and wondered where she could be. She wasn't worried, just curious. She realized how inquisitive Natalie was and was confident that she was exploring some new adventure. But it was time for the morning meal and Amora wanted to be sure that her daughter ate on time, as she had plans for them later that morning. She entered the kitchen and asked if anyone had seen Natalie, to negative responses. One of the slaves said that she would immediately go search for her, but Amora said it was not necessary. She was enjoying the fresh morning air and would look for Natalie herself.

Amora passed their fabric workshop and listened to the swish and boom of the loom. She peeked inside and observed Natalie intently watching the hands of one of their slaves move swiftly, working magic on the loom. One flick of the wrist, and the shuttle would fly, leaving a red thread as evidence of its crossing. Then the thread disappeared with a thump. In the blink of an eye, the shuttle retraced its journey across the expanse of red, blue and white threads to add another layer to the fabric. The woman glanced at Natalie and smiled.

"Would you like to help?" she asked politely.

"Oh yes!"

"Very well. Sit up here with me." She lifted her master's

child to the loom.

"Now, what color do you want to use?"

Natalie looked over the selection and noticed how the bright red thread seemed to jump out at her. "Red!" she said.

"Alright, take this little wood boat and launch it across this sea of yarn."

Natalie held the shuttle in her small hand and rocked it back and forth as if she were charging it with energy while she aimed the projectile. She let it go, only to see its voyage abruptly end in a web of threads close to its start. The slave laughed. Natalie frowned.

"That's all right. Now I get to guide it the rest of the way."

They both smiled when the boat landed on the far shore across the warp.

"Now help me bring this lonely thread home to its family," the laborer said as she lifted Natalie's hand up to the beater, which she had moved closer for Natalie to reach.

"Now on the count of three, help me bring this down so your little yarn can join its family. One, two, three." With a bang, the outstanding thread vanished. They both broke out laughing, joined by Amora, who, unbeknownst to them, had been watching.

They turned and looked at Amora as she joined the happy team, glad to see Natalie enjoying her first weaving lesson. Mastering this skill was important, as the materfamilias was expected to oversee cloth production for her estate.

"Let's save this piece and show Papa what you helped make," Amora exclaimed.

Natalie beamed with pride.

"Now that you know how to make fabric, do you want to go with me to the market and buy some exotic cloth that has just arrived from the East? Maybe we can find something for your birthday."

"Oh, may I?"

"Of course. But first we need to eat and then drop off some food on our way."

* * *

Mother and daughter ambled to the market hand in hand, followed by two slaves carrying baskets overflowing with food for a charity luncheon hosted by Senator Quintus's wife, Loretta.

"Mama, where are we taking this food?"

"Loretta is providing lunch near the market for people who are poor, and I am helping her."

"Why?"

"The gods have blessed us with so much that it is our duty to share." The conversation sparked a pleasant memory of when she was young. Amora smiled. "When I was about your age, I helped my mother serve a fabulous meal to a large group of people. They were so happy and excited. I didn't understand why, it was just some food. I was shocked to learn that many of them had never tasted some of the nice things we offered. That day my mother taught me that in order to be happy we need to be grateful. And, when we are grateful, we like to share. It was one of the most important lessons my mother taught me." And one, she admitted, she often forgot.

"I'm happy!" Natalie said with a smile. "So, I am grateful too."

Amora chuckled and said, "Yes, you are."

"I want to share too," Natalie implored.

"Then we will find a project we can work on together when we return home," Amora proudly replied.

Natalie stopped dead in her tracks, startling her mother. Natalie pointed across the street at two dirty young street urchins begging in the gutter. The older was a little girl dressed in rags around four years of age caring for her younger sibling, a two-year-old boy playing with a piece of trash in his hands.

"Mama, can we bring them to the luncheon?"

Surprised, Amora at first did not know how to respond. A myriad of thoughts and feelings raced through her mind. She was not hosting this affair and was not sure how Loretta would respond, yet Loretta had mentioned to Amora that she could invite deserving less fortunate persons to the luncheon. Amora was pleased that Natalie had taken her message to heart and wanted to help those in need. Yet, this just didn't feel right. But, if she denied her daughter's request, would that undo the lesson she had just taught? Amora, weighing all these factors, was interrupted by her daughter.

"Please, Mama. Look, they are poor and need food to eat. Can't we please help them?"

Amora looked at the innocent children, whose disheartened petitions were being ignored by the populace passing by. Moved by compassion, Amora replied, "Loretta said we could invite guests, so it should be all right."

"Oh, thank you, Mama!" Natalie exclaimed as she rushed over to the starving youngsters. Amora watched as the children looked inquisitively at Natalie as she explained her mission. Smiles burst through their despair, and Natalie reached out her hand to the little female guardian to lift her out of her solitary world of gloom into the joy of childhood friendship, oblivious to the boundaries of class. Natalie and her new companion laughed and giggled as they skipped along beside Amora with their little charge in tow.

Loretta spotted them in the distance as they approached and stormed out to meet them.

"Who are these despicable strays?" she demanded.

"These are the guests you authorized me to invite," Amora retorted confidently.

"I said you could invite guests worthy of my graciousness, not scum like this."

Amora realized that she had overstepped the bounds of social propriety.

Loretta continued, "Charity is supposed to elicit appreciation from those who can reinforce our position. What good can this worthless rubbish offer us? Heads, not hearts, must govern our philanthropy, Amora."

Natalie could not understand what was happening, but her new little friend knew all too well. She dropped her head, let go of Natalie's hand, and turned to walk away.

"Wait," Natalie enjoined. "Mama, can't they have some food?"

Amora was torn between compliance with social norms and her maternal instincts to teach her child compassion. She was not sure how to respond. But, her life's training as a lady of distinction took over.

"I apologize for my indiscretion. I misunderstood your invitation."

Loretta simply snorted as she raised her nose in the air.

"Here is the produce I promised to provide," Amora said. "Sorry, but we cannot stay." Amora then grabbed Natalie's hand, turned and walked away.

Amora watched the two dejected street urchins wandering off in front of them, their heads down as they meandered away, the little girl kicking a small stone along their path.

"Can't they eat lunch?" Natalie asked.

"No." Amora responded bluntly.

"But why?"

"It's just the way it is," Amora replied. "When you are older you will understand." But, Amora did not understand. This simple question by her innocent child was the chisel that cracked the façade of her life. For the first time, Amora wondered why the social conventions were the way they were. Who could be more deserving than those two dejected little children? She tried to dismiss these thoughts and questions by telling herself that she was just extra sentimental because she was expecting, but the image of those two ragamuffins walking away from them and the little girl kicking the stone haunted her mind.

Chapter 5

Esteban

Leo paused at the open door of Amora's room when he caught sight of the daughter he adored. Natalie stood in front of the large mirror watching Amora rummage through a huge chest full of fabrics. The room was a rainbow of colors from fabrics draped over the bed, the chair, and the lid of the trunk. Amora pulled a rich red piece of silk from the chest and laid it over Natalie's shoulder.

"Oh, this is gorgeous," she exclaimed.

Natalie smiled and glanced up at her mother as Amora stepped back and examined the fabric on her daughter.

"No, too formal for your birthday."

Amora tossed the red fabric over the chair and grabbed a piece of brilliant yellow silk from the chest. She held it up to Natalie's face and smiled. Natalie grinned adoringly at her mother, rubbed the silk on her cheek, and giggled.

"Do you like it?" Amora asked.

Natalie nodded her head. "It's sunny."

Amora grabbed Natalie's hand and spun her around, laughing while draping the yellow silk around Natalie as she twirled and squealed with joy, the end of the fabric flapping in the air behind her. Amora could not resist leaning over and embracing her daughter. Natalie rested her head on her mother's swollen pregnant belly and returned her hug. She beamed as she looked up at her mother. "I love you, Mama."

"I love you too, Natalie."

Natalie giggled and looked at her mother. "The baby moved!"

Amora smiled and stroked Natalie's hair. "It won't be long before you have a baby brother or sister."

"Papi!" Natalie exclaimed as she glimpsed her father and rushed to him. Leo scooped her up, threw her high into the air, and caught her securely in his arms as she came down.

"Hello, my pretty little princess."

Natalie flung her arms around her father's neck, and they embraced.

Amora smiled as she watched them spin around and laugh. Without warning, the first pains of labor interrupted the blissful scene.

Amora grabbed her side and took a deep breath as she began her descent into the valley of pain reserved for the "gentler" sex, since no man could endure the ordeal in which agony, death, and new life converge. It is the journey that each expecting woman anticipates with Janus's face of dread and eagerness. It is not a voyage one schedules, but is a trip that each traveler is compelled to take when beckoned, whether she is prepared or not. Indeed, no one is fully prepared for this excursion across the edge of mortality into the spiritual realm to escort her offspring into this world of pain. One hoped not to linger in this sacred sphere for fear that the gods would elect that your or your issue's life would pay the tithe that was required for passage by one out of ten who ventured into their domain, mother and child alike.

Hours later, Amora's bedroom was still a hive of activity as the midwife called out instructions to the two slave girls frantically attempting to assist her. Amora screamed, and the midwife reassured her.

"You can do this. Now, push!"

Amora screamed again, and a baby cried.

One of the girls left the room and notified Leo of the infant's birth. Leo rushed to her room but paused at the door. Amora ignored the commotion around her as she looked adoringly into her newborn's wet face. The baby grimaced, sealing his eyes shut more tightly as he stuck out his bottom lip and then let out a cry. Amora snuggled her babe tightly against her breast; his protestations between each breath diminished as she rocked him. He took a deep double breath, opened his eyes slightly, and promptly shut them again. A moment later, he opened his eyes, blinked, and stared up at Amora, who cooed as she embraced and rocked her new treasured offspring.

Leo smiled and entered the hallowed space.

"You have a son," the midwife proclaimed.

Leo beamed. The midwife lifted the baby out of Amora's arms and, according to their honored custom, placed the infant on the floor. Simultaneously, Leo knelt on one knee as he prepared to demonstrate his acceptance of the child by raising it up. However, Leo's smile evaporated when he noticed that the infant's leg was deformed. Leo stared at the shriveled leg and scowled. He did not know what to do, so he rose abruptly and walked out of the room as Amora implored him to stay. "Leo! Leo!"

Once out of the room, Leo stopped and leaned against the wall next to the door.

"We have to dispose of the child," the midwife said as she picked up the baby.

"No! No! You can't take my baby!" Amora exclaimed as she grabbed her newborn son from the woman.

"You know the rules," the midwife protested.

Amora ignored the remark and cuddled her babe close to her heart.

"But it is deformed," the midwife said.

"My baby. My sweet baby," Amora cooed, oblivious to all the chaos around her.

Leo turned and slowly walked away to the peristyle, conflicted.

A little while later, Amora instructed one of the slaves to bring Natalie to her room. Natalie, escorted by the slave, slowly entered and stopped, her eyes opened wide as they darted at images around the room. A large dark-haired woman wearing a gray tunic towered over her mother lying in bed. A slave was on her knees wiping up the floor in a corner of the room. Amora's dressers and tables had been cleared. The mirror over the makeup table reflected a view of the parrot in its cage across the room. Natalie smiled. At least something was normal. Light shone through the partially draped window next to the bird onto Amora's bed. Amora, exhausted, turned her head and smiled at Natalie standing near the doorway. Natalie stared at her mother. She had never seen her mother look so weak. Amora smiled and asked, "Do you want to see your baby brother?"

Natalie nodded.

"It's okay, dear. You can come over here," Amora said.

The slave gave Natalie a gentle nudge. She inched closer until she stood beside her mother and newborn brother. Amora laid the infant on the bed next to Natalie and stroked his head. The babe made a face and squinted his closed eyes.

"Why doesn't he open his eyes?" Natalie asked.

"Oh, he is very tired. He had to work very hard to get here."

"He's so tiny," Natalie observed as she leaned over and gently kissed the infant on his forehead. The babe smiled, opened his eyes, and looked up at Natalie.

"Mommy, he saw me! He saw me and smiled!"

"Do you want to hold him?"

"Oh yes, Mommy. Please."

"Now sit up here on the bed next to me...Yes, that's good. Now hold your arms out while I rest him on your lap...Very good."

Natalie sat up straight and beamed as Amora laid the infant in her arms. Her eyes were glued to her new sibling as she cradled the babe in her arms and gently rocked him for several minutes.

Natalie looked back up at her mother and declared, "Mama, you need to name him Esteban."

"It is a pretty name, dear, but that is your father's decision."

"But, Mama, you have to name him Esteban. His name is Esteban! I know it is!" Natalie insisted.

"It is a strong and handsome name. I will see what I can do."

"Oh, thank you, Mama! Esteban will be glad."

* * *

Natalie found her father sitting on a bench staring at the fountain in the central garden.

"Oh, Papi," Natalie said as she ran up to him and grabbed his hand. "You need to come and see." She tugged at his hand. "Hurry. I want to show you my brother." Leo hesitated. "Come on, Papi. I need to show you." Leo yielded and followed Natalie as she led him out of the garden to Amora's room.

"Hello, Leo," Amora said.

"Here he is, Papi."

"How are you feeling?" Leo asked.

"I will be fine."

"Papi, his name is Esteban."

"Leo, the Emperor Claudius had a limp."

"Do you like his name, Papi? Mommy said we can name him Esteban if you agree."

"The norms are not fixed, Leo."

"Papi, do you want to see him?"

"Your son could even become the emperor."

"I got to hold him. Do you want to hold him, Papi?"

Amora lifted her baby. "Here, Leo. Hold your son."

"No. You keep the child."

It was said. Amora would keep her son.

Chapter 6

Alone

A week later, Leo arrived at the public bath later than usual because of the lengthy morning *salutatio* where he heard requests for support from various clients and relatives. He looked forward to his time at this massive facility where male citizens bathed, relaxed, exercised, ate, studied, and above all socialized. He wanted to catch up on current events with his fellow patricians, so he skipped the activities in the other rooms and went directly to the main chamber where his friends would most likely be. Steam rose from the large tepidarium pool as Leo entered the expansive room with its lofty four-story domed ceiling. The pool was surrounded by spacious porticos under five-meter-high ceilings supported by large columns. Marble statues adorned the room along with mosaic designs on the floor and frescos on the walls. Dozens of men were relaxing and visiting in the pool while others in towels sat on chairs or stone benches along the walls, conversing with their associates. A masseuse labored over a large man as he lay on a stone platform. Several slaves throughout the room offered patrons towels, oils, and long *strigils* to scrape off sweat while others offered drinks and refreshments.

Quintus and Rusticus confronted Leo as soon as he approached.

"I heard you are allowing Amora to keep her deformed

infant," Quintus said.

"You are well informed."

"Leo, this does not reflect well on you and your leadership abilities. You need to take charge of your affairs and not let feminine sensibilities and weakness cloud your judgment," Quintus admonished.

"The gods will not be pleased that you are sheltering an affront to nature," Rusticus warned.

"You should abandon that deformed creature before your reputation is damaged any further," Quintus added.

"I have made my decision and do not want to hear another word regarding the matter." Leo turned and marched out of the room. He fell back against the corridor wall, dropped his head into his hands, and sighed deeply.

* * *

Amora was disappointed that none of her friends had dropped by to congratulate her on the birth of her new baby. She understood, though. Infants with physical defects were supposed to be abandoned. Even though it was legally sanctioned because Leo agreed to keep the baby, it was still contrary to custom. Regardless, Amora realized that her friends would not know how to deal with this unusual situation. So, she looked forward to her first outing with her cherished new babe to show her peers that she was happy, and that they didn't need to wonder whether they should offer their condolences for the child's defect or congratulate her on his birth.

She selected one of her favorite stolas, and a soft white blanket embroidered with royal blue trim to secure and display her treasure. She looked forward to sharing her joy with her friends and the positive reception she was sure her son would receive. She elected to stroll through the Porticu Liviae public gardens because it was an informal location that would facilitate this anticipated interaction. As they prepared to leave, the infant's nurse picked up Esteban, assuming she would carry the child during their excursion. Amora said that she could stay home. Amora wanted to carry her own son to clearly demonstrate how much she adored him. That way her friends would feel more at ease, she said.

Amora was exhausted by the time she had carried her child up the Oppian Hill to the garden, so she sat down to rest on the first bench that was available. She was excited to see Loretta and Julia approach, deep in conversation. How fitting, she thought. Two of her closest friends would be the first ones to see her new baby. Amora brushed her hair with her hand and tidied her stola, preparing for their arrival. Amora sat dumbfounded as she watched them walk right past her, without even acknowledging her presence. Shocked, she wondered, "What just happened?"

At first, she told herself that they must not have seen her. They never even looked her way. But they must have noticed her. "They were very engaged in conversation," she told herself. "So, they must have been discussing some very urgent and important private matter." But she knew that was not what really happened. She had been ignored! For the first time in her privileged life, she was struck by the harsh reality that the world did not revolve around her, and she was not exempt from its social norms. She was used to being the center of attention, and now no one even cared if she existed.

She walked home in a daze, sat down in the atrium and stared at the fountain. Confused, she tried to sort through her thoughts and feelings. She had been snubbed. As she pondered the experience, she recognized that her friends didn't really care about her at all. They were more concerned about their own position and enforcing social norms to keep everyone else in line. People didn't matter, only the state and the rules it dictated. Shockingly, women were its enforcers as much as its men at arms. She had never experienced this stinging bite of rejection before because she had always been a slave to tradition and its guardian without even realizing it. She was not greater than Rome, and now that she had strayed from its borders, she felt its crushing weight bearing down to coerce compliance.

That evening Amora walked over and looked down at her sleeping child in his crib. How could such an innocent peaceful little infant threaten Rome so much that it was determined to destroy him? He didn't have some infectious disease. He was just different. His defect would be his challenge, not Rome's. Sure, it would make things difficult for him, but he wouldn't be a burden on society. It may help build his character and make him strong. He looked so normal, so healthy, lying there under his blanket. Little Esteban began to suck the air in his dreams. "So sweet," Amora thought.

She had to protect him from this force intent on destroying him, even if it meant that she would suffer. No one was going to hurt her son on her watch! At least her husband was her ally. Her heart swelled with gratitude as she thought of Leo and his willingness to defend their son from these destructive forces.

Amora picked up her baby and held him close as he slept. She sauntered over to Leo's study to show Leo how healthy he looked and to reinforce Leo's hesitant decision during this trying time. However, as soon as she entered, Amora realized right away that something was wrong. Leo sat with his elbows on his desk and his head buried in his hands.

"What is it, Dear?"

Leo looked up and glared at Amora.

"You know what's wrong."

Amora stared at Leo in disbelief.

"That child is what's wrong. How can our life be right when we allowed that twisted creature to take over our world?"

"Leo, he is growing strong."

"I should have never let feminine sensitivities cloud my judgment. Now that I've announced my decision, it is too late to change or I will look weak and indecisive."

"Leo, what are you talking about?"

"Amora, I hope that infant dies. Do you understand me?"

"Leo, he is your son. He has your strength. He will conquer his adversity. Will you?"

"Don't question me, woman!"

"Leo, this will all work out. Right now, we need to be strong together."

"Don't lecture me. I am going out." Leo stood and made his way to the door.

"Out?"

"Yes. That is what I said."

"But where are you going at this hour?"

"I said, out!"

The next morning Amora was eating breakfast in the triclinium when Leo came in, stood next to her and said, "Good morning." Leo placed his hand on Amora's shoulder. Amora brushed it aside. Leo put his hand on her shoulder once more, and she emphatically pushed his hand away again. Leo grabbed Amora by her shoulders, lifted her up in front of him and said, "I am your husband. I demand respect!"

Amora glared at Leo and thought, "You are not the man I married. You are not a man at all. You run away from real responsibility like a, like a disgusting rat."

"Do you hear me?!" Leo demanded. Amora abruptly

broke his grip and stormed out of the room.

With that exchange, the intimate emotional connection between Leo and Amora was severed. They entered diverging paths where they increasingly lived separate parallel lives, interacting on a perfunctory level, each communicating with the other in their roles and not on a personal emotional level.

Amora's world had been turned on its head. She was alone, adrift in a turbulent sea in search of new moorings to secure her life. Her husband, to whom she had attached her future, was pursuing a course she could not follow, despite her vow. She was alone, abandoned by husband and her friends. She unexpectedly found herself in the middle of a bewildering life crisis. Who was she, really? A princess, a mother, a nobody? On what was her personal worth based? Was her self-esteem so vulnerable that it was dependent on the fickle assessment of her peers? Was she any different or better than her critics? Was her life just a sham? What was real?

She couldn't resolve these doubts and uncertainties, but the one thing that she resolutely concluded was that her children needed her. She always loved her children, but now she treasured them at a whole new level. More than ever, they became the focus of her attention and the center of her life. Nothing else really mattered. She still attended the obligatory social functions, but they no longer consumed her time and attention. She was a mother, and above all, she wanted her offspring to know and feel that they were loved.

Chapter 7

The Birthday Outing

Natalie fidgeted with excitement as she sat on the chair in front of Amora's mirror while Amora brushed and arranged her hair. She was excited that her parents were allowing her to wear a stola for the first time to celebrate her twelfth birthday. Girls were not allowed to wear stolas until they were twelve years old, so this was a very special occasion. She even helped Amora design her stola. It was bright yellow with distinctive blue trim, her favorite colors. Amora and Natalie chatted and laughed while Amora styled her daughter's hair in various arrangements. Amora stepped back, admired her creation, and proclaimed, "Now you look like a bride."

Natalie giggled. Admiring her mother in the mirror, she said, "I hope I am as pretty as you when I get married, Mama."

"You will be even more beautiful, dear. You are gorgeous!"

The sublime moment was suddenly interrupted when Amora grimaced and dropped her hand to her side. She moaned and turned to sit down, grabbing the back of Natalie's chair to steady herself. She felt nauseous, and faint. She sat down on her bed, and buried her head in her hands as she continued to groan. Natalie ran to her mother's side. "What's wrong, Mama? What's wrong?"

Sweat beaded up on Amora's forehead as she sat facing the floor, breathing deeply. "I'll be alright," she said between breaths. "My stomach just hurts…I must have eaten something bad…don't worry. I'll be better soon," she assured her daughter, who was stroking Amora's arm, concerned.

* * *

Amora felt quite a bit better that afternoon, after losing her breakfast, but she remained exhausted. She insisted that Leo still take Natalie and Esteban on their scheduled birthday outing, even though she would not be able to enjoy their company. Amora assured Leo that their slave, Monica, would be able to care for Esteban on their stroll, and that she would be fine at home. Reassured, Leo grabbed his son's little cane, which Esteban used as a sword almost as often as a walking stick, and handed it to his boy. They departed, Leo holding his birthday girl's hand with Monica accompanying Esteban behind.

As they approached the gardens, Natalie was the first one to spot Quintus and Gaius conversing near its entrance. Natalie liked Quintus. He always paid lots of attention to her when he would drop by their home to talk business with her father, and he often brought her little gifts.

"There's Quintus," she said, pointing. Looking up at her father, she asked, "Can I go show him my stola?" Leo nodded, and she skipped ahead to greet them.

"Hello, Senator Quintus and Senator Gaius. Do you see my new stola?" Natalie asked as she modeled it. "I'm a big girl now."

Quintus and Gaius smiled. "Just look at you, all grown up," Quintus said. He reached over, plucked a rose from the garden and handed it to Natalie as he leaned over and kissed her forehead. She beamed in delight as Leo reached the trio.

"Good day Senators," he said. Then, directing himself to

his daughter, he continued, "Natalie, the senators have important things to discuss, so we do not want to detain them."

"Nonsense," Quintus replied. "It is always a pleasure to see your beautiful daughter. Unfortunately, though, I need to leave, but I'm sure Gaius would enjoy your company."

"Oh, please do not leave on our account," Leo insisted.

"I'm not. I already mentioned to Gaius that I needed to be on my way." Turning to Gaius, he said, "I will let you know what I find out tomorrow. Good day." He shook Leo's hand. "Have a nice day, Leo." He then leaned down, took Natalie's hand and kissed it while he looked into her eyes. "Miss Natalie, I hope you enjoy your stroll. Goodbye, my little lady." Natalie giggled. With that, Quintus walked away.

By this point Esteban, waving his cane in the air, and his attendant holding his other hand, joined the small group. "Let go of me," he insisted. "I want to play."

"It is alright. Let him go play," Leo said to his slave. "Just watch that he does not disturb anyone."

"Certainly." She let go of Esteban's hand, and he immediately ran and hobbled down the path, laughing and zigzagging from side to side as he went. His caretaker followed behind, barking out orders: "Stay away from that man...don't hit those flowers...slow down." Leo and Gaius laughed as they watched the scene.

"Leo, what news do you have from Alexandria?"

"Our venture is doing well. I received a letter from Eusebius just the other day, and he informs me that the tax collections from upper Egypt were even higher than last year."

Bored, Natalie ambled over to a nearby bench and sat down. Leo watched her through the corner of his eye while Leo and Gaius continued their discussion. She played with her flower, leaned back and looked up at the clouds, and drew designs in the dirt with her sandals.

The tranquil atmosphere was abruptly shattered by a child's shriek, followed by screams of pain. Leo immediately recognized the voice as Esteban's. Leo bolted and ran to the far side of the gardens where he found his slave lifting Esteban up from the bottom of a long flight of stone steps, blood running down his forehead and face, drenching his tunic.

Leo rushed down the stairs as the nurse tried to comfort Esteban and stop the bleeding. Leo took charge immediately. He grabbed Monica's sash and wrapped it around his son's head. He took his son from his slave and ordered her to pick up Esteban's cane. Leo held his boy close to his chest as he ascended the stairs, telling him to be brave and reassuring him that everything would be alright. Esteban's cries of pain subsided to intermittent sobs as Leo reached the top of the stairs and came face-to-face with Rusticus, who had become the Prefect of Rome. Leo looked around and observed a crowd of people staring at him.

"Why did you bring this deformed creature to defile this sacred place and disturb our peace?" Rusticus demanded, oblivious to the suffering child's cries, which escalated with Rusticus's harsh inquisition.

"Can't you see the child is hurt?" Leo bristled as he handed the bawling boy to Monica and grabbed the cane.

"He is not welcome here, Leo. You should know this!"

"We are leaving!" Leo retorted.

"Be gone then!" Rusticus ordered.

Leo marched through the throng of people gawking to see the blood-stained man followed by his slave carrying the crying child. Leo fumed as he stomped toward Natalie's bench. "The nerve of Rusticus to accost me at a time like this!" Leo seethed to himself. "Why didn't that worthless slave watch Esteban? Can't anyone obey orders?!"

Even more enraged, Leo wondered, "Now, where did that girl run off to?" He scanned the horizon but could not see her. He stopped dead in his tracks. Monica and Esteban nearly collided with him. He turned and examined the dispersing multitude for any sign of his daughter. None was found. Fury converted into concern and then panic as he realized that Natalie was nowhere to be found. He spotted Gaius and ran to him.

"Have you seen Natalie?" he asked.

"No. We left her sitting over there?"

"I know. I can't find her anywhere," Leo exclaimed.

Leo and Gaius began asking people passing by if they had seen a little girl in a yellow stola with blue trim, all to no avail. Leo handed Esteban's cane to his slave and told her to wait by the bench with Esteban while he looked for Natalie. Gaius continued to ask bystanders about Natalie while Leo searched the area and then ran back to the stairs. He asked the lingering spectators about his little girl. Again, no one had seen her. He ran back to Gaius, who still had no information, and then back to the bench where Monica sat holding Esteban, who had stopped crying and was now watching all of the people scurrying about. Leo again searched the area around the bench and then ran partway back to his home, occasionally asking persons if they had seen his little girl. No one remembered seeing her except one old woman, who only remembered them walking up to the gardens earlier that day. Convinced that going farther was a waste of time, Leo ran back to the gardens and told his slave to return home. "Send me word if Natalie is there, and by all means, keep Amora home until I return."

Gaius and Rusticus arrived as the nurse and Esteban left.

Genuinely concerned, Rusticus ordered the *stationarii guards* of that post to look for Natalie and to immediately let him know of any information they discovered. He took Leo and Gaius back to his office to wait for any reports and to further review the details of the day's events in hopes of uncovering some useful clue. Nothing seemed out of place, except the incident regarding Esteban's fall. Leo sat in a daze, rehearsing the events of the day over and over again in his mind, oblivious to the activity around him. What had he missed? He searched his memory for any clue. Was there anyone lurking in the background while Natalie sat on the bench? He relived every detail—the way she held her flower and lifted it to her nose to smell it, the way her hair flowed down and swayed in the breeze as she watched the sky, even the designs in the dirt she had made. He examined it all, like pieces of a puzzle, looking, searching for something, anything that he had missed that would solve the mystery of her disappearance. He couldn't grasp the fact that Natalie was really gone. She couldn't have just vanished. She had to be somewhere, but where? Maybe she had gotten lost in all the confusion. Maybe she was calling out for him to find her? He was jolted back to the present when Rusticus placed a hand on his shoulder.

"Leo, it has been over five hours. All the patrols have reported back with no word. It is late. You should go home. Get some rest and comfort Amora."

Chapter 8

We Lost Her

Amora screamed with horror when she saw her blood-soaked son in Monica's arms. She ran to Esteban, grabbed him from her slave and ran to her bedroom shouting orders.

"Tell Cato to come immediately! Tell Sophia to start boiling some water! Grab some aloe and turmeric from the garden."

She gently laid Esteban on her bed. She began to remove his bloodied clothes to see his injuries before she attempted to remove the makeshift bandage around his head. His extremities displayed various scrapes and nasty bruises, but it did not appear that any bones were broken. Esteban looked up at his mother. Mixed emotions rushed through his little being as tears filled his eyes. Amora hugged her son as she lifted him up. The warmth and comfort from his mother's touch melted the cold defensive shield created by shock. Secure in his mother's embrace, he relived the terror of his fall and began to sob.

"That's alright...You can cry," she whispered softly in his ear. "You will be fine...I will take care of you." His sobs began to subside, and she laid him gently back on her bed. Cato rushed into the room followed by a half dozen slaves.

"Sophia's heating the water," Cato reported. "I also sent for some colostrum."

"Very good, Cato. Please send someone to bring clean

bandages," Amora said, while Cato was already pointing to one of the slaves and snapped his fingers before she darted off.

Amora continued, pointing to the heap of Esteban's clothes on the floor, "Please get rid of these soiled clothes and bring me something comfortable for Esteban to wear." Again, with a couple of pointing fingers and a nod of the head, two slaves were scurrying about doing their assigned duties.

"Send for Doctor Galen to come and examine the boy," she directed.

"Of course," Cato replied. With just a nod, the next slave was gone on her mission.

The first slave returned with an armful of white strips of fabric. "Well done, Veronica," said Amora. "Now go bring some soap, so we can bathe Esteban as soon as the water is ready."

"Yes, my lady," and she was off.

"Alright, Esteban, I want you to be brave and sit up tall while we take a look at your head," Amora said reassuringly as she lifted her son up. "Cato, come here and help."

"Certainly." He said as he stepped next to Amora.

Amora gently began unwrapping the bandage around Esteban's head. After unraveling several swathes of the sash, Amora noticed that the blood from the gash on his forehead had begun to dry, intermeshed with the fabric.

"Cato, bring me those scissors from my makeup table." Cato was back in an instant. "Now, cut the fabric right here," she indicated while holding the fabric in her hands. "That's enough. We need some water."

She had no sooner spoken than two female slaves entered the room carrying a large pot of steaming water. Amora and Cato dabbed Esteban's forehead with a wet cloth and tenderly removed the last remnant of the bandage. It was a horrible gash—close to two inches long—weeping a small amount of clear fluid. They washed the boy, dressed his wounds, clothed him in clean garments, carried him to his room and laid him in his bed.

With a sigh of relief, she turned to Monica and asked, "Where are Leo and Natalie?"

"I'm sorry, my lady, but in all of the commotion, we lost her." The words, "We lost her," hit Amora like a sledgehammer. The rest of the slave's report hardly registered, "Leo is looking for her, and said that you need to stay here until they return."

"We lost her."…"We lost her." The words reverberated in her mind over and over with increased intensity. She collapsed into the nearest chair and stared straight ahead.

"We lost her," she muttered in a nearly inaudible voice. Those words knocked her out of her hyper-conscious state into semi-consciousness. She was thrust into the ethereal world where time and eternity embrace to produce offspring of ghostlike images reflecting the material world around her. She sat in her chair staring into the far distance, repeating the words, "We lost her," while shadows of the mortal world danced around her. As much as she tried to object, the veracity of those words spoke so loudly that they drowned out all other temporal stimuli. She knew her worst nightmare was real, while the terrestrial world was just a dream. Time slowed down until it stopped. It remained only as a faint figment from her distant past.

She realized that the only thing she could do was to petition the proprietors of this alien world. She rose and walked to her room where she kept her ancestral gods. As she placed the idols on a waist-high dresser next to her makeup table, Natalie's brush seemed to jump out at her. She picked up the brush and held it close to her heart. It became a bridge between her and her lost daughter in this ethereal world. She arranged all the gods upon the dresser, and lit candles in front of them. The flames frolicked in front of the images, casting mocking shadows on the wall to match those in her mind. She knelt down in front of her idols, held the brush next to her breast, and pled, "Blessed ancestors, it is not right that a child precedes her parent into the underworld. Take me, so that Natalie may live. We will all eventually join you in eternity, but please, please, let Natalie exist in time for a while longer. I am here. Take me." Her petition was met with silence, while the dancing shadows continued to ridicule her desperation. She threw herself on the ground and continued, "I implore you, let our daughter live." And, so she persisted, appealing to her forebearers in vain as she lay prostrate on the ground, brush in hand, in front of her emblems of eternity. That is where Leo found her late that night before he put her to bed.

Morning brought no relief. There seemed to be little difference between sleep and her dreamlike state when she awoke. She went about her daily activities in a daze. Food had no appeal. All her senses were numb. She drifted in and out of her temporal existence like waves of time lapping up upon the shore of eternity, only to retreat again into the vast liquid expanse that separated the living from the underworld of spirits. She was trapped between two worlds and knew that there was no escape. Life seemed to slip out of Amora as she rested her head on her bed, too numb to cry. The only thing she could feel was her heart pounding, a constant reminder that she was still alive while her cherished darling was gone.

While Amora walked around in a trance, Leo took action. Leo was at Rusticus's office before he arrived and insisted that they interrogate every slave and plebeian in the vicinity. Leo filled his day meeting with officials and talking with potential witnesses. Even though he was running from one interview to another, his efforts were no more fruitful than Amora's.

Occasionally one would hear about a young slave or plebeian girl being abducted, but it was practically unheard of among the noble class. Everyone was talking about the incident and expressing their opinions. How did it happen? Who could have done it? Why did it happen? It was not long before people blamed Leo and Amora for bringing this bad fortune upon their family. They should have disposed of their deformed son. The gods were not pleased, and now Leo and Amora are paying the price for their disrespect.

Leo and the stationarii guards searched for two full days, with no results. However, the morning of the third day Natalie's naked bruised body was found hidden near the bank of the Tiber. No clues or trace of her stola were found anywhere. Upon receiving word, Leo was filled with rage. "What lowlife could do such a thing!" he exclaimed. He rushed to the scene only to be informed that Rusticus had ordered that her body be taken directly to the necropolis outside the city for cremation due to the length of time she was dead. They would have to forgo the custom of letting her lay in state in their atrium before transporting her to the cemetery with a *pompa funebris* funeral procession. They would hardly have time to arrange for the sacrificial offering and eulogy, let alone musicians and professional mourners.

Leo arrived home and informed Amora, who took the news in stride. It was simply confirmation of the reality she already knew, but had refused to accept. The rest of the day for Amora seemed to pass in a blur. Messengers were sent to inform family, friends and associates that there would be a simple procession to the cemetery that afternoon. Due to the short notice, only a few of their closest family and friends attended. Leo led the convoy wearing his dark *toga pulla*, with Amora by his side. When they arrived, Natalie had been dressed and placed on a pyre in preparation for her cremation. Quintus said the eulogy and spoke about what a shame it was that such a beautiful little princess would be taken so young. Leo then stepped forward and placed the *Charon obol coin* on Natalie's mouth as payment to the ferryman who would convey her soul across the water that separated the living from the underworld. The priest offered a sow to Ceres and placed a morsel on the pyre next to Natalie. He then placed the god's portion on the altar and gave the balance to the family for their memorial meal at the cemetery.

Leo and Amora sat down with the funeral company to eat the ceremonial feast that was intended to help the grieving parties bring closure with their loss and move forward with their lives. It did not work. As they ate, they watched the smoke from Natalie's cremation rise to the heavens. Leo stopped eating and stared at the smoke as the heat of indignation kindled a fire in his breast. He abruptly stood and stormed off in a rage. Amora was not moved. She continued to sit without eating through the whole meal, staring up at the smoke until it dwindled into faint wisps in the air while she felt the light in her own life being extinguished.

Chapter 9

A Solitary World

After a few weeks, the numbing fog that enveloped Amora began to lift, pushed out by excruciating pain that stabbed deep into her soul and pierced her heart. At times it was so sharp she found it hard to breathe. The intensity of the suffering scared her, especially because she could find no relief. The agony would not stop—second after second, minute after minute, hour after hour, the throbbing would not end. It was more than she could endure. Wine offered the only relief from this unrelenting grief and anguish. But it only dulled the pain for a short while before it would resurface to crush her soul once more. It never ceased.

Pain brought an unwelcome nauseating companion, guilt. "I should have been there, protecting my little girl," she accused herself. She often felt like vomiting to purge the guilt rotting inside her, but it did not help. "I should not have abandoned my family and stayed home. I was not really *that* sick. I was feeling better. I was just selfish and only thought about myself. I failed in my duty as a mother. I let her die!" And, so the self-accusations continued, day after day, week after week, until one day a new emotion exploded on the scene, anger.

Amora and Esteban had just sat down to eat their mid-day meal. Monica was serving Esteban's plate and dropped a spoon full of sauce on the floor, spattering their clothes.

Amora shot up and screamed at Monica. "You imbecile! Can't you do anything right? Just look at what you have done you worthless scum!" Amora, in a tirade, continued to berate Monica as she scurried about trying to clean up the mess as fast as she could while Amora, towering over her, pursued her every move.

Anger soothed the pain as it redirected it outward to others—to the monster who violated and murdered her little girl; to Leo, Monica, and the gods who ignored her petition. Amora began to lash out at others, even those who had nothing to do with the tragedy. At first the anger seemed familiar, but something was different. It seemed strange in some unidentifiable way. She began to recognize that instead of blinding her senses, as in the past, this anger was illuminating. First, she realized that in a strange paradoxical way, her anger became a bridge partially connecting her with Leo. From its vistas she could glance at Leo's position and sense his turmoil. She watched him vacillate between the emptiness of despair—which she knew so well—and the fire of anger that she was discovering. Occasionally, they would touch, even collide, while on this metaphorical bridge, but they would soon retreat to their solitary worlds.

As Amora embraced her anger, she discovered it building connections to other aspects of her emotional world. When she explored beyond anger's border, it dissipated, and she discovered a whole new emotional realm. Its neighborhoods were not happy villages, but they had more life and depth of feeling than she experienced in her world of pain and guilt. Sadness reigned in this new ethereal sphere, but a breadth of lesser emotions were its subjects, and occasionally she encountered a small oasis of respite. The more she explored, she found that these communities conjoined to form an inviting world where she found feelings that she had lost long ago. She even discovered new emotions emerging while on its turf. She found the strength to visit Natalie's interred charred remains and cry.

As she spent more time in this emotional terrain, she desired to share it with her lost companion, Leo. She missed their long-lost union. Each time she crossed the metaphorical bridge to reach her mate, she found a locked gate on the other side. She ached. She ached for him as well as herself. Why had he locked her out? This was not fair. Her anger flared, reinforcing her bridge and their connection. If he would not let her enter his kingdom, then she resolved to meet him on the bridge.

She did not need to wait long as Leo regularly paced its planks, guarding his perimeter, primed to jump on anyone who dared approach. Her overture started with a simple, innocent comment, "I think I will take some flowers to Natalie's sepulcher tomorrow."

"Why bother at this point. You weren't there when she needed you," Leo responded with contempt.

Amora looked directly into his eyes. "You were watching her, Leo. Not me." She regretted the words as soon as they left her mouth, but they were spoken and could not be recalled.

Leo glared at Amora, clenched his fists and gritted his teeth. She stared back, not knowing what he would do, until he marched past her and stormed out of the house, not to return until later that night, drunk. When he staggered into the house, he went directly to the slaves' quarters and found Monica, in her bed. He proceeded to savagely beat her, with all the slaves watching silently in horror as she screamed in pain. Exhausted, Leo left her a bleeding, moaning lump on the floor, and made his way to the door, where he stopped, looked at Cato, and ordered, "Dispose of her and purchase a slave worthy of my house." Leo stumbled out the door to his bed.

The next morning, he ordered that everything related to his deceased daughter be discarded and forbade anyone mentioning her again. She was gone, and he did not want to be reminded of her. Amora, however, secreted away her private collection of special memorabilia in her room.

Chapter 10

Maria

Monica was the slave Amora trusted to provide most of her personal services, so she was sorry to see her go and insisted that she be sold to a respected family. Due to the private nature of Monica's duties, Amora decided that she personally wanted to choose Monica's replacement instead of simply sending Cato to the slave market and being stuck with his choice.

An alternative to slavery had never occurred to Amora. It was simply a part of her world, but she now found going to the slave market repulsive. It was a dirty disgusting place where humans were displayed nude on circular pedestals, subject to examination and the gawking eyes of the passing public. The smell of disease hung over the market like a dark cloud, amplified by frequent whiffs of pungent body odor. Even though they were only slaves, the loud, crude language and demeaning activity of the dealers and buyers irritated Amora's refined nature. This typically was not a task for a lady. Mustering her resolve, Amora set out to find the domestic help she needed. It was late in the morning and the sun was beating down, but the heat was not yet unbearable.

She stood off in a corner near the entrance to the market and examined the scene. Nothing had changed since the last time she was there years ago. Slaves stood on large pedestals with placards around their necks stating their origin, age, education, and other pertinent information. Some of the more educated slaves destined for domestic or administrative duties were privileged to wear a semblance of clothing. Hordes of people flowed through the market like a wide, slow river. Eddies occasionally swirled around the edges where the more interesting prospects stood.

Merchants called out to the passing crowd, extolling the virtues of their stock. One lifted his slave's arm and pointed to his biceps. Another, displaying a young woman, stepped in front of a wealthy patrician passing nearby and solicited his interest in his wares. The patrician stopped and walked around the girl, then walked on. A woman examined a female slave. She looked in her mouth, grabbed her hands, inspected them, stepped back, and scrutinized her build. The press and hubbub of the throng, the shouts of the sellers, and the smells only added to Amora's discomfort. She considered leaving, but realizing the necessity of her purchase, she stayed.

As Amora continued to observe this spectacle of humanity from her vantage point near the entrance, the activity of a nearby stage drew her attention. A dealer was involved in animated and intense negotiations with a prospective customer regarding several male slaves on his platform. The merchant smiled when he was handed a bag of coins to close the deal. He congratulated his customer on his fine purchase, reassuring him that the slaves were well worth the price paid. Another group of slaves replaced those who were sold. Two young women who were walking through the crowd gawked at a muscular Ethiopian in the group, his ebony skin glistening in the sun. One of the girls said something to the other, causing them both to giggle as they moved on. Amora smiled as she recalled walking through the market years ago with some of her young schoolmates to glance at the male specimens on display.

The woman next to that booth purchased the slave she had scrutinized so intently, and a young mother and her small nine-year-old daughter took their place on the pedestal. They were dressed with tattered clothing but had fine pleasant features. Their dark hair framed the worried looks on their faces. The little girl clung to the mother's hand and looked up to her, seeking reassurance and direction. The woman's eyes darted from side to side. Without looking down she pulled her child close and held her tight to her hip.

The merchant attempted to sell them together, realizing that it would be difficult to sell the child alone. "Two for the price of one," he shouted. "How can you go wrong with such a deal?"

The passing potential buyers showed no interest. The dealer spotted a group of women approaching, stepped near, and engaged them in conversation.

"I have a great deal for one lucky lady—this fine young healthy woman and her bright ten-year-old daughter." He exaggerated her age, realizing that the small child was the objection for most buyers. "The child is a hard worker and can easily be trained for any task. Look," he said as he grabbed the child's hand. "Her hands are small and nimble enough for tasks in tight spaces." The women smiled and shook their heads. The innocent young girl pulled back her hand and looked up at her mother.

"Come now, ladies," the merchant cajoled as they passed his stand. "Just think how much further your money will go when you buy someone so young."

One of the women chuckled and replied, "And how much more I will have to pay to feed her until she is able to carry her own load?"

The women laughed as they walked on, and the anxious mother tried to reassure her young daughter, who was trying to make sense out of what was happening. Amora's heart ached for the woman as she watched the desperate mother struggling to reassure her daughter.

The dealer called out to the parting women, "You can just buy the mother if you wish. I will even lower the price to two thousand sesterces."

The women walked on without so much as glancing back, but a ponce from a brothel had been observing the exchange. He approached and eyeballed both of them.

"The girl is old enough to be of service," the merchant assured him. The procurer ignored the broker, and without saying a word, began to examine the mother, glaring at her face, figure, and arms. As he continued to evaluate the mother, he slowly slinked around the pedestal and looked at her child. He smiled and began to scrutinize the girl from head to toe. He reached for the child, but she hid behind her mother's robe, and the mother pulled her robe around in an effort to hide her child.

"Disrobe," the ponce ordered. "I need to see what I am buying." The mother slightly shook her head as she clenched the top of her tunic.

"You heard the man. Remove your robes!" the dealer yelled. Defiant, the mother shook her head as she pulled her daughter in more securely behind her. The merchant grabbed a whip and struck the woman. She shrieked in pain.

Amora sprang into action, shouting out, "I will buy the two of them," as she rushed over. "Here are twenty-five hundred sesterces. Do we have a deal?"

The merchant looked over to the procurer to see if he would better the offer, but he scowled and scoffed, "They're not worth it."

"Then they are yours," the dealer told Amora.

Before Amora could even pay the dealer, the mother was

kissing her feet, swearing her eternal loyalty and devotion. The new slave, Camilla, was true to her pledge. She and her daughter, Maria, served Amora devotedly and were attentive to her every need.

Chapter 11

The Theatre

As the first anniversary of Natalie's death approached, Amora shared some of her tender feelings with Julia and Loretta. To Amora's surprise, they showed little sympathy and said that she needed to move on with her life and be more stoic, like her husband. This surprised Amora. How could her friends be so insensitive? Besides, Leo was simply existing and not really living. Regardless, she had learned to brush aside such thoughtless comments. However, her ears perked up when they invited her to attend the theatre with them on the anniversary of Natalie's death and watch a play where justice prevailed over evil. She used to like to attend the theatre and had not been back since the tragedy. "Yes," she thought, this would be an appropriate way to face this daunting date. She looked forward to seeing justice triumph and hoped that it would ease her pain and sorrow.

The auditorium was nearly full of spectators when Amora and her female companions entered through the *vomitorium* passageway. The women sat in the upper level of the auditorium overlooking the male guests below and the orchestra near the stage. The theatre was elaborately decorated with a three-story set and large columns in the background.

The plot of the drama, with its conflict, was quickly established. A beautiful young maiden was being courted by two suitors bent on winning her affection. The first was a handsome young Roman warrior who had recently returned from conquest. The other was an older Greek merchant who tried to woo his prize with his affluence and flowery oratory. Eventually, the soldier was victorious. In a fit of jealous rage, the villain violated the heroine and left her for dead. She identified her attacker to the hero with her dying words. The soldier swore vengeance and carried his departed love from the stage. The hero returned and delivered a grand oration on the value of justice, and then proceeded to execute it on a slave wearing the villain's mask. With one broad swing of his sword, the soldier decapitated the slave, spraying blood on the spectators in the front rows.

The audience roared and rose in unison cheering, except for Amora who sat frozen in her seat, nauseous. Regaining her composure, Amora ran out of the theatre before she threw up. For the first time, Amora's sensitivities were offended watching death executed on stage. For the first time, it registered that death was real, disguised as a play. This graphic display of life and death confirmed that there is no real joy in life. It is all an illusion. Death is the reality. Life is a lie. As she walked home, she pondered what she had just experienced. The play seemed to be a metaphor for Amora's life. The love scene incorporated all the passion and promise of life that she felt when she married Leo, but the rape scene stole it all. Who was the villain—Leo, who falsely promised a life of bliss, only to abandon her to deal with the vicissitudes of life alone? No, he was simply playing his role. It was Rome. Its lust for dominance—its imperium, glory and blood—they were the culprits. But no, it was more than that, she realized. Life in general is full of disappointment and injustice. Life is full of misery for everyone. Life itself is the enemy and death is the solution.

As she neared her home, she reconsidered and concluded that it was the opposite. Death, not life, that was the archenemy. The uncertainty and shortness of life is what creates greed, tension and injustice. Yet, recalling the villain—who in her mind now represented death—being slaughtered, she realized that death cannot be defeated, for in the end, death conquers all. Killing death just demonstrates that death wins. All is hopeless. And, to make it worse, she realized tonight that she really was all alone. She had no intimate emotional connection with anyone, not her husband, not her friends, no one.

The sun had already set when Amora returned from the theatre. She found Leo sitting in the peristyle garden staring at the fountain, his back to the atrium where Amora stood, yet there was still enough of the afterglow for her to discern his distress. She did not immediately intrude on his vigil, choosing instead to grant him space and privacy as he wrestled with his heartbreak. She watched as the darkness of night enveloped them. She reconsidered her recent conclusion and realized that Leo shared her world of gloom.

Leo raised his hand and wiped tears from his eyes, then dropped his head in despair. Only then did Amora walk over to her husband, sit down next to him, and place her head on his shoulder. Leo immediately stiffened. Amora placed her arm around his shoulder and began to gently stroke his hair, but Leo pulled away.

"Leo, we both miss her. We need each other right now."

"I don't know what you are talking about."

"Please don't be so distant."

Leo stood up. "Am I some woman who bows to emotion? I am fine!" he exploded as he turned his back and stomped away.

Completely alone and deserted, Amora ran stumbling to

her room, her eyes welling with tears. She glanced over at her makeup table and noticed Natalie's brush. She picked it up and held the brush closely to her breast as tears streamed down her cheeks. All joy in life had evaporated, leaving only memories that Amora desperately refused to release. She grasped the brush, a token of happier times and a link to the fantasy that was no more.

The next morning, Leo announced that he would soon be leaving for an extended stay in Egypt to take care of business. Amora realized the half-truth in Leo's declaration. He was really running away from his sorrow, leaving Amora alone to assume his duties at home. She was agitated and ready to confront Leo on his disingenuous excuse, but paused and considered that it may actually be better for them to have some time apart. So, she kept her emotions in check and said nothing. She resolved to add this new burden onto her existing pile and just deal with it like all the rest of her challenges, one day at a time.

Chapter 12

Life's Revolving Door

Camilla and Maria were the most devoted and faithful slaves Amora had ever owned. Over the years Amora observed Camilla and Maria's close mother-daughter relationship with mixed emotion. On one hand, it reminded her of the relationship she longed for, but would never have. On the other hand, participating in their lives served as a balm to soothe the ache of her loss. In a curious sort of way, through them Amora vicariously lived the life she had lost.

A few years later, thirteen-year-old Maria frantically woke Amora. "Please come! Something is wrong with Mama! Oh, please help!"

"What? What's wrong?"

"She can't move. Oh, please come. Please help us!"

Rising from her bed, Amora asked, "What happened?"

"I don't know. She just can't move, and I can't understand her. Please hurry, my lady!"

Amora rushed to the slaves' quarters and found them gathered around the suffering woman's bed, some kneeling next to her while others looked on, aghast.

Cato stood up as Amora approached. "We found her on the floor by her bed, unable to stand. She tries to speak, but it is garbled. She has some movement in one of her arms and hand, but the other is completely limp."

Amora knelt next to her beloved and faithful servant,

looked into her eyes, and grabbed the one partially functioning hand. Maria stood over them anxiously hoping for a miracle. Camilla stared up at Amora with a look that pleaded for assistance more effectively than any words could invoke. She then glanced at Maria and squeezed Amora's hand before looking back at Amora, entreating her assistance with eyes that closed and sealed her petition as she took her last breath.

Maria threw herself down next to her beloved mother and wailed. Amora gently placed her arms around the girl's shoulders and held her close as Maria buried her head on Amora's bosom and sobbed. The helplessness of the grieving child in Amora's arms and the last pleading gaze of her mother stirred Amora's maternal instincts. Amora realized that this desperate mother had defied death in order to confer upon the one person she trusted, Amora, a mother's love for her offspring. Amora reflected on her musings after her excursion to the theatre and realized that, to some extent, death could not conquer a mother's love, and it lived inside her.

Even though it was never explicit, from that moment forward Amora assumed the role of Maria's surrogate mother. She realized, however, that Maria was also helping to fill the hole in her heart created by Natalie's death. Yet they maintained the charade that their relationship was nothing more than that of mistress and personal attendant.

Leo did not even notice their special relationship when he returned from his long escape to Egypt. Leo's natural tendency to bury unpleasant feelings fit nicely into the Stoic ideal of living a life of reason without passion. They taught that the superior rational mind needed to subdue the corrupting influence of emotions that moved people to do things that they would later regret. It was very convenient that Roman culture provided Leo with this ready excuse to stifle any feeling of love and tenderness in order to avoid further hurt and disappointment.

Amora on the other hand could not escape the painful reminders of the loss of her cherished Natalie, even though she hid her grief well. Death was an ever-present reality for all of the residents of Rome from the moment of their birth. The sieve of mortality randomly filtered out ten percent of the infants at birth, and, within ten years, half of the children who were fortunate enough to survive joined them. Mothers fared no better than their infants during childbirth. The stench of death, rot and decay were as inescapable as the cries of pain and the groans of grief that one encountered throughout Rome. One could be in good health on Friday and dead by Wednesday. And, so it was with Cato. An insignificant cut became infected and he was ushered to the underworld in a matter of days.

* * *

Maria was standing next to Amora in the atrium when Leo returned from the slave market with his new purchase. Maria was immediately struck by the commanding presence of this handsome, young dark-haired man who appeared to be in his early twenties. He stood erect, his broad shoulders and trim physique projecting his exceptional strength. He was of medium height, but his bearing exuded an air of authority that was unusual for a slave. Maria was captivated by the confidence radiating from him even more than his physical features. He appeared comfortable in his new environment. He was alert, keenly yet unobtrusively observing all of his surroundings, processing all of it instantaneously. Maria stared at this gorgeous specimen of a man as Leo spoke.

"Amora, this is Antonio. He is to be our new steward, but if we are not satisfied, I can return him within six months for a full refund. So, keep your eye on him and let me know of any deficiencies."

"I am sure he will work out just fine, Leo."

"I hope so. He cost me a fortune. He comes from Hispania and is educated. He knows numbers and speaks and reads Greek and Latin in addition to his native tongue."

"That will be very useful," Amora observed.

"The broker claims he has leadership qualities that will be useful in managing the other slaves. I hope he won't disappoint me."

Maria had not escaped Antonio's eye. He was enthralled by her natural beauty, the long brown hair framing her pretty face, her innocent happy disposition that seemed to make the room glow. Unable to resist any longer, he glanced over at Maria, smiled, and winked. Realizing that she had been gawking at him, she quickly looked away and blushed, but glanced back to exchange a coy grin.

Leo continued, "Amora, have your assistant help him get settled in and show him around." Then, directing himself to Antonio, "I will see you back here at mid-day."

"I will be here, Sir," Antonio responded, confidently.

Maria stood, frozen, looking at the ground while her heart pounded and her mind raced, "What should I say? How do I look? My hair is a mess. I wish I wore my other tunic. This one is so old and ugly. I hope he doesn't ask me questions."

Amora interrupted her rushing train of thought. "You heard him, now go show Antonio around," she said as she gave Maria a gentle pat on the shoulder.

Maria exited the atrium without looking up, followed by Antonio.

"What's your name?" Antonio asked.

Maria's mind was still racing so fast that it didn't have time to slow down and answer. "I looked like a klutz when I walked down that step," she thought. "Should I stop and answer him? What if he asks more questions? Just keep walking. Now he must think I am dumb, or worse, an imbecile. He is watching me. I really wish I had worn my other tunic today."

She reached the slave quarters without saying a word, and pointed to Cato's empty bed. As soon as Antonio walked past her to his new bed, Maria quickly brushed her hair with her hands and straightened her clothes. Antonio soon returned. Without looking up, Maria muttered in a nearly inaudible voice, "Maria."

Antonio extending his hand replied, "It is a pleasure to meet you, Maria."

Maria glanced up and saw Antonio beaming down at her. She smiled and said, "Hello," as she shook his hand.

Chapter 13

Shifting Winds

Time does not heal all wounds. Rather, it carries individuals along their trajectory in life until some force acts to change that destiny. Unbeknownst to Leo and Amora, forces were at work that would impact the course of their lives.

Marcus Aurelius sat alone in his study pondering the events of the past week. Emperor Antoninus Pius had died. For years he'd known this day would come, but now there was no escaping it. He rested his downturned head in his hands as a slave entered the room.

"Senators Quintus Marcellus and Gaius Maximus are here to see you, Sir."

Without so much as a nod, he replied, "Let them enter."

Marcus sat motionless when the two senators entered the room. Quintus boldly proclaimed, "Caesar, the Senate has confirmed your appointment as emperor."

Marcus glanced up at his visitors from his seat, and sighed, "I have not sought this position of power. As you well know, I would much prefer the simple life of a philosopher. But I see that this is my fate and duty." He rose to his feet. "Hence, let it be. Whatever your duty, perform it well. I do not trust Sextus as chief-of-staff. Please inform the Senate that I would like to replace him with Titus Clemens. Also arrange for double the usual bonus for the *Praetorian guard*, and I will address them shortly."

"Certainly, Caesar," Quintus replied.

* * *

The next morning Amora stood in front of a large mirror in her spacious bedroom admiring the simple yet elegant white gown she wore. Elaborate *Numidian* ivory and Syrian cedar furnishings adorned her room. Deep-green marble from Thebes along with the bright-red marble from Sparta complemented the splendid local white marble throughout the room. An exquisite makeup table sat next to the mirror, and Amora's parrot was perched in its cage next to a large open window that let in the fresh cool morning air. Maria watched her mistress admiringly as Amora styled her clothes and hair.

Amora reached over to the makeup table and picked up the brush she had treasured since her daughter's death. Following an oft-repeated ritual, she closed her eyes and held it to her breast before handing it to Maria who proceeded to brush Amora's long brown hair. Primping completed, Amora examined her image in the mirror from various positions. Both women concurred that Amora's robe was much more flattering than the traditional loose-fitting stolas and *pallae* worn at formal social affairs. Elated, Amora exited the room to model her newfound treasure for her husband.

She found Leo and Antonio walking past the fountain in the atrium. Eleven-year-old Esteban limped as he played with his monkey in the adjoining peristyle.

"Has the extra wine arrived yet?" Leo asked Antonio.

"Yes, sir, it came in early this morning."

"Good. When are the musicians and dancers supposed to arrive?"

"They are already here, sir."

Leo stopped and looked directly at Antonio. "It's not every day we get to celebrate a friend becoming the emperor."

"Understood, sir. I have made all of the arrangements."

"This party is important. With Marcus on the throne, I will have many more opportunities. So, don't disappoint me."

As Antonio reassured Leo, Amora crossed the atrium wearing the stylish and elegant white gown, with her long hair flowing behind her.

Leo glanced at Amora. "What is that you're wearing?"

"The new robe designed by Luciano that I purchased last week for this occasion." Amora spun around, showing the elegance of the robe.

"What a waste of money. Go put on something more appropriate."

"I believe that this robe is perfectly suitable."

"Well, I don't!" Leo bellowed. "Now go and change."

Esteban stopped playing and looked at his parents with trepidation and held his monkey tightly against his chest.

"Well, I like it!"

"You are a reflection on me, and that is all that matters," Leo declared.

"But it's beautiful and unique."

Leo grabbed the robe pulling Amora towards him, ripping its trim in the process. Amora screamed, broke free and rushed back to her bedroom.

"And wear your hair up!"

Amora growled.

Maria was picking up clothing and accessories when Amora stormed into the room and slammed the door. Amora glared at her parrot in its cage by the window. After a moment, she marched to the cage, opened it, and let her long-time feathered companion fly free through the open window as she watched longingly.

Below the bird, a long procession wended its way through

cheering crowds lining the streets and filling the plazas of Rome. Soldiers, followed by ragged prisoners in chains, marched past the cheering spectators. Gladiators rode in wagons and waved their swords and shields to their adoring fans. Caged wild animals followed, capturing the interest of young and old alike.

A plaza near the Colosseum was full of vendors hawking their wares to the crowd. Among them was a poor family selling fruit. The father, in his late thirties, had a pleasant demeanor and compassionate eyes. He was accompanied by his wife and strapping eighteen-year-old son. The grandmother, also dressed in rags, likewise had eyes that illuminated her wrinkled face. She moved among the crowd offering apples to potential buyers from the bag she carried.

"Apples! Only two *semis*! Apples!"

Quintus, accompanied by Crescens, walked through the crowd and grabbed a couple of apples from the old woman's bag. Tossing one to Crescens, he took a bite out of the other as they continued on their way. The haggard woman doggedly pursued them while her son intently watched from a distance.

"Please, sir. You must pay for the apples," the old woman insisted.

Quintus turned around and confronted her. "How dare you harass us!"

"But, sir, I need that money."

Quintus slapped the old woman, knocking her down.

"Learn your place!"

Her son jumped into action and called out to Quintus as he ran toward him. "Sir!"

The man stopped between Quintus and the old woman on the ground, followed by his wife and son. The crowd in the immediate vicinity turned to watch the commotion.

"Do your gods teach you to steal?" the man demanded.

"Who do you think you are?" Quintus inquired.

"Someone who knows that God does not condone stealing, regardless of your class."

"You must be a Christian," Crescens said with a sneer.

"As you say."

"Maybe the whip will teach you respect," Quintus said. He grabbed a flagellum from a nearby wagon. The man's athletic son stepped up next to his father and stared at Quintus, who hesitated as soldiers rushed to the uproar.

Noting the arrival of the officials, Quintus ordered the soldiers, "Arrest these Christians. They are creating a disturbance to mar the celebration of our new emperor!"

The soldiers grabbed the Christian family and dragged them away as they protested in vain.

"He stole our fruit!"

"We're innocent!"

"I say, we're innocent!"

* * *

Marcus Aurelius stood next to Titus facing the open double doors that led to the balcony high above Rome when the butler announced, "Your honor, Junius Rusticus, Prefect of Rome, and the philosopher Crescens are here to see you. Shall I tell them that you are occupied?"

"No, please show them in," Marcus replied as he and Titus turned to address their guests.

Rusticus was the first to speak as he and Crescens entered the room.

"Your Highness."

Marcus responded, "Rusticus, Crescens, I would like to introduce you to my new chief of staff."

"Congratulations, Titus," Rusticus replied and shook Titus's hand.

"What can I do for you, gentlemen?" Marcus inquired.

"There is a group of people undermining your imperial sovereign position, sir," Crescens blurted out.

Marcus furrowed his brow in concern and glanced at Rusticus, who supplemented Crescens's proclamation. "We have arrested some Christians who disrupted your procession, and others who refused to participate in the public sacrifice honoring your divinity, Caesar."

"Christians are strange," Marcus mused.

"They are a growing subversive cult," Crescens added.

Marcus glanced inquisitively at Crescens.

Rusticus quickly interjected, "Their teaching regarding social equality undermines our civil society."

"How to contend with Christians has been an issue the empire has struggled with for many years," observed Marcus.

"Yes, Caesar," Rusticus said.

"As a new emperor, I do not believe now is a good time to make any dramatic changes in policy. For decades we have treated the Christian question as a local matter. So, Prefect, you have authority to deal with your prisoners as you deem appropriate."

Chapter 14

Trapped

Rome's elite gorged on sumptuous cuisine while they conversed and enjoyed the entertainment at Leo's party honoring the new emperor. Quintus, Rusticus, Gaius, and three other senators reclined with Leo on the couches around the head table in the triclinium, while the other guests relaxed at tables underneath the porticos surrounding the peristyle courtyard. Amora, with her hair up and clothed in a gaudy chartreuse stola and palla, enhanced by an elaborate *instita and limbus*, entertained several of Rome's privileged women at her table that was situated across the courtyard from the triclinium.

The crowd had become quite boisterous as the alcohol flowed and the evening progressed. Even so, Amora was surprised when Leo yelled to her from across the courtyard. "Amora, come over here."

Annoyed, Amora, looked at Leo and motioned with her head that she was busy dealing with her guests.

"I don't care. I need you over here," Leo ordered loudly.

Amora's countenance reflected her displeasure.

"Well, it looks like the master of the house can't do anything without his wife," Amora told the women at her table, as they all chuckled. "Please excuse me."

"Go rescue the helpless soul," Loretta said. The women laughed, all recognizing the foolishness of masculine pride, though suffering from its dominion. Amora strode over to Leo's table while Maria poured drinks for his conversing guests.

"Spin around so we can see what you are wearing," Leo commanded.

Amora's gut wrenched in disgust, yet she constrained her visceral emotions. Maria looked up at Amora tentatively. Antonio, attending the guests at the adjacent table, likewise observed the exchange between Leo and Amora. Maria and Antonio glanced at each other and Antonio discreetly rolled his eyes. Maria nodded slightly in response as they communicated in the silent language of friends.

"Go ahead. We want to see your stola," Leo ordered.

Amora mechanically turned around, all the while winding the spring of anger within her tighter and tighter. Leo waved his hand and dispassionately dismissed her.

"That's all."

"Oh, that's all?" Amora rejoined, knowing full well that this was not going to be the end of the exchange.

She had started to march back to her table when she overheard Leo say to his guests, "Without me Amora wouldn't know what to wear."

Amora stopped in her tracks, turned and glared at Leo, who was again drinking with his companions, oblivious to Amora's reaction. She felt her hands begin to clench, and this time she refused to restrain the reflex. Amora could not stand it any longer. Her heart pounded. She was about to explode. She had made progress in rebuilding her life after Natalie's death, but since Leo had returned from Egypt, he made it impossible. She had perfectly played the role of dutiful wife for what seemed like an eternity. Yet year after year, dinner party after dinner party, she felt her life slipping away, suffocating under layer upon layer of disappointment and confinement. The light of her life was fading, and she knew that soon it would be snuffed out. Life was not supposed to be like this. She had done her part. Her misery was Leo's fault. She was sure of it. He was the one smothering her. He was the source of her pain and loneliness, and she despised him for it. Something had to change, but now was not the time.

Later that night Leo and Amora bid farewell to their last guests to leave as Antonio shut the door. The click of the locked door was the trigger that unleashed Amora's fury.

"Leo. Do not ever embarrass me like that again!"

"Oh, don't get so excited, woman. I just wanted our guests to admire you."

Leo started to walk away, but Amora marched right after him.

"You liar! I'm sick and tired of you treating me like just one more piece of your worthless chattel."

"Oh, be quiet, woman."

"That's all! That's all! You're exactly right! That's all I am to you. That's all you see, you blind, ignorant, pompous ass!"

Leo stopped and faced Amora. Several servants scurried out of the room, leaving Antonio and Maria with their masters.

"You're drunk," Leo observed.

"I am perfectly sober."

"Then remember your place, and do what I say."

"You're just a scared little boy, afraid of what will happen if you don't control everything."

Leo moved closer to Amora as she also stepped forward. "Why, you ungrateful little slut. I've taken care of you for over seventeen years."

"No, you stole the best years of my life."

Nose to nose, they continued.

"I am the same person you married. You are the one who has changed," Leo insisted.

"I was only sixteen. You knew I'd grow up to become a woman instead of that child you married."

Leo stepped back and pointed his finger at Amora. "You admit it. You've changed. You've turned into a critical old bitch."

Amora roared, "You treat me like a dog, so no wonder I bite."

"You're lucky you don't have four legs, or I would have dispatched such an ill-tempered companion a long time ago."

"Not even a dog would put up with your abuse."

Leo threw both of his hands in the air. "It is impossible to please you," he said as he turned and staggered away.

"That's fine. Run away and hide in your lair, you impotent counterfeit of a man."

Maria glanced over at Antonio with concern.

Amora looked around at the vestiges of the elaborate party and shook her head. Dirty plates and platters with half-eaten food covered the tables, and scraps were strewn all over the floor. She shook her head and defiantly pulled a horribly gaudy hairpiece from her hair allowing it to flow down to its natural style. Amora stared at the ornate hairpiece with its many feathers and gemstones. She slowly turned to the sideboard on which a partially consumed goose remained. In silent rage, she defiantly plunged the hairpiece into the carcass and stomped out of the room.

Chapter 15

The Martyrs

The crowd roared. A fallen fair-skinned gladiator quickly rolled to his side as a glistening blade flew past his head and struck the ground where he had been. He tried to get to his feet, but his dark-haired opponent pressed him to the ground with an unrelenting foray from his short sword that the fallen combatant barely deflected with skills he had honed through years of combat. The crowd rose, not wanting to miss the fatal blow to end the contest. The muscular contestant towered over his foe as he moved in for the kill. Unable to repel the barrage any longer, the seasoned warrior resorted to a desperate move. He grabbed his opponent's foot with his two legs in a scissor-hold as he stepped forward, his momentum propelling him to the ground.

Both gladiators scrambled to their feet and resumed the fight. The powerful dark-haired gladiator relentlessly assailed his opponent, pushing him towards the wall while he endeavored to maneuver out of danger. Then, with a sudden twist of his sword, the retreating contestant spun around and disarmed his aggressive foe, who collapsed backwards to the ground. The victorious gladiator stood over his disarmed opponent, who rose to his hands and knees, looked up at his victor and sneered. The crowd went wild when the defeated gladiator defiantly extended his neck to meet his antagonist's sword.

"That was amazing," Martin said. "Thank you for inviting us."

"Of course. I wouldn't think of celebrating without you," Titus replied as he slapped his cousin's knee.

"I have never had such a great seat before," Justin said as the victor jogged past him holding his vanquished foe's head high in the air for the cheering crowd to see while he took a victory lap around the arena. Across the field the *libitinarii*, entered the arena to remove the corpse laying on the ground close to their seats. The libitinarii's job was less dramatic than usual, as there was no doubt that the contestant was dead, yet they tried to enliven the spectacle regardless. One of the men dressed in a winged hat and winged sandals representing Hermes, a god who helped escort the souls of the dead across the vast waters of the Styx to Hades, waved his red-hot poker in the air as he pranced toward the lifeless body. He was followed by a man dressed as a bird of prey wearing a mask with a large yellow beak and carrying a large wood mallet that he spun around as he leaped and hopped towards the remains. Charon was a birdlike god who also escorted the deceased to Hades, and his job in the arena was to finish the job not completed by a gladiator so that the soul could proceed on its journey.

Hermes stood next to the corpse, slowly stooped down and hesitantly poked it. He jumped back as if he were startled and looked up to his audience, drawing laughter from the crowd. He then turned back to the lifeless form on the sand and poked different areas of the body as he circled the corpse, to the amusement of the laughing horde. Charon kneeled next to the dead gladiator and raised his hammer high above his head and smashed it down where the head had been. He acted astonished and pretended to look for the missing head on the ground as the crowd roared with laughter. The two clowns then took hold of the lifeless arms and dragged the body from the arena, stopping occasionally to bow to the spectators while they applauded with approval.

"I think the next fight is the top seed," Martin said excitedly.

"I'm willing to wager that the champion from Philippi will best the Ethiopian," Rusticus announced.

Crescens eyed the well-built Ethiopian as the two contestants entered the arena. His oiled dark skin shone in the sun. He was a retiarius carrying his net and trident, with a gladius strapped to his waist. "How much are you willing to gamble?"

"Twenty *denarii*," replied Rusticus.

"Make it thirty, and you have a bet."

"Agreed. Prepare to lose your money."

"We shall see."

The crowd cheered as the gladiators began their contest of strength and skill. The retiarius dropped his net as he used his trident and sword while the champion deflected the trident blows with his shield and matched swords with his opponent. At first the contestants seemed to be sizing each other up as they wielded their weapons. The Ethiopian gladiator used his superior strength to advance with rapid, heavy blows and jabs from his trident that the Philippian champion expertly deflected as he was forced to retreat under the barrage.

Then the Philippian quickly stepped to one side and swung at the Ethiopian, who defended the attack with his trident. The agile champion advanced with quick strikes that the Ethiopian strained to deflect in time. The brawny Ethiopian made a dramatic thrust of his trident at his opponent, which the experienced champion was able to deflect, putting the darker-skinned aggressor at a disadvantage as he stumbled to the side.

"Get ready to pay up," Rusticus said.

"Don't count your winnings yet," Crescens replied.

The Ethiopian recovered but was now fighting a more confident opponent vigorously pursuing his rival. The black contestant held off the blows from the Philippian, and then made the same aggressive move that previously had put him at a disadvantage. His opponent countered with his previous maneuver as well. However, this time the Ethiopian was waiting for this reaction and countered by spinning inward toward his opponent. The Philippian, not expecting this move, swung his sword wildly and missed his mark.

The Philippian gladiator stumbled backward to avoid the close proximity to his advancing foe, seeking more room to use his sword. Now the champion was at a disadvantage, and he realized he had been lulled into a false sense of security, which the challenger had manipulated to his advantage. Terror filled the Philippian's face when his foe caught his sword in his trident and disarmed him.

Rusticus threw down his drink and jumped up. "You idiot!"

The crowd jeered and booed when the Philippian bolted in panic. Rusticus flopped into his seat. "What a coward."

The Ethiopian grabbed his net and pursued his foe until the vanquished champion was cornered and tangled in the net close to where Justin and his companions were seated. Cowering, he met his doom at the point of the victor's trident. The crowd erupted into cheers.

"Well, look who has to pay up," Crescens smirked as he held out his hand.

Rusticus took some coins out of his bag and thrusted them into Crescens's hand. "Stop your gloating," he grumbled.

The victorious gladiator strutted around the arena while the libitinarii removed the body.

"Did you see the terror in his eyes?" Martin exclaimed.

"Wasn't that great?" Titus asked.

"I must say, that was impressive," Quintus said. "I have never seen a champion behave like such a coward."

"Even lions flee from hunters. Survival is our most basic instinct," Justin observed. "It is only natural to express fear when faced with certain death."

Martin patted his companion on the back and jovially said, "Leave the philosophy in your classroom, Justin. Relax. Enjoy the entertainment!"

"What's next?" asked Crescens.

"I think it is the lions," Martin answered.

"This will be boring," Quintus complained.

"Really? I would think it'd be quite entertaining," Martin said.

"It can be," Quintus replied, "but sometimes the criminals are Christians, and they just stand there and do nothing."

Soldiers escorted four individuals into the arena. Justin observed their composure as they walked toward him, unruffled by the heckling crowd. The man who led the way appeared to be ten years younger than Justin's fifty years, followed by a woman near the same age, an old woman and a young man in his late teens. Intrigued, Justin sat forward and intently observed these individuals as the soldiers released them. The condemned prisoners did not bolt but serenely looked into one another's eyes, slightly smiled, and nodded as the soldiers withdrew. The man hugged the younger woman, who Justin surmised to be his wife, while the older woman hugged the young man, who appeared to be her grandson. The old woman held her grandson's hands, looked up to heaven and began to sing. The man and woman calmly knelt in front of Justin and prayed.

"Dear God, please forgive them, for they know not what

they do," the woman implored.

Three lions were released and began to stalk their prey. While the rest of the spectators stood up, Justin remained frozen in his front-row seat, astonished that these victims showed no increased level of anxiety. He raised his hand to his chin and listened in amazement as the man in the arena prayed, "Father, into thy hands we commend our spirits."

At that point the man turned and looked directly into Justin's eyes. He smiled serenely and nodded. Justin felt the man's gaze pierce through his whole being and burn an indelible image on his soul. At that very moment, a lion attacked, mauling the man to death, the same fate shared by each, who, astonishingly, made no effort to escape.

Shaken, Justin jerked around to face his hosts. "Who are these people?"

"Christians," Crescens sneered. "They're a superstitious cult."

"Amazing," Justin said. "They've conquered man's most basic instinct."

"What are you talking about?" Martin inquired, somewhat embarrassed by his friend.

Justin motioned to the arena and asked, "Didn't you see that? All of them faced death with peaceful resolve."

"I told you it would be boring," said Quintus.

Justin leaned toward Quintus, shook his hands in the air, and exclaimed, "No! No! I have never heard of people who actually accept death with such serenity."

"I thought that previous gladiator showed tremendous courage," Quintus said.

Justin, pointing to the arena, said, "His bravado merely mimics the courage of those Christians."

"You view this as a great accomplishment?" Martin inquired as he glared at Justin, trying to calm him down.

"Yes!" Justin declared unrestrained, again gesturing with his hands to emphasize his point. "This is the greatest achievement man can realize."

"Dying?" retorted Martin.

Astonished, Justin wondered aloud, "Where did they find the power to conquer their fear? They must be students of some great school."

"No. Most are uneducated, and some are even slaves," Crescens said.

Dumbfounded, Justin stared at the arena, slightly shook his head and muttered, "This is unbelievable. How did they conquer their fear?"

Chapter 16

The Lady in the Mirror

It was a bad day from the start. Esteban had gone out front to play with his monkey. Amora was glad that Leo had brought this pet for Esteban back from Egypt. Not only did it provide Esteban with companionship at home, but it also served as the means for her child to connect with other children in the neighborhood, who previously had excluded and even harassed him for his disability. She was pleased that today Esteban had wanted to venture out of the comfort and security of their home to look for his newfound playmates. Oh, how she wanted her son to have friends and enjoy a normal childhood.

Maria looked out a window to check on Esteban and noticed him standing in the middle of the cobblestone street surrounded by six older boys. One of the boys grabbed the monkey and held it out in front of Esteban, taunting him.

"Give him back!"

"It's right here. Come and get it."

Esteban reached for his pet, but the bully stepped back out of his reach.

"Yeah, go get it," one of the boys shouted.

Esteban limped after the kidnapper, who mockingly sprinted out of reach whenever Esteban approached.

"What's the matter, don't you want it?" another boy chimed in as he mockingly limped behind Esteban.

"Yeah, I'll just keep it if you don't want it," the first boy taunted.

"Please give him back," Esteban pleaded.

The bullies were laughing and pointing fingers at Esteban when Maria came running out of the house toward the boys. "Leave him alone!" Maria screamed as she ran to Esteban with Amora right behind her.

The larger boy dropped the monkey, which scampered over to Esteban and jumped into his arms as his tormentors scattered.

It wasn't long before Amora was in Leo's study, demanding that he console their son. Amora was tired of Leo's disinterest in their son and knew that Esteban needed to feel his father's influence and support, especially now that he was approaching adolescence and Leo had returned from such a long absence during Esteban's childhood. She was irritated that upon hearing the news of his son's persecution, Leo just sat there reading his papers, without even looking up, hardly saying a word. "How can you be so cold and detached?" she said. "He needs you. He's your son!"

"And that is precisely why he will be just fine in spite of that lame leg he inherited from you."

"Leo."

"The power is within him to overcome this challenge. If we coddle him, he will grow up to be weak."

"I'm not talking about coddling him. I just think he needs to know that his father cares."

"We won't always be around to rescue him. He needs to learn to stand on his own."

Maria, standing behind Amora, hugged the back wall and quietly slipped out of the room.

"You may very well be right, but it's still not helpful," Amora replied. "He still needs our support while he's growing."

"You don't make any sense, woman. I'm done discussing it." Amora sighed angrily. Too many of their conversations ended this way.

That night Amora sat alone and dejected in her cold study, accompanied only by her bottle of wine. Glass in hand, she mused over the events of the day, which seemed to encapsulate her whole life. Her best efforts to nurture and protect her children had proved worthless. Natalie was dead, and her son had been terrorized before her own eyes. Her husband couldn't stand to be around her. Yes, sitting here all alone in the dark with this bottle of wine was the sum total of her life, she surmised. She was exhausted, tired of trying day after day, year after year, all to no avail. What was the use? Nothing ever changed. She felt powerless. How could she accomplish anything when her husband blocked all her efforts? He wouldn't even talk with her. She sighed, hopeless. Numb, she dropped her head into her hands.

Maria did not notice Amora when she first entered the dark room. Amora hardly had the energy to look up. Maria stopped in her tracks when she saw her mistress.

"Oh, I'm sorry. I will come back later."

"No. Please stay."

Maria walked over to Amora.

"Today's her birthday, you know?" Amora sighed.

"Natalie?"

"She would be sixteen if she had survived."

Maria tenderly put her hand on Amora's shoulder. Amora looked up at her and said, "I picture her as pretty as you."

"I'm sure she would be as beautiful as her mother."

"It's probably for the best. Avoid all this misery," Amora muttered as she dropped her head into her hands again.

"It will all look better in the morning," Maria assured her.

Amora glanced back at Maria morosely. "No. I'm all alone. No one really cares," she said and looked away.

"You have lots of friends."

Amora shook her head. "No, not really. If I was gone, they wouldn't miss me at all."

"I would," Maria declared.

Oblivious, Amora continued, "I really can't blame them. What good am I anyway?"

"Please don't talk like that. The wine has clouded your mind."

"No. I'm all alone and worthless."

"My lady, you just need your rest."

Maria helped Amora stand and accompanied her to the door of her bedchamber. Amora glanced in the mirror. "Who am I? I don't even recognize this person I've become."

"You are a talented, amazing and caring woman," Maria insisted. "Shall I help you get ready for bed?"

"No. I will manage."

Maria watched Amora with concern before exiting reluctantly. Amora looked at her makeup table, staggered over to it, picked up the old brush, and held it to her breast as tears streamed down her cheeks. Even though she had performed this ritual for many years, tonight her loss felt particularly acute. Through the tears in her eyes, Amora noticed a pair of scissors among the items on the table. Slowly, Amora laid down the brush and picked up the scissors. She stared at them, transfixed, contemplating her fate. Her focus shifted to glimpse her image in the mirror behind the scissors. She lowered the scissors slightly and gazed at that pathetic reflection, a haggard woman with haunting eyes, far from the beauty she used to be. Amora dropped the scissors, collapsed into her chair, and sobbed.

Chapter 17

Clashing Worlds

It was a typical day as Maria entered the busy plaza carrying a basketful of produce that she had just purchased at the produce market. Amora had asked her to look for some candles while she was out, so she stopped by the plaza to complete her task. She was too absorbed in her errand to at first notice a small group of people gathering around the pottery booth, until Justin jostled her as he rushed past her toward the crowd. Crescens was mocking a teenage Nubian slave girl in the booth, generating laughs from the onlookers.

Justin called out loudly, "Come, now, Crescens. Are you so desperate that you now engage illiterate slaves in debate?"

"Ah, here comes the great philosopher, Justin, who has become a Christian," Crescens said. "It appears that a nightingale has turned into a bat to rescue this little rat."

The crowd cackled as Justin walked directly up to Crescens. "I'm afraid that your ignorance has blinded you to the truth, not me."

"Truth? Like people live after they die?"

"Why should our existence end with death?"

Maria reflected on Amora's grief as she approached and listened intently.

"Whether it should or not is immaterial. It simply does," Crescens declared.

"I thought you were a skeptic who teaches that we can't

really know anything for certain."

"Yes, but some things are so implausible that they are pure fantasy. I don't know anyone who has seen a resurrected being."

"But others have, and their written testimonies remain with us today," Justin asserted as more spectators continued to gather. Maria was surprised to hear that there were written reports from eye witnesses who had seen individuals who were resurrected from the dead.

"So, does our soul ever die?"

"No. The essence of our being, our spirit, is eternal."

Justin stepped over to the next vendor's booth, picked up a glove, and put it on. He wiggled his fingers and proclaimed, "Our spirit is what gives life to our body, just as my hand animates this glove."

He then took off the glove and let it drop while he held it up. Maria pressed forward through the crowd to get even closer to Justin so she could hear him more clearly.

"Death is nothing more than the separation of our spirit from our body," Justin added.

Crescens smiled and declared mockingly to the crowd, "So, according to Christians, at some point our body will jump up out of the grave and wander the earth looking for its lost spirit."

The bystanders burst into laughter and howled as Crescens scurried around as if he were looking for his spirit—under the booth's canopy, under a table—and then grabbed a lady's robe as if he were going to look underneath it before she yanked it away.

"No. Our body does not have life without our spirit," Justin replied. Justin put the glove back on and said, "Resurrection is simply the reuniting of our spirit and body, never to be separated again."

Maria was convinced that Amora needed to hear this message.

"Then how does this work after the body has decomposed? If a dozen moths eat your glove, does your spirit split into a dozen pieces to chase each moth to get a portion of its body back?" Crescens asked as he waved his hands about like fluttering moths.

The crowd chortled and heckled Justin but was silenced by his response.

"I don't see why you think this is so incredible. When you look at a drop of man's seed, there is no indication that it will turn into a human, yet it does. God can likewise take the smallest particle of our dissolved body and regenerate the whole, just as He did when He gave us life in the first place."

"It's unbelievable because we see evidence of conception all around us, but we don't see resurrected beings buying meat at the market," Crescens said as he pointed to the meat vendor.

The boisterous horde nodded. Crescens smirked.

The entertaining dialogue was interrupted when a soldier on horseback galloped into the plaza. The people scurried out of his way, all eyes looked to the young man as he pulled up his horse near the fountain in the plaza's center.

"The Parthians have overrun Armenia! We are at war!"

Chapter 18

Dashed Hope

"Now look at what Festus can do!" Esteban exclaimed excitedly to Amora as she sat under the portico surrounding the manicured gardens. Esteban affectionately grabbed his monkey, Festus, who was crawling on his back and head, and sat the monkey down in front of him. He clapped his hands, and his pet did a backflip, then jumped into Esteban's arms.

"That's wonderful! And you trained him to do that?"

"Yes. I taught him another trick too."

"You did?"

"Let me show you. Festus, pay attention."

Esteban sat the little primate down in front of him again and then made a ring in front of his body with his two arms. Festus jumped through the circle on Esteban's command, then jumped back up to his arms and stood atop the ring for a moment until his master ordered him to fall, at which point the monkey fell backward but caught Esteban's arm with its tail and swung as Amora burst out laughing.

"How did you teach him to do that?"

"Look! He can do another one too!"

Esteban excitedly set the monkey down again and tossed him a ball. Festus caught the ball and threw it back to Esteban. After playing catch for a few throws, Esteban bounced a second ball over to his pet. The monkey threw the first ball to Esteban and caught the second ball.

"That's amazing! You're a remarkable trainer."

Esteban looked glowingly at his mother. "I love you, Mama," he said as he rushed over to give her a big hug.

"I love you too."

Maria interrupted their embrace when she called excitedly from the entrance. "Amora, are you here?"

"Yes, Maria, I am out back."

"Oh good. I want to introduce you to a philosopher."

Esteban, holding his monkey, followed Amora into the atrium and saw Maria standing next to a man.

"This is Justin. He's educated just like you and teaches many fascinating things."

"Welcome to our abode," Amora said as she walked over and greeted him. "I'm Amora."

Justin gently shook Amora's hand with both of his. "It is a pleasure to meet you."

"I'm afraid Maria overstates my academic qualifications," Amora said as she motioned to the seating area in the atrium near the fountain.

"That is nothing to be concerned about. I myself have recently learned that no person is so great that he cannot learn from everyone he meets, and no one is so insignificant that he cannot contribute something to each individual he encounters."

"Spoken like a true gentleman," Amora said while Esteban and Maria watched Amora lead Justin to the concrete benches surrounding the atrium pool. "May we offer you some refreshment?"

"Thank you, but I cannot stay long."

"I'm sorry if she has imposed on your time."

"It is not a problem at all," Justin replied as they sat down. "Maria mentioned that you have lost a daughter, and she hoped I might be of some assistance."

"It is no longer an issue," Amora lied. "That was a long time ago."

"A mother's love never dies," Justin said. "I am sincerely sorry for your loss and hope my message provides some comfort."

Amora tried to hide the sensitive emotions swelling in her breast.

"Amora, I simply want to let you know that your little girl still lives. Her spirit, or soul, did not die but has returned to God, who sent her to you. And you will have an opportunity to not only see her again, but also embrace and hold your sweet child once more."

Amora could hardly control her feelings as tears welled up in her eyes. She turned aside. The consoling touch of Justin's hand on her shoulder burst the dam holding back a flood of tears. Amora rested her head on Justin's shoulder and sobbed uncontrollably while he comforted her. "Go ahead and cry. It is good for the soul."

"I'm so sorry...I only wish it were true," Amora said between sobs.

"I assure you that it is," he declared. She sat up and faced Justin squarely. "God," Justin continued, "the creator of all things, came down to earth to live as a human being, to show us the path to happiness and to break the bonds of death."

"That is a phenomenal message if it is real."

"It is real."

"I don't see how one can be sure."

"I invite you to attend our services this Sunday evening to learn more about it."

"I'm sorry, but I will need time to consider it."

"I understand. But please be assured that you are welcome to attend any time. You can communicate with me through Maria, and I will guide you to our meeting. I must be going, but it has been a real pleasure to speak with you." Justin stood up.

Amora escorted Justin to the door and opened it. "You have given me a lot to think about. Thank you." She then gave him an impulsive hug.

"I hope to see you at our service."

Amora watched Justin depart around the corner before she shut the door, unaware that Leo was stomping toward the house from the opposite direction. Amora stood in a daze, pondering the message she had just heard, as a smile formed on her face.

She glanced over at Maria. "Thank you for introducing me to the philosopher."

Leo burst through the front door and demanded, "Who was that man?"

"That…that was a philosopher. He was sharing a religious message."

"Religion? Bah! So, you entertain men while I am gone?"

He noticed Esteban retreat against the wall and silently slip out of the room while Amora answered. "You are mistaken. Nothing inappropriate happened here."

"What? I saw your embrace."

"It is not what you think."

"Creeping into homes to seduce women while their husbands are away."

"I was simply showing gratitude for his message of hope and life. Maria was here the whole time."

"You will never see that man again. Do you hear me?"

"Don't tell me what to do!"

Leo slapped Amora across the face. She ran from the room, weeping. In her haste she knocked over a vase, shattering it on the floor. Startled, Leo chased after her, but she had already reached her room, slammed the door shut, and locked it. She threw herself on her bed, awash in tears.

Leo banged on the door with his fist. "Open up! Come out here!"

Amora ignored Leo's insistent demands, but he continued to pound on the locked door. Esteban cowered in the shadows of the corridor, terrified, and tried to slip out of sight, but Leo noticed him. Father and son stared at each other for a moment before Leo abruptly turned on his heel and left in a huff. He stormed past Maria, who was cleaning up the broken vase.

"Hurry up," he ordered as he stomped over to a small *amphora* on the shelf and took a long swig directly out of the bottle. For the next several minutes, Leo paced back and forth, amphora in hand, periodically drinking from the flask before he threw it across the room, shattering it against the wall and spewing wine in every direction. Incensed, he stormed out of the house.

Esteban gently knocked on Amora's bedroom door. "Mama? Are you all right?"

Amora opened the door, knelt down, and embraced her child. "Yes, my sweet boy. I'm all right." She held her son close to her breast and stroked his hair. Esteban nervously twirled a lock of Amora's hair with one of his fingers. "Everything will be fine. Don't worry, dear. We will be all right."

Chapter 19

Diverging Paths

Leo witnessed a maddening scene when he entered the war room. The large open window on the back wall filled the expansive room with light. It was a hive of activity, with men coming and going, consulting one another and looking at documents on tables strewn with papyrus scrolls, manuscripts and wax tablets. Marcus stood next to Titus staring down at the map of the area surrounding the Caspian Sea that was unrolled on top of a large table. Another large map of the entire Mediterranean area hung on the wall next to several astronomical charts.

Rome was in shock at losing Armenia to the Parthians. Emperor Trajan had decisively defeated Parthia over forty-five years earlier when Rome conquered this territory. Since then, Rome's Emperors had ruled with an iron fist throughout the empire without any significant difficulty, except for an annoying Jewish revolt thirty years earlier. Now the Roman army had not only been challenged, but defeated in an important strategic location. This crisis early in Marcus Aurelius's administration grabbed his full attention.

Seeing Leo approach, Marcus walked around the table to greet his old friend. "I'm glad you were able to come so promptly."

"I am honored to be summoned by my Emperor."

Marcus tapped the map on the table with his forefinger.

"Leo, I would like you to meet with Lucius Maecianus, governor of Egypt, to arrange sufficient provisions for our forces on the front and to replenish the grain reserves here in Rome that were exhausted after the flood. I also desire Lucius's report on how the eastern provinces are reacting to the war." Marcus handed him a scroll and continued, "I want you to deliver this order recalling him to Rome. He is to return with you as soon as arrangements for the shipments of grain have been secured."

"Yes, Caesar. I'm honored to accept this charge."

* * *

"I hope to be back in about six months," Leo informed Amora. "But it could take a lot longer depending on whether we start back before the winter storms begin."

"We will miss you," Amora said, feigning affection.

Leo ignored Amora. Instead he continued to examine the contents of a travel chest that Antonio had placed on a bench.

"I will pray to the gods for your success and safe return," Amora continued in an effort to elicit further conversation.

Leo grunted.

Amora bristled without saying a word. She wondered how much longer she could maintain this charade of a loving, supportive spouse. She was tired of always being the only one exerting an effort to make this relationship work, she told herself, simply to be rebuffed over and over again. She hated him for it. She was actually glad to see him leave. Maybe he would stay away a long time, she silently hoped. Regardless, it was her duty to play the role of doting wife, so she obliged. Of course, her unspoken true feelings had not escaped Leo's detection.

As Amora leaned forward to kiss Leo goodbye, he turned his cheek. She turned and stormed out of the room, all of her negative feelings confirmed. Leo slammed the chest shut and threw it towards the door behind her.

Chapter 20

The Columna Lactaria

The day was already hot and sticky. Amora had hoped to avoid the uncomfortable humid heat by leaving early, but the bright morning sun was bearing down on the merchants and shoppers, making this excursion to the produce market most unpleasant. Amora tried to ignore the putrid smell of spoiling discarded fruit and vegetables strewn on the ground from the previous day's activity, and began to second-guess her decision to personally select the exotic food for a luncheon she was hosting the next day. Was this detail really so important that it demanded her personal attention, she wondered.

Amora, accompanied by Maria, made her selection hurriedly. Now that her mission was accomplished, Amora wanted out of this disgusting environment as quickly as possible. However, it proved to be no easy task. The market was full of customers meandering from stand to stand, examining the produce and haggling with the vendors, while slaves wended their way through the crowd carrying baskets overflowing with foodstuffs.

As they headed toward the exit near the Temple of Pietas, they approached the Columna Lactaria, a site for hiring wet-nurses and where parents often abandoned newborns in hopes that their infant would be pitied and find nourishment. A real-life drama unfolding at the site caught Amora's attention. A half-dozen nutrices surrounded the column, nonchalantly resting on its base while a young mother holding her infant pleaded for mercy.

"Please take my baby! Please."

The wet-nurses continued to ignore her petitions. Frantic, the mother ran up to a woman walking close by. "Please save my baby!" she implored. The woman turned her head and walked on.

A brothel's procurer sauntered over and closely examined the mother's looks as he walked around her. "I will take it."

The distraught mother recoiled, pressing her infant to her breast. "No! You can't have her!" In a panic, the mother turned around, dropped to her knees in front of the wet-nurses, and offered them the babe in her arms. "Please! Please take my baby!"

"But, ma'am, how can we afford to nurse her every day if we aren't paid?" one of the nutrices replied.

"Please! My husband doesn't want a daughter. Please have mercy!"

"I would like to help, but who will feed my children if I'm not paid?" another wet-nurse asked.

"I can't pay. My husband won't let me bring her home. Please, someone save her."

"I said I'd take her," said the irritated panderer.

The mother held her child more tightly. "No! I will not let her be raised in the brothels."

"Then you are condemning her to die," the procurer charged.

The young mother dropped her head and sobbed, "Please...Please have mercy...Oh gods, please have mercy."

Amora approached the distressed young woman and touched her shoulder. The mother gazed up at Amora. "Your daughter will be fine," Amora assured her. Directing her attention to the last nutrice to speak, Amora asked, "What is your fee to nurse and care for this child?"

"Five semis a day, my lady."

Amora handed the wet-nurse a few coins from her bag. "Here. Come back next week at the same time, and I will pay you again." Amora reached down and tenderly lifted the infant out of her mother's arms and gently handed her to the wet-nurse. She knelt down and put her arm around the distraught young mother. "She will be all right."

The young mother sobbed on Amora's shoulder as Amora compassionately held the heartbroken woman in her arms. When the flood of tears began to subside, the young woman looked into Amora's eyes and thanked her. Amora squeezed the woman's hands, reassuring her as they parted.

Amora and Maria walked home in silence, this poignant scene occupying their thoughts. Maria wondered if this emotional experience had created an opportune time to broach the subject of Justin's invitation to attend their worship service and broke their silence. "The Christian meeting is tomorrow night. Do you want me to ask the philosopher to guide us?"

"No. I'm not interested."

Maria looked at Amora in disbelief as they walked on.

* * *

A group of the most influential women of Rome enjoyed the luncheon Amora hosted at her home. The women relished the juicy tidbits of gossip exchanged at each table as much as the exquisite food. Near the end of the banquet, Amora stood up at the head table and announced the reason for the gathering.

"Sisters of Rome, I have decided to create a home for abandoned foundlings in honor of my daughter, and I solicit your support."

Such an announcement was not to be taken lightly.

Charitable activity was common, even expected of aristocratic women in Rome, but one's choice of which charity to support reflected greatly on one's standing in society. As Loretta had warned Amora, the culture's whole system of patronage demanded that those with means exercise wisdom in selecting those worthy of assistance, which was measured by the honor these clients would bring to their benefactors. Anything less would be a waste, highlighting the donor's foolishness and diminished standing in society. This practice maximized the beneficial distribution of resources throughout the empire.

The guests exchanged glances, trying to read one another's thoughts in order to gauge their own reactions to Amora's grand declaration. Loretta broke the silence. "Would this home be just for patricians?"

"No, it would be open for every mother who cannot keep her child."

"Even slaves and plebeians?" Julia asked incredulously.

"I doubt they love their infants any less than we do."

"But what honor will plebs bring us?" scoffed Loretta.

"I feel that there is a sisterhood between all mothers."

"No slave or pleb is my sister," Loretta insisted to the general agreement of the guests.

"But, Loretta, hundreds of infants are abandoned every year, and most of them are females."

"There are nutrices to suckle infants at the Columna Lactaria," maintained Julia.

"Yes, but most of the babies die."

"Then let the brothels raise them," Loretta proclaimed.

* * *

Amora sat in her peristyle garden reflecting on her unsuccessful luncheon. At first, she felt dejected. This experience accentuated how forlorn she had felt for years.

Yet underneath all this despair was a seed of hope reawakening sensations that Amora had long forgotten. Despite the rejection by her friends, Amora felt an awakening sense of optimism and purpose, a new spark for life.

The next morning Amora awoke happy with a zest for life, something she could not remember feeling since Natalie's abduction. Sure, there were days when she felt good and appreciated the beauty of nature surrounding her, but this was different. She actually felt a level of excitement that roused her senses and energized her soul with eager anticipation as she greeted the new day. She committed to move forward with her charity in memory of her daughter without the assistance of her peers.

How refreshing, she thought, to rediscover her independent nature. It was actually quite liberating, she mused, to realize that she was not fully constrained by the shackles of society's protocols. The power was within her, not others, to realize her dreams. She was amazed at how bright life now seemed once she changed her perspective and looked outside herself. She felt a renewed determination to press forward with her endeavor to save the lives of abandoned infants, regardless of what her socially confined friends thought.

Chapter 21

A Risky Venture

"Are you all right, Antonio?" Maria asked when she entered the room. She was surprised to see him in a daze, staring out a window. Even her presence did not disrupt his trance. Something certainly was wrong, as Antonio was always attentive to her cares and observant of every detail taking place around him.

Finally turning to look at Maria, Antonio responded, "Yes. I'm fine."

"Surely something is bothering you?"

"Oh, I'll be fine," Antonio insisted. "It is just that my brother leaves today, and I couldn't go see him off."

"Where to?"

"He is heading off to war with other slaves."

"I'm sure Amora won't object to you saying goodbye."

"There is no need to bother her."

Maria started to leave as she impulsively declared, "Well, I'm going to ask Amora to let you go."

Antonio reached out and grabbed her hand. "It's too late. He's already gone." Maria turned and looked up at Antonio.

Antonio looking down at Maria smiled, and said, "Just look at you." Maria grinned adoringly at Antonio. "Your beauty certainly helps a man forget his troubles."

They drew closer together while gazing into each other's eyes. His arm slipped around her. She closed her eyes as their lips brushed, only to be parted by the abrupt appearance of Amora at the door.

Startled and quite a bit flustered, Antonio made his exit the best he could. "Excuse me, my lady. I was just leaving."

"That's quite all right, Antonio." Amora smiled reassuringly.

Antonio, however, was not in any condition to risk further embarrassment and left the room without further delay.

Likewise, befuddled and unsure of what to do, Maria attempted to follow his lead. "I should be going as well."

"Maria, please sit for a moment?"

Amora motioned to a bench nearby and put her other hand on Maria's shoulder to escort her personal attendant to the site for a private interview. Once seated, Maria looked down at her feet, not knowing what to say.

Amora took a deep breath, held Maria's hand reassuringly, and asked, "Dear child. You care for him, don't you?"

Hesitantly Maria said, "Yes."

"Have you been seeing each other often?"

Maria's head snapped up. "Oh no! I would never betray your trust, my lady."

"I was not trying to imply anything improper, Maria. I was just wondering if he also shares your feelings."

"I think so."

"Antonio is a good man, but be sure he cares enough to let you blossom into the woman you are meant to become."

"I think he will, my lady."

"You're probably right."

Amora gazed past Maria as her thoughts drifted off to those blissful days of youthful love with its unrealistic hopes and dreams. How naive she was then, yet there was still something appealing in that bygone era.

Sensing the intimate nature of the dialogue, Maria felt safe enough to broach anew a subject not mentioned for weeks. Maria, mustering her courage, broke the silence. "Amora, why don't we see if the Christians will help with your charity?"

"I've already said I'm not interested."

"I've been talking with a Christian friend in the plaza."

Amora looked directly at Maria. "Maria, I don't want you associating with Christians anymore."

Shocked, Maria collapsed to her knees and pleaded. "Please. Please just meet with them."

"Maria, life is full of disappointments. I don't want you putting too much confidence in those charlatans."

Unbeknownst to them, Loretta and Antonio had come to the doorway and were observing their conversation.

"Didn't you feel something when you talked with the Christian philosopher?" Maria asked.

"No," Amora lied.

"You are as obstinate as Leo."

Amora jerked back in shock. "How can you say that?"

"Pleeease, Amora. Please just consider it."

Loretta marched into the room. "She should be whipped!"

Startled, Amora and Maria turned to see their visitor approach in a fury.

"Be gone," Amora ordered Maria, who promptly left.

"What arrogance," Loretta proclaimed. "This Christian disorder will be the end of all of us if we don't squash it soon."

"Who are they?" Amora inquired.

"They are a superstitious cult that meets at night amongst the graves in the catacombs, where they eat human flesh and drink blood while siblings profess love to each other in incestuous orgies."

* * *

That evening Amora sat alone in the courtyard pondering the events of the day. Despite her denial, she could not escape the thoughts and feelings evoked by Justin's visit. They haunted her every day. As much as she tried to ignore them, they were always there, lurking in the back of her mind, gnawing away at her complacency, enticing her to investigate and discover more. Yet she had to resist this influence. This group was held in disrepute. There must be a reason the authorities had outlawed this religion.

Besides, her social standing would be further jeopardized by even remotely associating with such a disfavored group. Social norms served a purpose. She acknowledged that she had pushed their limits, but who was she to turn centuries of order on its head? Yet, she could not ignore how comforting the idea of holding Natalie again made her feel, and how the Christian philosopher's words haunted her thoughts. She had to know if it was true. But was this just a trap to lure defenseless women into their grasp? Loretta had described some bizarre and horrific practices. One must be cautious.

Amora shook her head, stood, and set out to find Maria. She found her cleaning up the vestiges of the evening meal. Maria glanced at Amora and promptly looked away, downcast.

"Maria, you need to be careful. I've heard that this cult teaches some very strange and evil things."

Maria set the plates on the counter and faced Amora. "It's not like that at all. They talk about all of us being children of God and that we should love each other."

"Just words. I doubt that they really believe that."

"Then maybe we should investigate to find out for sure."

"Don't be so naive, Maria. Humans are selfish and corrupt by nature, and flowery words won't change that."

"But people talk about how their lives have changed. How they used to drink and fight and cheat, and now they don't do those things."

Sarcastically, Amora said, "That would be a sight. A bunch of reformed miscreants sitting around praising God and talking about love."

"Please don't poke fun at them," Maria pleaded. "They really are nice people. They might even be able to help with the foundlings."

Amora was surprised to feel that same warm, calm feeling sweep over her that she had felt during the philosopher's visit. Mystified, she continued to look at Maria in silence.

"Please," Maria again pleaded. "They are not at all like what you hear."

Amora continued to look at Maria intently, trying to sort through her own thoughts and feelings. Despite all the warnings that the Christians were strange and dangerous, she still felt drawn to find out for herself. But it would be very dangerous. A mistake could cost her life or, at a minimum, the remaining standing she held in society. However, her life was miserable regardless, and something had to change. "Perchance this might be what I have been seeking," she speculated to herself. The concept of the immortality of the soul and a physical resurrection had constantly been on her mind. Yes, she must find out the truth regarding this message or her mind would never be at peace.

"All right," Amora said. "I will go, but only to expose their deceit."

Chapter 22

Light in the Catacombs

"The Christians are undermining the war effort with their pacifist ideas," Rusticus contended.

The accusation piqued the interest of his associates at the bath, but Quintus had other worries. "Let Marcus deal with the war. I'm more concerned with their impact on our social order here in Rome," he declared.

"Christian slaves act like they are gods," Crescens said.

"They seem quite harmless to me," Gaius confessed to the consternation of his peers.

"They are traitors," Rusticus insisted.

"We have been saying that for years," Crescens added.

Quintus, being a man of action, had little patience for nonproductive chitchat on urgent matters, chimed in, "Then do something about it."

Rusticus continued, "The plebs think the gods of nature cursed us with the flood and earthquake because these Christians no longer believe in the gods."

"Then blame them for every disaster," Quintus interjected.

Gaius leaned back and crossed his arms as he wondered where this attitude would lead. Did the end always justify the means, or should actions always be based in truth?

Crescens did not leave him much time to ponder these issues before he announced, "I have heard rumblings that the plebs feel Christians are to blame for these new cases of pox."

"The more upset the masses are, the less they will sympathize with this cult," Rusticus argued.

"Then we need to stoke public opinion against them," Quintus said.

* * *

A few days later, three figures moved through the dark evening shadows on the streets of Rome, making their way to the city wall near the aqueduct. They stopped at an intersection and pressed against the building wall as eight soldiers marched by on the cross street. Once past, the group quickly traversed the public thoroughfare and silently disappeared into the darkness.

"We are almost there," Justin whispered to Amora and Maria. "It's just outside the city walls."

Justin held a small oil lamp as he led them down a tight dark tunnel into the catacombs. Dim light fell from the occasional lamp placed in depressions carved into the dark gray walls between the burial vaults. The musty air at times seemed suffocating as they crept along single file. Amora was constantly looking around, wondering what she had gotten herself into. If Loretta found out, she would never let Amora live this down...that is, if she survived the night.

She jumped with a start when seven other parishioners emerged from a side tunnel and joined them. Her heart pounded so loud that Amora feared it would reveal their presence.

"Don't worry," Justin reassured her. "The soldiers won't bother us down here."

Unconvinced, Amora continued to survey her surroundings anxiously.

A faint light in the distance became stronger as their group approached. Soon Justin led the party into a small cavern moderately lit by several lamps and candles. A small congregation sat on the ground and on a few large stones. Amora noticed that a man, a priest of some sort, stood in front of the gathering. She would later learn that he was the bishop of Rome.

"What's the purpose of life?" the bishop inquired rhetorically. Looking at a middle-aged woman seated near the front, he asked, "Do you know?" Pointing to a parishioner at the far side of the room, "How about you?" He directed his attention to a young man sitting near the rear of the congregation close to Maria's friend, Kassinda, from the pottery booth. The bishop questioned, "Maybe existence has no meaning at all."

Kassinda spotted Maria, rushed up, gave her a hug and led her by the hand to where she was sitting. Justin and Amora followed closely. All of Amora's senses were on high alert, her glance bouncing around the room.

"We exist to glorify God, which occurs as we exercise our free will to allow Him to glorify us," the bishop proclaimed.

Amora continued to observe her strange surroundings as she sat down next to Gloria, a Christian woman, and her ten-year-old daughter, Sabina. Shadows created by the light of flickering candles and lamps danced around on the walls and ceiling. A reverent silence filled the cavern as the audience watched the priest in rapt attention, but Amora fidgeted nervously. Gloria smiled serenely at Amora and gently squeezed her hand as the bishop continued.

"As we choose to accept God's grace and follow Him, more love and goodness exists in the eternities, so God is glorified. As we allow the light of Christ to enter our hearts…" The bishop picked up a bright candle and lit another one as he resumed. "We become a conduit of His love to shine as a light for others to see and follow, just as one candle lights another until the whole room is bright."

The bishop set the candle down and motioned to the light throughout the room. "Love is the key," he averred. "Jesus said, 'A new commandment I give unto you, that ye love one another as I have loved you.' So how has Christ loved us? He extended his grace and forgave me, and at the same time he felt the pain that I caused others through my sins and misdeeds. What love! What mercy! What debt of gratitude is mine?"

A tall man on the far side of the room exclaimed, "Amen."

The bishop smiled and nodded to the parishioner, then continued, "In order to become unified with God, we need to follow Jesus's teachings to love our enemies, bless those who curse us, and do good to them who hate us."

By now Amora's anxiety had dissipated. She sat transfixed, focusing on the bishop and his message.

"But," the bishop continued, "we need God's help to raise us up to this higher level of love. We can't do it by ourselves. It is possible only as we open our hearts to let God fill them with His love. I pray that we will always seek God so that we can become conduits of His love to bless both our friends and our enemies. Amen."

Chapter 23

The Mentor

Amora was surprised to see Justin standing in the doorway of her home, and she was even more stunned when he announced, "I have come to offer assistance with your foundling charity."

"You are?" Amora asked.

"I spoke with several Christians to see if they would also help, and most of the nursing mothers are more than willing to do what they can."

"That's wonderful."

"Others said they can provide some of the labor."

"I don't know what to say. Come in."

Amora motioned for Justin to enter and escorted him inside. They walked past the ornate carvings, tapestries, and statues in her vestibulum. Maria shut the door and followed close behind. "Why are you doing this?" Amora queried.

"God is working through you, and I want to help."

"I don't see what God has to do with this."

"After all these years, why do you think you are now interested in forming a charity?" Justin asked as they entered the atrium surrounded by opulence.

"Because it is needed."

"That's not new. No, God's word has taken root in your heart, and it will continue to grow until it bears fruit."

"Like your priest's message?" Amora said.

"What do you mean?"

"I have never heard a message like that before—to love your enemies—and I felt something I can't explain," Amora said as she motioned to Justin to sit on one of the carved stone benches in the atrium.

"Please try to describe the feeling."

Amora sat down on a bench facing Justin. "It was so strange. I felt warm and secure like I was a little girl who had come home."

"You felt like you were embraced in the arms of love?"

"Yes. Yes. That is it."

"What you experienced is God's love caressing your soul. God is not some abstract concept detached from humanity. He is your loving Heavenly Father. He cares for you personally. He wants to bless you, His daughter."

"Strange. I've never heard that before, yet it sounds so familiar."

"It feels familiar because you are a daughter of God. You have a spark of His divinity inside you, and because God is love, you also have an innate need to love and to be loved. This is your inheritance from God."

"So, love is divine."

"Yes, but we all have been disappointed in this life. Some of us have had a harder time than others, but we all have been hurt to some degree. This lack of love creates an emotional void in our soul that longs to be filled."

"We certainly all want more love," Amora said.

"But many people do not realize that the emptiness they feel is caused by a lack of love. So, they go through life trying to fill the void in their life with all sorts of things, but nothing actually satisfies this yearning that haunts them."

"The feeling that something is missing?"

"That's it," Justin said. Sweeping his hand in front of him,

Justin continued, "Look at all your possessions, yet you still feel that something is missing. Material things cannot fill the emotional hole caused by a lack of love."

"All these things are nothing more than props for my cage," Amora bemoaned.

"Are you sure they are not the bars?"

Shocked, Amora jerked back and stared at Justin.

"You can't serve both God and your possessions."

"What do you mean?"

"If your hands are clenched shut trying to hold on to wealth, they are not open to receive the treasures God offers you."

"Are you saying I need to become a pauper?"

"No, just that you must be willing to lose your life in order to find it."

Amora furrowed her brow and leaned her head slightly back. "That is a hard doctrine."

"The gate to spiritual freedom is as narrow as the catacomb tunnels, and few find it. But those who do are born again into a fuller and more abundant life."

"I don't understand."

"The void in your life is God's way of calling you to come home to Him and His love."

"And the child should leave her toys when called by her father?" Amora concluded.

"Exactly. While material things occupy your heart, they block the space for you to feel God's love, so you remain emotionally empty. Only God is great enough to fill the void in your heart and heal your soul."

"What should I do?"

"Consider being baptized."

"What is 'being baptized'?"

"Meet me at midday on Sunday by the South Bridge and

find out. We will be holding a baptismal service, and you can see for yourself what it is all about."

* * *

Rusticus, sat in his marble office overlooking the city as the centurion delivered his report, "My spies have informed me that the Christians plan to hold one of their baptismal services at the south bend of the Tiber on Sunday."

"Very good. I want you to take half of your century and arrest the whole lot of them."

"It will be done, sir."

Chapter 24

The Right Question

By Sunday morning Amora still had not decided if she would attend the Christian service. Being a dynamic person, it was rare for Amora to delay making decisions, but she realized that this choice was seminal, one that might change her life forever. Consequently, it was worth deliberating over. Sure, she had felt drawn to investigate this strange religion, but was she getting sucked into something she would later regret? Last time she attended one of their services she was protected by the cover of darkness; now she would be venturing out in the full light of day. To be honest, she admitted to herself, she was also fearful that she may continue to find this Christian message appealing.

The morning had slipped away, and she knew she had waited so long to make up her mind that she would be late. Yet she was still intrigued. "What should I do?" she asked herself. She was not one to let others dictate her choices, even time. It would be her choice. Finally, she decided what she must do.

Meanwhile the centurion dutifully examined his troops—forty well-trained young men of the regular army itching for action. They stood erect in their full armor, ten rows, four abreast in the center of the compound surrounded by brick-and-concrete barracks. Finding them satisfactory, the centurion mounted his horse at the front of the column, raised his arm, and motioned forward. Even though bystanders were accustomed to seeing troops tramp about the city, it was not every day that they witnessed so many troops march out of the compound's gate in the center of Rome on an apparent military mission.

In the meantime, Justin continued waiting for Amora on the large stone bridge over the Tiber south of the city. It was past noon and Amora had not arrived, yet still he waited. He felt that she would eventually come, and he was right. Soon she appeared in the distance, scurrying down the road toward him. He greeted his anxious, out-of-breath invitee. "I'm so glad you decided to come. It's this way."

Amora joined Justin as he led her down the road next to the river. She constantly looked around and over her shoulder. "I'm so nervous," Amora confessed.

Justin smiled. "Fear is the root cause of most of our problems."

Amora jumped when a dog barked in the distance and anxiously looked over her shoulder again. "You act as if it is not a problem to openly defy public authority."

"It most certainly is," Justin admitted. "But if fear controls your life, you will never really live."

"Maybe fear helps keep us alive," Amora responded.

Justin chuckled. "People think they are so independent, but they are just puppets, controlled by their fears."

"Puppets?"

"Of course. We go through life reacting to what other people say or do instead of enjoying life."

"I don't see what fear has to do with it."

"Think of the last time you were upset. Was it because you felt rejected or abandoned, not respected or not in control of your circumstance?"

Amora sighed and admitted, "All of them."

"But why did it even matter?"

Amora looked inquisitively at Justin. She was unaware of her decreasing anxiety level as she became more engaged in the conversation.

"It is because the genesis of those emotions is the fear of losing love."

"So, feeling God's love frees us from the puppeteer's strings?"

"It certainly helps. Notice how the love you have felt from God has already empowered you to do something you would not have dreamed of doing a short while ago."

"I'm not so sure that is a good thing."

Justin laughed. "Oh, don't worry, Amora. God will watch over us today," he promised as he led her into a grove of trees next to the road.

Justin continued his instruction as he guided her through the brush and trees. "I believe there is more sorrow and heartache in the world caused by damaged relationships than by all of the wars throughout history."

"Everyone suffers from some heartache."

"That is the point. Once God heals our souls with His love, we are no longer slaves to our fears and weak behavior. We are freed to love others more deeply."

Justin and Amora emerged from the thick underbrush to a clearing under the trees next to a horseshoe bend in the deep river. The serenity of this natural setting with the soothing sound of running water and a cool breeze swaying the leaves calmed Amora's anxious mind.

Many of the Christians she had met at the worship service sat on the ground under the trees, including Kassinda, Gloria, and her daughter, Sabina. Intrigued, Amora watched as the bishop stood in the river and immersed a female convert in the river.

"Baptism is the symbol God has ordained to represent the spiritual reality that we have been born again in Christ," Justin explained. "Just as Christ was crucified on the cross and lowered into the tomb and then rose again as a resurrected being, we likewise enter into the water, where we offer our old sinful self to be sacrificed and washed clean. We are buried into a watery grave, which also represents the womb from which we emerge a new creature born again in Christ." The new convert in the river gave the bishop a big hug.

"And that is how one becomes a Christian?" Amora asked.

"Yes. It is how we make a covenant with God to take upon us the name of Christ and to follow his teachings. God in turn welcomes us into His family to become joint heirs with Christ to inherit all that He has."

Gloria greeted the soaking-wet convert when she stepped out of the river as a couple of other Christian women rushed forward to hug and congratulate her.

"So that is why Christians call each other brothers and sisters?" Amora inquired.

"Yes. Once you are baptized, you are no longer a stranger to God's love but a fellow citizen in the household of God, where we are all brothers and sisters in Christ. All equal— slave and master, rich and poor. We are all one in Christ and strive to bear each other's burdens."

"That is a big commitment," Amora observed, thinking about her slaves. "I will need time to think about that."

The serenity of the scene was shattered by the blare of a horn and the centurion barking out his command. "Advance!" The shouts of soldiers crashing through the trees startled everyone. Several of the women screamed, and everyone jumped to their feet. A few of the terrified women hugged each other as Amora grabbed Justin's hand and looked into his eyes in horror.

Three groups of soldiers emerged from the brush on the opposite side of the deep river. The centurion and soldiers rushed forward but stopped at the water's edge and stared at the fleeing Christians across the impassable river.

"I said advance!" the centurion yelled, whipping his horse and plunging into the river with the hesitant soldiers following suit. The centurion's horse was able to navigate the river, but the warriors in their armor struggled to cross, some with less success than others.

As soon as the centurion emerged, he pursued the Christians scurrying off in all directions, focusing on Kassinda's group. Most of his soldiers remained in the water trying to save themselves and their comrades-in-arms from drowning in the swift, deep current. A few soldiers successfully navigated the river crossing but stumbled coming to shore. One soldier slipped and planted his face in the mud. None of the warriors were in any condition to effectively chase the Christians, even though they continued to make the attempt.

As the centurion on his horse approached Kassinda's small group, the Christians split up to seek individual escape routes. He pursued Kassinda, grabbed her, and dragged her beside his horse.

In the midst of the commotion, three soldiers were swept downstream despite the efforts of the others to save them from drowning. "Centurion! We need your help!" one of the soldiers called out in despair.

The centurion looked back at his soaked and drowning troops, dropped Kassinda to the ground, and rushed to the river to help his men. Kassinda laboriously rose to her feet and hobbled away.

Justin and Amora ran through the woods until they realized that they had escaped. Amora collapsed, exhausted. Justin fell down beside her as she caught her breath.

"I haven't had so much excitement since I was a young maiden," Amora exclaimed.

"I told you God would protect us."

"Why would anyone join your religion when it is so risky?"

"Now that is the right question."

Chapter 25

Natalie's House

"That is the house," Amora told Justin as she pointed to a three-story stucco building with an arched stone doorway situated along a narrow cobblestone street. "I was able to buy it with part of my inheritance. It is close to the Columna Lactaria."

As she opened the door, Justin strained to make out the interior through the darkness, but as his eyes adjusted, he was able to detect broken cupboards, beams leaning against the back wall, and part of the ceiling that had collapsed. He needed to be careful where he stepped as he entered the room due to the debris strewn around the floor.

Amora walked over to the window and opened the shutters, flooding the room with light, its rays reflecting on millions of disturbed dust particles dancing in the air, revealing that the building had been abandoned ages ago in the midst of interior demolition.

"It will take some work to fix up. But I got it for a very good price."

"Yes, it will take a lot of work," Justin acknowledged as he rolled his eyes.

"I am going to call it 'Natalie's House,'" Amora walked over and opened the door at the far end of the room. "Back here is the kitchen, and it even has a small courtyard for the children to play in."

Justin shook his head and followed Amora out of the room.

"We are going to need a lot of help," he mumbled under his breath.

Over the next few months, Natalie's House consumed Amora's attention. She was there on site directing her slaves, volunteers, and skilled laborers nearly every day as they demolished and remodeled the interior. Justin and various Christian volunteers assisted on a regular basis, tearing out a cupboard here and a wall there, all under Amora's discriminating eye and direction. Justin often worked side-by-side with Omerus, an old man, and his daughter, Gloria, who Amora met in the catacombs. Gloria often brought lunch and refreshments for the workers with her daughter, Sabina. Amora and Gloria soon became friends, but what pleased Amora most was that Sabina had befriended Esteban.

Esteban often accompanied his mother to the remodeling site, especially after the major repairs were completed. His newfound friend played with Esteban and his monkey while the workers assembled cribs and added finishing touches. Their childish laughter rang through the house as they watched Festus try to pick up the tops they had spun. It warmed Amora's heart to watch her son play with another child his own age who did not seem to notice or care about his disability.

Amora took an instant liking to Gloria from the moment she met her in the catacomb. She was confident, yet very open and friendly. She never seemed to care what other people thought about her, while always seeming to be interested in what was important to them. She was very observant of her surroundings and things that needed to be done. She had a passion for life that was contagious. Amora loved her frequent spontaneous laugh. Amora began conversing with Gloria when she would drop off the lunches for the workmen, and was surprised that even though she was not of aristocratic birth, she was well-educated and familiar with current affairs and various philosophies. Amora began to look forward to their visits as their children played. Their conversations covered the gambit—family, health, fashion, weather, religion, and life's trials. Amora appreciated this refreshing new friendship not burdened with pretense.

The wet-nurse, Esilia, stopped by Natalie's House every week for her pay. It wasn't long before she began to linger, asking questions and conversing with Amora and Justin. She started coming by the facility more frequently to listen to Justin teach her about Christianity while she nursed the babe that Amora had entrusted into her care, and occasionally Amora joined their conversations.

One morning Amora overheard Esilia complaining to Justin about how some Patrician had unjustly treated her and how mad it made her feel. She continued to complain about the arrogance and injustice of the upper-class. Familiar with injustice, Amora listened with interest as Justin responded, "Learning to forgive is one of the most important life lessons we need to learn. It is how we become united with others and with God. Beyond forgiving his crucifiers while they were in the very act of killing him, the Savior also forgave you and me at the same time. The pain he felt for his personal injuries during this ordeal were only tokens of the infinite pain he felt from all of the sorrow we cause each other as he literally bore all our grief."

Amora didn't understand how that was possible until Justin explained, "His atonement was infinite because he truly took upon him all of our sins and the pain that we cause each other, yet he still offers us forgiveness while he bore all of our sorrows, so that through his stripes we can be healed."

For the first time in Amora's life, she felt a personal connection with deity. God knew her. More than that, Jesus felt her pain when Natalie died. He felt the hurt from being rejected by Leo and her friends. He was currently feeling her insecurities and fears. She never imagined a god so personal and intimate before.

She liked Justin's lecture up to this point, but that all changed when Justin said, "Through his suffering, we sold our claim for justice to God in exchange for His offer of grace to us. That is why we are required to forgive everyone." How could she be required to forgive the monster who abused and killed Natalie? No, this was not something she could bring herself to do.

All that day and into the next Amora struggled with Justin's message. How could anyone forgive the beast who murdered her daughter? No, she could never do that. Yet, she could not escape the nagging feeling that it was something she needed to do. This was possibly why she was so disturbed by Justin's lesson. But forgiveness was impossible. No, she needed justice for all of the pain she and Natalie had suffered.

Amora found it hard to concentrate while supervising the finishing touches of the remodel, so she took a break. Gloria noticed Amora leave, but continued to fold linens while she watched her daughter, Sabina, hide behind the curtains next to the window as she and Esteban played hide and seek. She chuckled to herself, but felt concern for Amora. She had not been her normal self all day. When Amora did not return after a while, Gloria decided to go see if she could be of any assistance. She found Amora sitting alone in the overgrown unkept garden behind the building. She sat down next to Amora. "Are you alright?"

"Oh, I will be fine."

"Something is troubling you, Amora. Do you want to talk

about it?"

"It's nothing really...I just can't believe anyone would expect me to forgive the twisted fiend who killed my daughter!"

"Who said that?"

"Justin. He said that we have to forgive everyone. How can he say that? He doesn't know what it's like to have your child murdered. It's not fair to expect me to forgive. I don't care that your God suffered Natalie's pain. It just makes it all the more unfair—one more innocent person suffering due to this beast. This whole talk about selling our claim for justice sounds like men negotiating some business deal. It doesn't help me. I hurt! The pain has never stopped from the day she was abducted. Sure, some days are worse than others, but the hurt is always there. I understand why Leo has run away from this agony. I wish I could. There is no way that I can forgive the depraved creature who did this inhuman thing! How can anyone even ask me to?" It felt good to unload her pent-up anger and frustration.

"I am sure Justin didn't intend to cause you more pain. He was only trying to help."

"How can it help?! I can't just pretend that it never happened."

"Of course not!" Gloria said.

It helped Amora to feel that Gloria was validating her pain and loss, unlike all her friends and Leo who told her to forget about it.

"Amora, you need to own your grief and pain before you can give it to God. Do you want to talk about it?"

For the first time since that fateful day, Amora felt free to share her feelings. They gushed out of her like a dam that had burst. She related the details of that day—how she loved brushing Natalie's hair, became ill, the horror of seeing

Esteban injured, the shock when Monica reported that they had lost Natalie, the funeral. She described the flood of feelings that overwhelmed her, the numbness, the emptiness, the loss, her anger, her guilt. As Amora poured out her soul to Gloria she felt relief, as if a huge boil had been lanced releasing the pressure of poison and rot that had been eating her insides for years. It felt good to get it all out.

Gloria sat listening to Amora's story intently. She recalled the pain when her mother and brother and his family were killed in the arena, but said nothing. She realized that this was Amora's time to reconcile with her loss, not Gloria's. So, she sat there for hours as Amora unloaded her burden. She expressed her empathy and sincere interest in Amora's welfare, encouraging her to verbalize all her pent-up feelings.

Once Amora was done sharing her story and feelings, she took a deep breath and sighed. "Thank you for listening, Gloria. You are a true friend." They hugged and wept together.

Gloria took a breath, and said, "Amora, I would like to tell you a short story about the ancient Jews when they escaped from slavery in Egypt."

"Alright."

"There were thousands of them traveling through the hot dry desert. To make matters worse, there were these poisonous serpents that were biting a lot of the people. The bite would burn horribly and then most of the people who were bitten would die. Their leader was a prophet of God named Moses. God told him to make a brass snake and put it on a stick and hold it up in the center of their camp. He promised the people that they would be healed if they would simply look up at the brass serpent on the rod when they were bitten. Those who looked were saved, yet some did not even bother to look, and they died. This story may even be the basis for the legend of the healing *Rod of Asclepius* in Greek mythology, and foreshadows Jesus being lifted up upon the cross to save us. Now, why do you think some of the people didn't even bother to look?"

"I'm not sure. It doesn't make sense not to look."

"It's simply because they did not believe it would work. They did not trust God. Maybe they were preoccupied about being bitten again and wanted to watch where they stepped. Regardless, they just did not believe. It is the same with us. All God wants is for us to trust Him with whatever little we can start with, even if it is just a desire to believe, and then we will feel His love, which will help us endure and even enjoy the rest of our journey. If we truly believe, God has promised to wipe away all of our tears. He has extended His hand to us, but we need to accept it. It is that simple."

"I really do want to believe, Gloria. But it is hard. I just can't get over thinking how much Natalie suffered, and I can't forgive the vile creature who did this."

"I understand, Amora. But, once you trust that God is good as well as just, you will realize that God's goal is to set things right and make people whole again—to reconcile His children with Him so that they can experience all of the love and joy that He has to offer them. I am sure that He has already healed Natalie and that she wants you to be happy too."

Amora began to cry. "Do you really think so?"

"Yes, Amora. I can imagine Natalie up in heaven playing with her friends, happy."

"I'm sorry, Gloria, but all I see is Natalie's little bruised mutilated body lying on the rocks by the river. I can't get that image out of my mind."

"Once you can trust God's goodness, you will know that this is true. You will know that Natalie is happy," Gloria reassured her.

"I want to know this more than anything."

Gloria took Amora's hands in hers and said, "Then ask God. He will answer you in His own way and in His own time, but He will answer."

Amora closed her eyes and prayed, "God, I want to believe. Please help me…Oh, God, I miss my little girl. I love her. Oh, please take good care of her." Amora threw her arms around Gloria and buried her head on her shoulder and wept some more.

Chapter 26

At Home with Christianity

Once the facility was ready, it did not take long before Natalie's House was caring for a dozen infants. Amora was so busy that she had little time to be troubled by the concerns that just a short while before had overwhelmed her. Gloria and her daughter, along with other Christian women, were regular volunteers helping to care for the infants.

About a month after they opened the facility, Amora was surprised to see Maria, distraught, enter the door carrying a newborn wrapped in a small gray blanket.

"I found him abandoned at the Columna Lactaria," Maria exclaimed. "They said no one could touch him because he was deformed. He could hardly cry and no one was helping him!"

"Let me see the baby," Amora said.

Maria handed the infant to Amora. "They said it was forbidden to take him. But I couldn't just leave him there to die!"

Amora examined the newborn and noticed that he was very small, obviously born premature, and one of its arms was nothing more than a stub with fingers. The baby was in distress and having a hard time breathing. With each exhale his little chest collapsed, only to expand with each gasping breath.

"They can't take him away, can they?"

"The baby is safe here. But, Maria, he is very sick and may not survive."

"Please don't let him die!"

"That is up to God, but we will do our best."

"Oh, thank you, Amora. Thank you."

"What are you going to name your boy?" Amora asked as she handed the infant back to Maria. Maria stood in silence, shocked that she, a minor female slave had the power to name someone.

"The father abdicated his right, so you can name the child."

Maria looked down at the babe in her arms. The infant opened his eyes and smiled up at Maria. Maria beamed, looked over at Amora and said, "Marcus. His name is Marcus like the Emperor."

"So be it," Amora declared with a smile.

Maria labored over the infirm child night and day with Amora's permission. The newborn hardly had the energy to nurse, and would tire quickly. But, over the next two days the short frequent feedings became longer as he began to recover. Between feedings Maria would hold and rock the baby until he fell asleep and she would then gently lay him in his crib. At the slightest stir, she was there at his side. The infant would smile without even opening his eyes when he heard Maria's voice. The visible bond between the babe and Maria grew with each difficult breath.

After three days, the babe took a turn for the worse. He stopped nursing, his breathing became more labored and he didn't even open his eyes. But he would still attempt to smile when he heard Maria's voice. Maria was exhausted, and Amora said that she should go home and get some rest, but Maria pled with Amora to allow her to stay the night with the baby.

In the morning Amora found Maria sitting on the floor in the corner holding her little Marcus, tears in her eyes. "He didn't make it, Amora," Maria whimpered.

"Oh, sweet child!" She leaned down in front of Maria. "Hand me the child and I will see that he gets a proper burial." Maria handed the lifeless babe to Amora, dropped her head into her hands and sobbed. Amora handed the child to Kassinda, sat down next to Maria, put her arm around her and pulled her close as Maria buried her head on Amora's shoulder and wept.

After time stood still for what seemed to be an eternity, Maria looked up at Amora and asked, "Why didn't God save Marcus?"

"We will never know in this life, Maria. But God is good, so we know that He is taking good care of little Marcus."

Maria tried to smile between sobs. "I love him."

"I know you do, and more important, little Marcus knows it too. Thanks to you, he felt love in his short difficult life. You made his life worth living, and I'm sure you will feel his love again."

"Do you really believe that, Amora?"

"I am sure of it, Dear." With those words, Amora received the answer to her sincere prayer offered weeks before. Now Amora was sure that Natalie was fine and was happy.

"He suffered so much. His body just didn't work right," Maria said.

"Remember what Justin taught us the other day. Our physical bodies are flawed temporary homes for our spirit, like a tent, but when Jesus comes again, we will receive our perfect resurrected bodies which will become our permanent home like a palace where God can dwell. Little Marcus will receive a perfect body in the resurrection and he will enjoy all of the happiness he missed out of in this life."

"Oh, I sure hope so," Maria sighed.

A worker approached and mentioned that there was someone outside wanting to talk with Amora. When she stepped outside, she was surprised to see Justin and Omerus standing beside two handcarts overflowing with foodstuffs. Justin smiled.

"As you know, Christians don't have much money. So, we held a fast and are donating this food we would have eaten."

"Oh! This is wonderful!"

"That's not all." Justin grabbed Amora's hand. "I have something else to show you."

Justin and Amora navigated their way through the busy plaza while Crescens sat nearby on the edge of a fountain conducting an experiment surrounded by six teenage pupils. Crescens spotted Amora with Justin, stopped his instruction, and watched them for a moment in disbelief before standing up and rushing over to confront them. His students followed close behind.

"Amora, do you realize that you are dealing with a Christian?"

"Certainly."

"You dishonor your husband and your position by such behavior."

"Good day, Crescens. We are occupied by important business." She turned her back and continued on her way.

Justin led Amora through the produce market toward the Columna Lactaria. Gloria and Esilia stood in front of a small group of women, including the mother of the infant Amora had rescued. Esilia was the first one to spot Amora and Justin. She jumped for joy and excitedly pointed to them. "They are here!"

All the women rushed over to greet them, Gloria lagging

behind with a small chest. They circled around Amora as Gloria arrived and opened the empty container. The grateful mother stepped forward and poured some coins out of a small bag into the empty chest, followed by the other women, who each in turn emptied their bags of coins. With the ring of the last coin falling into the overflowing coffer, Gloria stepped forward and presented it to Amora. Amora's eyes filled with tears as she was overwhelmed with gratitude. She handed the chest to Justin and hugged Gloria, weeping tears of joy. Between her sobs Amora struggled to form the words to express the feelings that enveloped her. "Thank you…Thank you" was all she could manage to say. She extended her arm to welcome the infant's mother and Esilia into her embrace. "Thank you all."

* * *

Amora watched with interest as a number of Christians entered her home, nearly filling her atrium and courtyard.

"It is very kind of you to offer your home for us to meet," Justin acknowledged as more Christians arrived.

"I am glad to do it," she assured him.

The bishop stood in front of the assembly as silence fell over the congregation. He welcomed the guests and profusely thanked Amora for her hospitality. She was intrigued when the congregation knelt on the ground, and the bishop held up two large round loafs of flatbread, stepped forward to place the bread on a small table, knelt, and prayed. "Remembering then His death and resurrection, we offer to You the bread and the wine, returning thanks that You have judged us worthy to stand before You and to serve You. And we ask You to send Your Holy Spirit in the offering of the Holy Church, in gathering them together in one, give to all the saints who partake of it the fullness of the Holy Ghost to strengthen their faith in the truth. Amen."

Amora continued to watch with interest as the bishop stood and invited the Christians to partake of the bread. "We invite those who wish to reaffirm their baptismal vow to come forward and partake of the emblems of the Lord's flesh, the bread of life."

Several persons in the congregation approached the bishop, who broke off pieces of bread for them, after which the individuals returned to their seats. Amora watched intently as Justin, Kassinda, Gloria, and Sabina stepped forward to participate in reverential silence.

What a strange ritual, she thought. Yet she was struck by the veneration demonstrated by all involved. This was quite different from the loud and boisterous sacrificial meals she was accustomed to in the state-sanctioned ceremonies. Then it occurred to her. The bread and wine were physical tokens that they could touch and feel to help them remember a loved one who had passed away, just as Natalie's brush helped Amora. Now she realized why everyone was so reverent.

Chapter 27

The Past Returns

A few days later Amora was surprised to find Crescens and Quintus at her front door. Quintus wasted no time in informing her of the purpose of their visit. "While Leo is gone, we feel it is our duty to warn you about some of the people you are associating with."

Crescens quickly added, "The Christians are a subversive cult and an enemy to the state. Even socializing with them will damage your position in society."

Irritated, Amora informed them, "I am fully capable of taking care of myself while my husband is gone."

"He will return soon, and I am sure he will not be pleased to discover that you have invited this cult to meet in his home," Quintus warned.

Amora surprised even herself as she tossed out a cursory sendoff, "Good day, gentlemen," and slammed the door shut in their faces. It offended her that these men had the audacity to confront her on her own doorstep. She realized that she may have acted too strongly. Such disrespect, especially by a woman, would eventually have consequences. Amora wondered if she had been pushing herself too hard, and perhaps this had led her to overreact. She decided that a change of pace was in order; she would take an evening off to relax and enjoy some entertainment.

Amora looked forward to a relaxing evening watching a

comedy at the theatre. She had been so busy lately that it had been a long while since she had last attended. Strange, she thought, comedies used to be one of her favorite pastimes. It was one of the few means she had to escape the misery of her life, yet a lot of time had elapsed since she had enjoyed an evening out. Yes, she thought, tonight's show would be a wonderful break, and she began to feel her customary eager anticipation.

As Amora entered the theater's women's upper seating area, several of the ladies stared while others whispered to each other. Amora sat down next to Julia, who acted as if Amora did not exist. Loretta, sitting behind Julia, whispered something into Julia's ear. Julia snickered.

"What is so amusing, Julia?" Amora asked.

"Oh, nothing...well, just that Christians are helping you fill your foundling house with abandoned infants."

"And this is entertaining?" Amora asked.

Loretta interjected, "No, but the fact that your husband consorts with all sorts of providers in the brothels in Egypt at the same time—now, that is amusing."

Amora recoiled in dismay while several of the women sitting close by scoffed and laughed.

* * *

Leo stood in the vestibulum after his return from Egypt, his hands on his hips. "Where have you been?" he demanded as soon as Amora stepped through the front door.

"Working at my charity."

"I hear you have been associating with Christians."

"They are helping me."

"You are to cease that immediately."

"No!"

Leo stood speechless. "What insolence. What has become of her?" he wondered. "I forbid it!" he ordered loudly.

Unfazed, Amora said calmly, "I have decided to become a Christian."

"Are you insane? Do you realize what that will do to my political future?"

"That is irrelevant."

"What?"

"Is there any truth to the rumors I hear of wild escapades at the brothels in Alexandria?"

"Yes. What of it?"

Amora dropped her head in disgust.

"Don't act so shocked. All men engage in these activities when they travel."

Amora looked directly at Leo, shook her head, and said as calmly as she could, "I am sorry, but this is something I cannot deal with. You have destroyed our marriage, Leo. It is over. I want a divorce."

Amora marched past Leo into the atrium. Stunned, Leo recovered enough to yell, "You can't divorce me!"

* * *

Even though Esteban was not privy to the prior evening's exchange between his parents, he still felt the suddenly heightened level of anxiety now that his father had returned. He had a foreboding premonition. Perhaps that was why he watched from an upstairs window, holding Festus closely, as Amora and Maria left. The scene of his mother disappearing into the distance was indelibly engraved on his young mind.

Amora and Maria rushed down the gently sloping cobblestone street past slaves carrying produce and a few wealthy women engaged in conversation, oblivious to the starving children begging at their feet. Amora and Maria stepped aside as a chariot rolled past and were startled when they nearly stepped on a man's body in the gutter, his face, arms, and hands covered with sores and flies. An elderly woman wept next to him, reminding them of the terrible toll the pox had taken on the residents of Rome. Distressing as it was, they were accustomed to this scene, having witnessed it in a multitude of variations every day as they walked to Natalie's House.

In the meantime, inside the facility Esilia was comforting a crying babe while Kassinda, Gloria, and her daughter attended the infants in two rows of cribs. Omerus and one of the workers were assembling a new crib near the door when the ten soldiers burst into the room.

"Arrest them!" the centurion ordered, positioning himself by the entrance.

Four of the soldiers rushed over and grabbed Omerus and the worker. The other soldiers rushed toward the screaming women. Sabina quickly hid behind the window curtain as the soldiers seized Gloria and Kassinda. One soldier tried to capture Esilia, but she avoided his grasp by quickly stepping behind a crib while simultaneously dropping the infant inside. The soldier grabbed her and, in the struggle, knocked over the crib, spilling the screaming babe onto the floor. The soldier nearly stomped on the child as he struggled to contain Esilia.

Amora and Maria burst into the room.

"What is going on?" Amora demanded.

The centurion seized Amora. One of the two soldiers holding Kassinda let go and grabbed Maria. Amora resisted vigorously, insisting that the centurion free her, but to no avail.

Sabina darted from her hiding place, snatched up the baby, and rushed out the door as the centurion tried to grab her while he struggled with Amora.

"Let go of me!" Amora yelled as he dragged her out of the building, followed by the other soldiers hauling off their prisoners. "Let go of me! You brute! Stop it!"

* * *

Leo was sitting under a portico overlooking his spacious courtyard, chalice in hand, when Antonio burst through the atrium. "Leo! Amora and Maria have been arrested!"

"Well, there's nothing I can do," Leo casually responded.

Antonio stood dumbfounded until his blood began to boil. "You had them arrested! You arranged this!"

"Now calm down. I simply complained about disruptive Christian meddling. I had no idea they would be there."

"Then use your influence to get them released."

"Why? All Amora needs to do is renounce this religion, and she will be fine."

"But what if they won't?"

"Then it is not my problem. It is her choice. She's free to choose what she wants."

"But they will be killed, Leo."

"If she prefers to lie in a tomb instead of my bed, I cannot stop her. It is all up to her, not me."

"But you could intervene."

Now irritated, Leo barked, "I told you, it's not my choice. If she dies, she chose to be her own executioner. Don't bother me about this any further! Now, go find a replacement for that girl, Martha or whatever her name is."

Leo felt sure that this disturbance to his orderly existence would soon pass and everything would settle back to normal. Amora would renounce this ridiculous new religion and resume her role as his gracious wife. He was sure of it. It was her only logical course of action. It would not take long for his peers to overlook her bizarre behavior. Everyone knew that women were prone to eccentricity, he thought. They would not hold it against him. After all, he had been away for several months. Yes, this unfortunate episode would not be laid to his charge and would soon blow over. Life would soon be back to normal. He was sure of it. It just had to be. Any other outcome was unimaginable.

Chapter 28

Time and Eternity

The day after their companions were executed, Amora awoke to the sound of sniffling. She turned over and saw Maria in the corner of their prison cell sitting in a fetal position, her head buried between her knees, crying. Amora sat down beside her. Maria looked up, tears streaming down her face. Amora looked into Maria's wet eyes. "What is wrong, Dear?"

"I'm just sad."

"You miss them, don't you?"

"Ah ha. They helped keep my spirits up."

"They were wonderful people."

"Amora, I'm scared."

"I know, Maria."

"It's just not fair. They were such good people. Why did God let them die? It just doesn't make sense."

Amora gave Maria a big hug and looked deep into her eyes. "I don't have all of the answers, Maria. But, sitting in this cell over the past year, contemplating our fate, has given me time to think, and I have begun to understand a few things. It is interesting that the more time slows down the more I realize that this life is but a small instant, a flicker of time in the vast expanse of eternity, but life is amazing."

Maria wiped tears from her eyes as she looked at her mistress.

Amora continued, "God could have created a world that only sustained life, like this cold concrete and iron cell, but He didn't. Instead, He created this marvelous beautiful world as a physical manifestation of His love for us."

Maria nodded and wiped away her tears.

"Maria, once, when I was depressed and couldn't sleep, I sat on a hillside by our country villa watching the sunrise. Everything was cold and dark, but ever so slowly the black sky began to grey and I could begin to discern the images around me, trees, stones, and the distant horizon taking shape. As the sky began to lighten to a brighter blueish-grey hue, I began to hear the birds sing. Soon, color displaced the grey as the sky became a panorama of red, orange and yellow on a canvas of blue. The whole world around me began to come alive. The sound of small critters scurrying about and the aroma of pine needles woke my senses to the life around me. And, then the sun burst over the horizon, casting its rays of light on the scene before me that exploded with vibrant color—multiple shades of green leaves, brilliant red and yellow flowers, deep brown earth, purple grapes in the valley. As I felt the warmth of the sun's embrace, I realized that even though I was in a very dark place emotionally, a new day would dawn. Life was worth living."

Maria smiled. "It sounds beautiful."

"It was. I cherish that memory."

"I like the countryside too."

Amora grinned. "Way too often I have been oblivious to the rejuvenating beauty of nature—the hummingbird drinking nectar from the cherry blossoms, the bouquet of honeysuckle, the sound of the brook running by our villa—it all is amazing to me now.

"Me too."

"What are some of your favorite memories, Maria?"

Maria smiled. "Feeling the bread dough squeeze through my fingers while I knead it." They both chuckled.

"The cool morning breeze in the hot summer," Amora said.

"How clean it smells after it rains."

"The smell of bacon in the morning."

"Watching a mother sparrow feed her hatchlings last spring."

"Going on holiday and watching the sea," Amora said. "It is always changing. The power of the crashing waves in the storm, and the peace and beauty of the sunset over the tranquil sea. I love it."

"Going to the villa last fall during the grape harvest and dancing with the other maidens in the vat to make wine. It was so much fun. Laughing and holding hands with the girls as we stomped the grapes to the music, splattering the red juice over our clothes. That is one of my favorite memories." Maria laughed.

"Life is wonderful, isn't it?"

"Yes, it is."

"Maria, what is even more phenomenal than this physical world," Amora said, "Is that God has given us an opportunity to develop personal relationships, to experience love and disappointment, joy and sadness, the whole spectrum of emotions generated from our connection with other individuals, like you and me. It is all so valuable to me now. All of it. The hard times and the fun times. It all is phenomenal."

"But some memories are painful,"

"Yes, pain is an integral part of life and our connection with others. But it plays a role in how our relationships grow. Looking back, I realize that I have learned much more during my hard times than the pleasant ones. Even though they were very painful, and I don't wish to go through them again, I value those difficult times even more than those blissful moments we cherish."

Maria looked at Amora with a puzzled look. "I don't understand."

"Suffering, especially by innocent persons, does not make sense from our limited temporal perspective. Pain and death seem to be the worst thing possible. But, the seeds of life are found in the death of a flower. From an eternal view, you can find reason in this madness. It is all about our personal growth and eternal development, which is even more important than having a pleasant life. No, suffering is part of life. None of us escape it. From the moment of our birth we feel pain."

"I still don't see what it's good for."

"Most of life's lessons are associated with some sort of pain and suffering. Apparently, there is a connection between the two. If nothing else, we appreciate our good times more."

"But it is so hard sometimes."

Amora smiled and nodded. "I know it is, Maria. I thought I was helping those abandoned infants in Natalie's House, but I now realize that through our service and sacrifice, God was accomplishing His greater purpose, drawing us closer to Him by increasing the amount of love we feel for others. I learned that when we serve those in need, it is as if we are investing part of our self in the other person, creating a bridge between us that enables love to flow. Didn't you feel a special love for little Marcus?"

"Oh yes! I miss him every day."

"You have developed an eternal bond with that suffering child. Love is divine. Love is eternal. Your love for little Marcus will not evaporate when you die. You will always love him, and soon you will have the joy of seeing him again."

Maria smiled as the thought of seeing her infant charge once more helped to alleviate the fear of her pending death.

"That joy comes from love." Amora continued as Maria nodded. "But Love is an expression of free will. Love cannot exist without free will, so, unfortunately, we can't feel love without the possibility of feeling the pain that comes from wrong choices. Like in nature, this tension between opposites creates the environment for change, growth and development. And, that is God's objective or goal for us. He wants us to grow and develop more love so we can experience greater joy."

"But it still hurts."

Amora smiled. "Yes, it does, but God does comfort us. Maria, He loves us. When we suffer, He is there, offering us His support to sustain us through our trial. He feels our suffering and wants to ease our pain. He does not abandon us, but stays by our side to sustain us. Don't you feel His presence now?"

"Yes."

"Maria, I have come to realize that our whole eternal existence is more integrated than I had ever imagined. Time and eternity are not opposites. Time is consumed in eternity. God lives in time as much as He lives outside of time. Likewise, this physical universe is not the opposite of the spiritual metaphysical realm, it is simply an extension of it."

"I never thought of it that way before."

"The logos, the intelligent energy, the essence of God, is in everything. It is in you, me, the sun, the sky, the earth and the sea. We are all connected with God. He simply converted part of His infinite energy into physical matter that He organized into various forms and levels of intelligence. He experiences what we do as we experience it—our joy and pain, our hopes and fears, our love and heartache—He feels it all at the same time we do. He is always here to comfort us."

Maria, listening intently, said, "I'm not smart like you, Amora. So, I don't understand such complicated things. I just know that I feel a lot better when I choose to do the right thing."

Amora chuckled. "Maria, you just expressed the concept better than all my fancy words."

"You humor me, my lady."

"No, it's true, Maria. You have grasped the essence of the profound in your simplicity."

"I still don't understand everything you say, but it is helping me. But I still don't see how pain is valuable."

"Maria, this mortal existence increases our capacity to love through our association with our families and others. We develop our capacity to love by showing love through sacrifice and through forgiveness. That is partially why we live in this unjust and imperfect world. We need to interact with pain and suffering so that we will have an opportunity to develop love and become more unified with God and the universe so we can experience greater joy."

"Can't there be a better way?"

Amora laughed again, causing Maria to feel a bit dejected.

"I didn't mean to belittle you, Maria. It's quite the opposite. I find your comments very insightful."

Maria smiled.

"I don't know Maria. I suppose God could have created a universe that would have accomplished His purposes in an easier way for us, but I trust that He knew what He was doing when He created things the way they are."

"I suppose you're right."

"Maria, I believe that when we are living in eternity and

look back on life, we will realize that our pain and suffering were just small moments, even though they seem overwhelming to us now."

"We have gone through some difficult times together," Maria said. "I am glad you were there for me."

"Maria, you inspire me." Maria looked up at Amora with a doubtful look. "You really do, Dear." Maria grinned.

Their conversation was cut short by the approach of the jailer accompanied by four soldiers. "I love you, Maria."

"I love you too, Amora."

The two forlorn women, master and slave, united in love, hugged as the soldiers entered their cell.

Chapter 29

The Quarry

Marcus faced the crowd beyond his outstretched arm, waiting, as a hush began to fall over the Colosseum. All eyes were glued to Caesar. The crowd erupted with a cheer of approval when he signaled death with his downturned thumb.

Amora closed her eyes and tilted her head up toward heaven, a serene smile on her face. She opened her eyes, looked directly at Marcus, and then scanned the cheering horde behind him. As she scanned the crowd, she realized that they were not one huge mass of humanity but instead were individual spectators and participants in the game of life. Each one was struggling to find hope and meaning as they were manipulated by the forces around them. Compassion filled her heart for these lost souls.

A small door in the stadium wall opened, allowing two lions to enter the arena behind Amora and Maria. One was a large male, and the other one was its mate. At first the cats were distracted by the light and noise in the arena and hugged its wall in the safety of its shadow. They soon forgot their trepidation when they spotted Amora and Maria. The hunters began to stalk their prey.

Amora stepped forward to face Caesar, her gown glowing in the sunlight. Her majestic appearance commanded the attention of the whole arena. Amora raised her hands to her mouth and blew a kiss to her family friend, Marcus Aurelius, and the section of the crowd behind him, pacifying the mob. Amora turned to face each of the remaining sections of the Colosseum and blew kisses to the spectators in hopes of creating a bridge so that they, too, could feel the love that Amora had received from her God.

A hush fell over the crowd as the lions slowly approached their quarry, placing one paw in front of the other. The large male lion fixed its sights on Amora as it inched toward her. The smaller female cat made a slightly wider berth while it focused on Maria.

Amora looked at Leo, placed her right hand over her heart, and offered it to him as one last gesture of her eternal love. Leo collapsed to his knees, buried his face in his hands, and sobbed.

Amora, triumphant, with her chin up in regal dignity, knelt, looked up to heaven, and smiled. She closed her eyes and bowed her head to pray.

The lions pounced.

* * *

"She has to be here." Antonio said as he watched the burly, bloodstained worker tug on a mangled body stuck in a heap of corpses on the far side of the room.

"Oh, she's here, all right," the worker replied. "The dead don't just walk away." He chuckled. "It's been a busy day up there," he continued as he rolled the body down the heap. "It's always busy when the emperor is here." He grabbed another corpse and pulled it aside. "The more they cheer, the more we work," he grumbled as the other worker in the Colosseum's morgue joined him in sorting through the remains.

"I need to find her," Antonio insisted.

"Don't rush us, kid," the second worker barked. "You'll wish you hadn't seen her soon enough."

Antonio, oblivious to his surroundings, stared at the workers as he moved closer, as if his proximity would expedite the process. He hardly noticed Amora's mutilated body lying on a table in the center of the room or the pile of weapons and armor that he passed as he approached the pile of cadavers. He did not hear the three guards conversing by the door or the cranking of the huge gears, pulleys, and counterweights as the large elevator next to the pile of bodies began to rise.

All his senses were focused on the mass of human flesh in front of him. Nothing else mattered now. His life had been so intertwined with Maria's that all interest in life had died with her. His only desire now was to find the remains of his deceased young love to ensure she would receive the dignity in her burial that she was denied in her execution.

"Is this her?" the first worker asked as he slid Maria's mauled body and dangling head down the heap.

Antonio moaned as he threw himself down next to her body. He gently caressed her lifeless form and tenderly began to raise her up when her head flopped to the side.

"Oh, Maria, Maria!" he sobbed.

At that moment, the guards jumped to attention and moved aside as Leo entered the room. Antonio glanced up at the source of the commotion that had interrupted his private bereavement. Hatred displaced the tears in his eyes.

"You killed her!" he roared.

Antonio jumped up and grabbed a sword from the pile of weapons as he lunged toward Leo. An attentive guard struck the sword out of Antonio's hand while the other two guards rushed past Leo and grabbed Antonio. The first guard raised his sword to execute Leo's impetuous steward, only to be stayed by Leo's raised hand and command.

"Stop! Spare him."

"Kill me now! For if I live, I swear I will have my revenge!"

"Take him to the quarries," Leo said, nodding over his shoulder dismissively.

With a jerk, the guards dragged Antonio away as he bellowed, "I will have vengeance! You will pay for this!"

Leo approached the table bearing Amora's lifeless body, reached out, and gently took her hand as he collapsed to his knees. His mind raced as he recalled the hopes and dreams extinguished with her death. Leo stared at Amora's limp hand in his. He watched as her hand slipped out of his and dangled below Amora's lifeless form on the table above. Leo dropped his head.

Chapter 30

The New Steward

Leo paced back and forth in the peristyle of his villa. Nothing made sense. When he had denounced Amora, he'd felt sure that she would abandon this ridiculous new religion and resume her role as his loyal wife. He'd been sure of it. It was her only logical course of action. But the unimaginable was now his reality.

He stopped and gazed at his manicured garden in the center of the peristyle and wondered what had become of his orderly world. He tried to reconcile what had just occurred in the arena with his understanding of reality. How could she choose death instead of a privileged life with him? Sure, there was some tension in their marriage because of Esteban's disability and Natalie's death, but that didn't explain her choice to die. Especially when he had felt her love in the arena. Nothing added up. All Leo could think of was that Amora must have been bewitched by the sorcerers of this new religion. There was no other explanation. Even so, what was he going to do now? Had he fallen from favor because of Amora's indiscretion? How would his business partners react to this turn of events? That was what worried Leo the most.

Rome was ever present. Everyone knew their place in this society, and noncompliance called down the crushing powers that sustained order, regardless of whether you were an insurgent state, a defiant slave, or an insolent noble. Order must be maintained at all costs, and honor and respect were the glue holding this world together. Patronage was the model that sustained society. Vassal states paid tribute to Rome for its protection while the inhabitants paid homage to their patron gods in hopes that they would bestow blessings on their mortal devotees. Slaves served their masters, and citizens honored wealthy patrons who doled out benefits to worthy clients. Position in society dictated one's role and the benefits one received if that role was played well. The life of a patrician never wanted for intrigue in the best of circumstances, and now he wondered what would befall him.

While Leo contemplated his fate, Senator Quintus, one of Leo's investors in his lucrative Egyptian Publicani operation, approached Leo's door accompanied by his slave, Prometheus.

"Now remember, Prometheus, I chose you for this mission because you are my most shrewd resource," Quintus said, "and if you perform well, you will be richly rewarded. Keep your eyes and ears open, and let me know if you learn of anything that may be helpful. I will inform you when we are ready to strike."

"You will not be disappointed."

One of Leo's slaves opened the door and greeted the guests. "Hello, Senator Quintus. Thank you for coming by on this sad day. Unfortunately, I do not believe my master is in any condition to entertain guests."

"You need not be concerned. I have come to provide practical assistance. Step aside."

Quintus found Leo pacing back and forth in the peristyle near the atrium. "Hello, Leo."

Leo looked up and scowled. "They have to be stopped!" he growled. "These Christians are destroying us. Just look at the curse they have put on my house. I can't believe they bewitched my own wife. We have to eliminate them, Quintus."

"I agree."

"Your home could be next. They have some foul power, and once they enter your home, they jinx it."

"They wouldn't dare come close to my home."

"I was gone. It wasn't my fault."

"I understand, Leo. That is why I have come to offer you assistance."

"I knew you would stand by me."

"Leo, you will need a new steward, now that your old one has betrayed you. I am giving you Prometheus," he pointed to his slave, "to serve as your new steward. He is my most astute worker."

"Thank you, Quintus, but I insist on paying for him."

"Nonsense. What are friends for if you don't let them help you when you need them?"

"I really appreciate it—this gift and your support."

"Of course, my friend," Quintus said as he patted Leo on the back. "I do not want to intrude any longer on your mourning. Just let Prometheus know if you need anything, and I will be there for you."

"Thank you, Quintus," Leo said as he escorted him to the door. "You have been a real encouragement."

Walking back to the atrium after Quintus had left, Leo noticed that his crippled son, Esteban, was about to leave.

"Where are you going?"

"To see one of my friends."

Surprised that Esteban had friends, Leo continued his inquisition. "And who is that?"

"Sabina. She helped at Natalie's House."

"A Christian?"

"Yes."

Leo exploded into a rage, grabbed Esteban, and shook him while he yelled, "You will never see another Christian! Ever! Do you understand me?"

Esteban nodded his head and eked out a weak yes.

Leo tossed him aside like a rag doll and stormed out of the room.

Prometheus watched the scene from the peristyle, taking mental notes without saying a word. Esteban, in pain, glared at his father.

Chapter 31

The Ludus

Antonio leaned on his shovel and caught his breath. Seven months of back-breaking labor hauling large blocks of stone and clearing the hillside adjacent to the open quarry were taking their toll. He worked from sunup to sundown every day exposing the valuable marble below the soil, with only a very short break for a sparse midday meal. At least the work was not as dangerous as in the quarry itself, but soon the hillside would be clear of dirt, and he would surely be put to work in this new extension of the quarry. He would be fortunate to live another twelve months once that work began. He had to figure a way out of this death sentence. Escape was impossible, and those who tried were summarily executed. No, he could not risk a futile escape attempt. He needed to live to execute his revenge on Leo. But how?

His thoughts were abruptly disrupted by the crack of a whip and the cutting sting on his back.

"Get back to work, you lazy scum."

Antonio hated this guard, who made no effort to disguise his pleasure at watching his charges wince and cower under the pain he inflicted whenever possible. Maybe he would be able to smash the guard's head during his escape. That would be sweet justice, Antonio thought as he thrust his shovel into the hard, dry surface.

The loud snap of wood breaking, shrieking screams, and

the crash of stone exploding as it hit the ground grabbed everyone's attention. A portion of the four-story-high scaffolding had fractured under the weight of the huge slab of marble being lowered onto it. Several workers had fallen to their deaths as their section of support collapsed, leaving one man dangling from a broken board, swaying precariously. While the hanging worker yelled for help, a half-dozen workers scurried below and disappeared into the dust to slowly reappear as the dust settled. A couple of the workers were carefully climbing the skeletal remains of this platform; the others were desperately trying to rig up a rope and pulley to rescue their colleague. It was a vain effort as their fellow worker lost his grip and fell to his doom with a thud.

Antonio closed his eyes and sighed. More senseless death caused by his master's irrational demands and disregard for safety. "Now we will pay for their loss by starting long before dawn and working well into the night for at least a week," he thought as he shook his head. It was pointless to try to improve his working condition, and escape was hopeless, yet he still imagined that some miracle would emerge. So, he remained vigilant for any sign of its advent.

That same day General Sulla Pompeianus appeared with his entourage. He had just returned from the war with Parthia and regularly visited the Carrara quarry when he was at his estate in Tuscany. He was a successful *lanista* who owned the largest *ludus* for training gladiators in the area. Unlike most lanistas, he was primarily an absentee owner who allowed his *doctorii* to run his facility, except on the rare occasions when he was present. Yet, as a general familiar with fighting, he maintained an intense interest in his investment, and his commanding influence was felt even from a distance. It was not uncommon for him to purchase potential gladiators while on assignment and send them to his facility. Now he was here and looking for more stock.

The quarry's overseer lined up the workers for his review. General Sulla, in his gleaming *lorica segmentata* armor, walked down the line with the quarry overseer. He stopped and looked over a buff worker, examined his teeth, and walked on. He stopped in front of another large worker and turned to the overseer.

"What is his story?" he inquired.

"He came from Gaul about three months ago. He is a hard worker and is as strong as a team of horses."

"I will take him for five hundred denarii."

"Agreed."

General Sulla continued to walk down the line, his keen eye quickly spotting potential talent. Occasionally he would stop, ask the subject a few questions, and move on. He selected a couple of large, bulky men before he passed by Antonio without even giving him a glance. "This cannot be happening," Antonio thought. "This is my opportunity. The gods have ordained it. I must do something."

Antonio looked around; fixed his vision on the largest, burliest man nearby, and sprang into action. He charged and slammed into the colossal mass of muscle before the man had a chance to react. The stunned worker stumbled back and then regained his footing. All the while Antonio was pummeling him with blows that seemed to bounce off his foe's tightening bulk. Antonio grabbed a broken timber from the collapsed platform and swung it at his target, who snatched the board in midswing. In his wrath, the enraged giant broke the plank in two over his knee with his bare hands. He tossed one piece to the side and charged Antonio, swinging the other fragment above his head.

Antonio stood his ground until the last second when he

dove for his storming assailant's feet. The hulk's momentum slammed him to the ground. Antonio spun around and grabbed the bouncing broken beam that the Herculean worker had dropped during his fall. Antonio charged the shocked but furious man attempting to get back on his feet. Again, he grabbed the board with one hand in midswing and tossed it to the side, along with Antonio, who refused to release his grip. By then several of the guards had rushed to the brawl while the other guards alertly watched the slaves and prisoners with drawn swords.

The guards seized Antonio and his rival and hauled them before the general and the quarry overseer.

"Quite a show," the general said. The combatants knew better than to speak. The general studied the large worker, turned to the overseer, and asked, "What can you tell me about him?"

"He is a slave from Germania that I purchased only last month. He is as strong as a bull but does not have much training."

"I will take him. Our regular price, agreed?"

"Yes, Your Honor."

"Now, what shall we do with this passionate young man?" the general said as he gazed into Antonio's eyes staring back at him without flinching. "Focused determination. That's good…I see anger driving your passion, but you have the wisdom to control it. That's even better." Still staring at his subject, he asked, "Why is he here?"

"He's a prisoner, sir. He tried to kill his master."

"A rebel slave, then?"

"No. He was the steward of a respected patrician. I believe his master sent his betrothed to die in the arena."

"Ah. Vengeance. Yes, that is what I see. You say he is educated?"

"Yes, he came from Hispania, is good with numbers, knows letters, and is fluent in Latin and Greek, as well as his native tongue."

Slowly nodding his head, Sulla observed, "He is quick and decisive. I like that. I will take him as well."

"Oh, I can't, Your Honor. He is condemned to die here in the quarry."

Sulla gave him a wry smile and whispered, "Then no one will know of my generous gift, will they?"

The overseer glanced from side to side. "Very well," he mumbled sheepishly.

* * *

The hard, wooden bench in the wagon made the trip over the bumpy road uncomfortable. Worse yet, the chains around their hands made it difficult to keep their balance as they rocked back and forth, slamming into the prisoner next to them. Antonio shared his bench with three other future gladiators. He glanced across the wagon at the large fellow he had attacked a short while ago. His rival sat between two other acquisitions on the bench facing Antonio, continually nodding, half-asleep. Antonio grinned. Yes, the gods had smiled on him today, or at least they were amusing themselves as they watched him pursue his quest for justice. Yes, today was a sign that providence was with him.

Antonio slightly nudged his combatant's foot. "Hey, you."

The husky man looked up. "Yeah."

"I didn't mean anything personal today," Antonio said.

"Yeah."

"I didn't see any other option."

"I understand." He smiled at Antonio and nodded his head. "Thank you for getting me out of that death trap."

"I'm not sure it will be any safer in the arena," Antonio

said.

"At least I will die with honor."

Antonio smiled and nodded his head in agreement. "My name is Antonio."

"I am Adolf, but they call me Adolphus here."

They exchanged nods, acknowledging their new connection. Adolf closed his eyes and lowered his head to rest. After a while, Antonio followed suit and leaned back as the inescapable cherished memories of Maria flowed into his mind.

* * *

The massive gates of Sulla's compound creaked as they opened, allowing the wagon carrying Antonio and his companions to enter the complex. Antonio scanned his new surroundings. It was a large facility, about one hundred meters square, surrounded by a two-story-high stone wall with numerous guards strategically placed on the thick wall to watch the activity below. Cells with iron bars lined the far wall facing the interior courtyard, with additional cells along the wall they had entered through. A round arena was in the far-right corner of the courtyard. A half-dozen training stations, containing a variety of mechanisms and apparatus, were occupied by gladiators engaged in various forms of training under the watchful eyes of their trainers. To his left were the barracks for the guards and trainers, a mess hall, an office, and a nicer residential facility for the doctorii. A formidable statue of Mars stared down over the facility from the roof. Antonio concluded that there was little chance of escape. That did not concern him, though, as he planned to put the training he received here to good use.

The driver and two guards jumped down from the wagon and were soon joined by General Sulla and Commodus, the facility's head *doctores*, along with several more guards. A guard began to unchain the prisoners one by one.

"Here are your new trainees," Sulla said. "See if you can turn them into gladiators."

"That's what we do, sir."

"Yes, you do a fine job of it."

As the new arrivals jumped down from the wagon, they lined up in front of General Sulla and Commodus. They released all the prisoners except Antonio. Sulla turned to inspect his trainees and introduce them to their new master.

"This is Commodus. He will be your new guardian," Sulla began as the last trainee and the guard releasing him joined the group, leaving Antonio chained in the wagon. Antonio's head began to spin. What was going on? Had he been forgotten? Weren't they going to train him to be a gladiator? What was in store for him?

Sulla continued. "If you learn well, you will gain fame and riches. If not, you will die. Now, you all need to swear your allegiance to me according to the gladiator's oath. Commodus?"

Commodus stepped forward and faced his new trainees. "Swear to be loyal even as you are bound, beaten, whipped, burned, and killed with steel."

"Excuse me, sir," Antonio said. "Am I not to join them?"

"Oh no, my boy. You would not survive in here long enough to even make it to the arena."

Several of the guards and new arrivals laughed. Antonio's blood boiled at the insult yet he held his tongue. Maybe the gods had better plans for him.

* * *

"Antonio, I introduce you to your new constant companion," General Sulla said with a smirk as his villa's blacksmith permanently fastened the shackle to Antonio's ankle. Sulla handed Antonio the heavy ball connected to the shackle by a thick chain, laughed, and said, "Someday you may become so attached that you will name her." The weight of the ball sank all hope of escape. Not only would his new companion slow him down, the ball and chain would be even more obvious than the slave brand on his heel.

"You will work under Marcellus keeping my books. In light of your interest in gladiators, the ludi's accounts will be your responsibility, unless you prove incompetent."

Antonio didn't even try to hide his disappointment. "A boring accountant," Antonio thought, "and mocked every day by useful training just beyond my reach."

"You will be on-site four days a week. The rest of the time, you will be here. I expect you to learn every aspect of that business and not be distracted by the action."

Antonio mused, "The gods certainly have a sick sense of humor, dangling hope in front of my nose and then tossing it into the midst of the desert of despair. Curse them and their injustice."

"Do you understand me?" General Sulla bellowed.

"Yes, sir."

Two days later, Antonio sat at his desk, pen in hand, staring out the window at the horses running in the field, ignoring the ledger and stack of letters beside him.

"Sulla's black stallion is such a beauty. It reminds me of the Arabians we used to own back home," he reminisced. He envisioned himself free, racing on the stallion's back through the trees, down the road past the vineyard, and back to Rome to execute judgment on Leo.

"Come, show me your ledger," Marcellus said.

Snapped back to his dreary reality, Antonio said, "Yes, sir." He grabbed the ledger, stood, and started to take it over to his supervisor. "Ouch!" he yelled as the shackle cut into his ankle when the chain tugged on the iron globe under his desk. Antonio threw the ledger down. "Enough," he said as he jerked the chain and ball toward him. He picked up the ball and scanned the room.

"What are you doing?" Marcellus asked.

Ignoring Marcellus, Antonio continued to examine his surroundings until his eyes fixed on a cloth runner and brass bowl decorating a side table. He marched over to the table, grabbed the fabric, and ripped it off, tumbling the brass bowl to the floor with a clank and jangle. Antonio wrapped the runner around his waist like a sash, secured it tightly, and pulled open the top edge to create a pouch to hold the ball. "This stupid weight will not rule me," he declared once the ball was secured in its pocket.

noticed, Esteban waited inside the kitchen, in the dark, and listened.

"Any better luck with your wagers today, sire?" Prometheus asked.

"Quiet," Leo said. "It's all the Christians' fault. They have cursed me. Cursed me, do you hear?"

"Yes, sire."

"How else can you explain my bad luck ever since they set foot in my house? Can you? Can you? No, that is the only explanation. Cursed."

"Yes, sire."

Stumbling toward the kitchen, Leo continued. "My own wife abandoned me. Imagine that. She chose to die…die for that Christian god, instead of staying with me," he said as his voice trailed off, until he spotted Esteban cowering in a corner of the kitchen. Pointing at Esteban, he said, "She abandoned you too. Imagine that. A mother abandoning her own child, so she could die. It's not natural. It's a curse, I tell you. A curse."

The next day, Esteban sat on the edge of his bed again, sulking. "Father is right," he thought. "It isn't natural for Mama to choose to leave us and die. Maybe she really didn't love me at all." The thought stung. For years he had known that his father didn't care for him, so Esteban tried hard to win his love. But his mother was always there, comforting and reassuring him. The constancy of her love was something he had relied on. Now he began to wonder if it was all just a mirage. "Maybe I really am not worth loving. Maybe Mother was just pretending so she wouldn't have to deal with all the problems I cause," he thought. "Maybe I really am just a broken kid that they should have thrown away." He dropped his head and stared at the floor. He saw an ant crawling along, and then another one, and then a few more. "Even ants have a better life than me," he thought. "They have each other, but I am all alone. I really don't have anyone who cares for me." Tears welled up in his eyes, dripped down his cheeks, and fell to the floor.

As Esteban continued to stare at the ants and his tears on the floor, his mind traveled back to the dungeon and the last time he saw his mother. He began to relive the experience, recalling every detail of that fateful day. He remembered Antonio asking him if he wanted to see his mother in prison; his immediate positive reply; the long tiring walk to the jail; sitting on the hard bench, waiting while Antonio sought permission from the guard to enter; how scary it felt walking down the long, dark, narrow halls; going down countless stairs on the way to their cell, and then the joy when he saw his mother.

* * *

"Mama!" Esteban exclaimed.

Amora spotted her son and rushed toward the cell's iron gate. "Esteban! Esteban!" she called. The jailer pointed his spear at Amora. "Stay back," he ordered. Amora retreated, and another jailer unlocked their cell door.

He then grabbed Esteban, pulled him back, and ordered, "Only one at a time." Motioning to Antonio, he continued. "It's your turn. You have three minutes." Esteban felt devastated. How could he wait when his mother was right there in front of him, but he had no choice, so he listened intently. Every word was engraved on his memory.

"Antonio!" Maria exclaimed as she ran up to him. She threw her arms around his neck, and they kissed passionately.

Then Maria looked up at Antonio. "I'm scared."

"Just renounce this silly new religion, and they'll let you go," he urged.

"Oh, I could never do that."

"I cannot bear to lose you," Antonio said.

"But we can be together forever. There is life after death."

"You have always been such a sweet optimist. But, Maria, this is real. Once you are gone, it is over. And I cannot handle that."

"You are strong. And God will help you."

"How can you allow me to suffer like this if you really love me?"

"Oh, Antonio. I do love you. I'm willing to die so we can be together in heaven."

Antonio became angry. "This is Leo's fault. He set this up."

"Antonio. Please don't let hate fill your heart."

"If I lose you, I will kill him."

In tears, Maria pleaded, "Antonio! Please don't talk that way."

"No one who arranges your death deserves to live," he insisted.

"Hate breeds hate. I don't want to lose you forever. If you love me, please try to forgive."

"How can anyone forgive this senseless killing?"

"Antonio, none of us has a right to revenge," Amora interjected.

"What? Your own husband just arranged for you to die."

"Yes, his betrayal was devastating. But God has healed my soul."

"Do you plan to go back to him?"

"Of course not. I just don't feel animosity toward him anymore."

"How can you say that?"

"Once I was willing to forgive, God opened my mind to understand Leo better, and now I feel compassion for him."

"I understand him, all right. He is an egotistical, selfish

tyrant," Antonio proclaimed.

"Yes, but he is much more than that. We are all a mixture of good and bad, and Leo is no exception. God is the only one who can correctly judge."

Maria chimed in. "Antonio, Christ has felt all our pain, so He can take it away and replace it with peace and love."

"If I lose you, it will take more than some sweet talk to stop me from getting revenge."

"Please try. If you really love me, you will try."

"For your sake I will try, but it will take a miracle to take the sword out of my hand if I lose you."

"Antonio," Amora said, "I can assure you that God is a God of miracles. In Leo's house I was a prisoner of hate, anger, and self-pity. Now, in this dungeon, my soul is free to feel love and joy. If you seek God's love, you will find it."

The jailer approached and unlocked the cell door, announcing, "Time's up."

"The Christians have rescued the infants at Natalie's House and have taken your charity underground, but it continues to grow," Antonio mentioned to Amora.

"Oh, thank God," she exclaimed.

"I love you," Maria said.

"I love you too. I will do what I can. I heard that Titus is trying to arrange a stay of the execution."

"I pray he succeeds," Amora said, quietly.

"We all do," said Antonio.

Antonio and Maria attempted to embrace but were blocked by the jailer, who separated them.

"I said, 'Time is up.' You need to go. Now!"

The jailer pointed his drawn sword at Antonio, who reluctantly retreated from the cell, leaving Maria in tears.

Esteban ran to his mother as the jailer locked the door behind him. Amora fell to her knees in front of her son and wrapped her arms around him, showering him with kisses.

"Oh, my boy! My boy! I love you! I love you!"

Crying, Esteban exclaimed, "Mama. Mama."

Making an effort to compose herself, Amora held Esteban in front of her with her hands on his shoulders and stated emphatically, "Now, Esteban. I need you to be strong. I am sorry that you have to grow up so young." She fought back tears as she continued. "I know this will be difficult, but you can do it."

Esteban struggled to pay attention as he rubbed his eyes fighting back his tears and intermittently sobbing.

"Remember, I will always love you. My spirit will never die," Amora declared. "We will just be separated for a while, like going on a trip. But I will always love you. I will be in heaven watching over you."

"I miss you, Mama."

"I know you do, Esteban, and I miss you too. But you will always be able to feel my love in your heart. Love never dies. Our love is stronger than death. Do you understand that?"

"Yes, Mama."

Amora enclosed Esteban's hands within hers, holding them tightly. "Now, whenever you feel alone or sad," she instructed, "I want you to think of me smiling at you. I love you. Now close your eyes. Can you see me in your mind? Am I smiling at you? Do you see me?"

"Yes, Mama."

Amora gave Esteban a big hug. He began to open his eyes, but she said, "Don't open your eyes yet. Can you feel my love?"

"Yes, Mama."

"I want you to always remember this. Remember you are not alone. Whenever it is hard, remember my love for you. My love will give you strength. Oh, please remember."

"I will, Mama."

Amora released her embrace and held Esteban by his shoulders again. Esteban opened his eyes, and tears streamed down his cheeks.

"Now, Esteban. I want you to attend the Christian services as often as you can."

"I will, Mama."

The two jailers approached, and one unlocked the cell door. "Time's up. He needs to leave."

"God bless you," Amora said to her son. "Be strong. God will give you strength. I will always love you."

Amora stood, but Esteban fell to his knees and wrapped his arms around one of Amora's legs, sobbing inconsolably. "No! No! They can't take you!"

One of the jailers used the end of his spear to separate Esteban from Amora as he continued to sob. The jailer dragged Esteban away as he screamed while the other jailer locked the iron bars behind him.

"Don't hurt him! He is only a boy," Amora cried out. "I love you! Esteban, I love you!"

Antonio tried to help Esteban, but the jailer pulled him away and dragged Esteban out of sight while the boy wailed.

Amora looked up and reached toward heaven with both arms. "Oh God! I can't do this!"

She collapsed to the floor and sobbed uncontrollably as Esteban howled in the background for his mother.

Amora looked up with tears streaming down her face. "Please, God. Oh please, help my boy." She dropped her head into her hands. "Oh God. Please help me."

* * *

As Esteban recalled the events of that day, a warm feeling began to flow from his heart throughout his body. He remembered. He remembered it all. He remembered how it felt when he opened his eyes and saw his mother kneeling in front of him, her eyes full of love and concern. He remembered her telling him to recall that experience whenever life became hard. He remembered her promise that she would never be far away and that she would watch over him. In that moment, he felt her presence, even though he could not see through the veil of eternity.

He had been wrong. His mother really did love him. He smiled. He realized that it was the first time he had smiled in quite a while. "Yes, Mama does love me, and she tried to prepare me for this day," he thought. He vowed to keep his promise to his mother. He would be strong.

Then it occurred to him that he had also promised his mother that he would attend the Christian worship services as often as possible. The problem was that Father would never allow it, and Prometheus wouldn't either. Regardless, he resolved to keep his promise to his mother. There had to be a way, even though Prometheus rarely left the house when his father wasn't there. He would figure out a way. He was sure of it. Now he had a goal, an objective to work toward, and he would focus his attention on finding a way to accomplish it.

Chapter 34

Friendship Renewed

Esteban closely observed the comings and goings of the household for two weeks. He had a plan, and now he needed to test it. The Christians usually met at dusk on Sunday evening, so he hoped to take advantage of his father's disinterest and frequent drunkenness, as well as Prometheus's preoccupation with reviewing his father's affairs in the evening while he was gone.

"I am going to bed," he told Domitia, the slave who had replaced Maria. "I'm not feeling very well," he said as he walked to his room.

She followed right behind him. "What is wrong?"

"I just don't feel good."

She put her hand on his forehead. "Well, you don't have a fever."

"My stomach hurts, and I feel tired."

"Alright, just rest. I will be back to check on you in a little bit."

Esteban lay down in his bed. As soon as Domitia left the room, Esteban jumped up and ran to the *clepsydra* he had set up on the table across the room. He quickly started the water clock to measure how long it would take for her to return and jumped back into bed. It was not long before Domitia returned with a cup of hot mint tea.

"Now, sit up and drink this tea. It will help settle your

stomach."

"I don't want it."

"Come, now. It will help you feel better." She reached down to help raise him up.

"OK." He sat up and took a sip, then handed the cup back to his slave and laid back down. "I don't want any more."

"I will just leave it here," she said as she set the cup on the stand next to his bed. "Get your rest, and I will be back later to see if you want any dinner." She patted him and left the room.

"Next time I will tell her I don't want any dinner," he told himself as he jumped up to check how long it had been. He reset his clock and lay back down. He tossed and turned, going through every detail of his plan to help pass the time. It seemed like an eternity, waiting for her to return. Finally, he heard the door open, so he lay very still, pretending to be asleep. He heard someone walk toward his bed and pick up the empty cup. She seemed to be standing there forever.

Domitia didn't know what to do. She hated to wake him, but Prometheus would want to know where he was and if he was going to eat his evening meal. Prometheus was such a demanding overseer that she feared his wrath if she disappointed him. So she leaned down and gently shook Esteban. He feigned waking up.

"Master Esteban. Do you want to eat your dinner?"

"Ugh. No. I'm not hungry," he said as he rolled back over to face the wall.

"Very well. Get your sleep."

As soon as she left the room, Esteban ran over to check and reset his water clock. It had been nearly an hour. Everything else was still in its place, so she must not have seen the clepsydra on the table or suspected anything. His scheme to escape his domestic prison without detection might actually work!

He lay back down to wait and see if they would come back again. It was hard to wait. It was so boring that he began to tire. He sat up with a start. "What if I fall asleep," he thought. "I won't know if anyone came in. I can't stay awake all night." He continued to sit pondering his predicament until he hit upon the idea of putting a feather in the door. He examined his pillow and was able to extract a feather and secure it between the door and its frame so that it would fall when the door was opened.

He lay back down, proud of his ingenuity. He tried to review his plan again, but it was too hard to concentrate. He didn't want to fall asleep, so he tried the mental number games his teacher had taught him, but that was much too boring. His thoughts finally drifted off to pleasant memories of his mother—the comfort he felt in her arms as a child after a nightmare, her care after he fell down the steps at the park, playing games together, showing her his pet monkey's tricks, the fun times he had with her and Sabina at Natalie's House. He missed Sabina and looked forward to seeing her again. Soon his memories drifted to become a pleasant dream with his forlorn friend.

Morning came quickly. He immediately looked at the door. The feather was still secure in its place. "Yes, my plan will work," he thought. He determined to execute his strategy the following Sunday if his father was not at home in the late afternoon.

Esteban had had to wait an extra week, but now he was ready. At first his idea played out exactly as he had planned. He went to bed. Domitia brought in a cup of tea. He told her he did not want any dinner. She simply looked into his room, and he appeared to be asleep. He waited until the evening meal when Prometheus and most of the household would be occupied, and then he got up and put on his outer robe over his tunic. He stuffed some clothes under his blanket so it would appear that he was asleep.

He silently cracked open the door to see if anyone was around. The coast looked clear. He snuck out the door and was tiptoeing out through the atrium when his pet monkey spotted him and started to screech in his cage near the triclinium. "Not now, Festus!" he thought. The one thing he had not tested was going wrong. The monkey continued to screech and jump around his cage. He made such a ruckus that Domitia came out of the kitchen to see what the matter was.

"He's sleeping, you noisy beast. He can't play now."

She noticed that Festus continued to jump from side to side in his cage, stop and look toward the atrium, screech, and then jump around again. Domitia turned and scanned the atrium. Everything seemed in order.

"OK, I will bring you some fruit," she said as she went back into the kitchen.

Esteban quickly stepped out from behind the potted plant in the corner of the atrium where he had been hiding and slipped out the door.

It was darker than it used to be when he would go to the catacombs with his mother, but he still easily remembered the way because of the number of times they had gone before. He realized that he was running late because of his delayed start, so he hurried along as fast as he could, trying not to draw attention to himself. He finally arrived at the graveyard where the catacomb tunnel began. The location was so dark and forbidding that he hesitated to enter. Mustering his courage, Esteban began to make his way through the dark cemetery. He froze when he heard troops approach. He didn't breathe as the soldiers marched past without noticing him.

Esteban slowly crept forward, stopped, and looked around. He made out a few familiar crypts in the dim moonlight and slowly inched forward to the tunnel's opening.

"Who goes there?" a gruff, deep voice said.

Startled, he answered, "Esteban Atticus, sir."

"Come closer so I can get a good look at you."

Esteban was too scared to move. The obscure image of a large, bulky man appeared as a basket covering a small oil lamp was lifted. A large rugged hand came sharply into focus, reaching out, picking up the lamp, and holding it toward Esteban, as the ominous figure approached.

"Are you Amora's boy?"

"Yes, sir."

"Well, I'll be. What an honor," he said as he shook Esteban's hand. "Come, I will escort you."

Relieved, Esteban followed the man down the stairs into the tunnel and down its narrow walkways, lit only occasionally by dim lamps placed into small cavities carved into the walls. Esteban tried to stay close so he could see where to step while his guide rushed forward, babbling incessantly.

"I can't believe I am the first one to meet you. Won't the bishop be surprised? I can hardly wait to introduce you. Everyone will want to meet you. Watch your step. The service has already started, but they won't care. What an honor. I can hardly wait to tell my family that I met you when I go home tonight. Will you come next week? I'm sure to bring my wife and kids if you do."

Esteban wondered if the man would ever stop jabbering. When he spotted the light in the cavern where the services were held and noticed a crowd of people standing outside the worship service. "What are all those people doing standing outside the meeting?" he wondered.

"Move aside. This is Amora's boy," Esteban's guide said as they approached. The people crowding around the entrance to the room straining to hear the sermon all turned and stared at Esteban, making him feel uncomfortable. They parted, opening a tight pathway for Esteban and his guide to squeeze through. Everyone continued to gawk at Esteban as he walked by. One old lady reached out and touched him as he passed, giving him the creeps. Then several more people touched him as he passed by, causing Esteban to contract his shoulders in an effort to shrink out of people's reach.

They entered the chamber, and it was crammed with people standing everywhere. This was not at all what Esteban remembered or what he expected. "Who are all these people?" he wondered. He scanned the horde to find familiar faces and finally spotted Sabina's father, Darius. He strained to see through the crowd and thought he could see Sabina standing next to her father. Meanwhile, the bishop stood on a small raised lectern giving a sermon.

"Jesus said, 'Love your enemies, bless them that curse you, do good to them that hate you, and pray for them which despitefully use you and persecute you.'"

The catacomb guard led Esteban through the crowded assembly toward the front where people were sitting on the ground. Esteban scanned the crowd.

The bishop continued. "This is only possible as we open our heart so God can fill it with His love."

"Excuse me, Bishop," Esteban's guide said loudly. "This is Amora's boy."

The congregation gasped and turned to look at him.

"Is it? Yes, it is Esteban!" the bishop said as he stepped down from the lectern and walked toward Esteban. "My, you have grown this past year. I am so glad you were able to join us," he said as he shook Esteban's hand.

The bishop turned and faced the assembly that was now curious about this newcomer. "Praise God. This is Amora's son, Esteban. He has suffered a great loss through Amora's sacrifice. Let's pray for his comfort and well-being."

Esteban was surprised that most of the congregation fell to their knees and started praying while others gathered around him, thanking him and simultaneously offering their condolences.

"Your mother is a saint."

"I am so sorry for your loss."

"Thank you, Esteban."

"I pray that God will bless you."

All the voices fused into one unintelligible pounding noise that increased as the gathering parishioners pressed in on Esteban. This was not at all what he had expected or desired. He simply wanted to sneak into the back of the room, find Sabina, sit by her during the service, and let her know that he missed her. He had never liked being the center of attention. This was all very uncomfortable.

People again started to reach out and touch him. He started to breathe faster as he felt people pressing in all around him. Every way he turned he saw hands reaching out to touch him. He could not breathe. They were smothering him. He had to get out of there. He had to escape. He turned and made for the door, his arms thrashing, and his head gyrating as he swam through the mass of humanity. He finally broke free into the dark tunnel. He ran as fast as he could, gasping for breath—past the dim lamps—up the long flight of stairs—into the fresh air at last. He took a deep breath, and ran.

Sabina found Esteban sitting on the steps of Natalie's House. Esteban's head was buried in his hands. Sabina could tell that he had been crying. She sat down next to him without saying a word. She reached over and put her hand on his knee. He raised his head and looked over at her.

"How did you know I would be here?" he asked.

"I just thought this is where you would go."

"I miss all the fun we had here."

"Me too. I think a lot about you, Esteban."

"I miss you too.

"I am glad you came to the service tonight."

"Who were all those people?"

"They are new believers. Most of them became interested because of your mother's example in the arena."

"I don't like the way they touched me."

"They didn't mean any harm. Your mother is like an angel to them, so you are the closest thing to something divine that they have seen."

"I still don't like it."

"They were just trying to honor your mother."

"She is my mother, not theirs. I miss her more than they ever will. Life has been horrible since they killed her. I am all alone, Sabina. No one cares for me. Sometimes I wonder if she even loved me. Why would she choose to die and leave me all alone? Father hates me. He blames me for Natalie's death, and I think he blames me for this too. The new steward gives me the creeps. They never let me do anything. They are always hovering over me, telling me what to do. I can't stand it. And I can't see how it will ever change. I hoped that coming here tonight would help, but it didn't. Maybe I should just die."

Sabina sat silently, wondering what she could say to comfort him. Finally, she said, "I understand. I miss my mother too. But I have learned that even when things look hopeless, they get better."

"That is easy for you to say. At least you have a father

who loves you."

"I know you have it worse than me, but I still suffer, Esteban. I can't get over feeling guilty."

"Guilty? Why would you ever feel guilty?"

"I know it doesn't make sense, and I know that Mama is glad that I survived, but I still feel guilty that I am the only one who escaped."

"You do?"

"Yes. Your mother helped me, Esteban."

"She did?"

"I wouldn't be here without her. It was horrible, Esteban. My mother and grandfather were with me, along with other workers when the soldiers burst into the room. The centurion stood in front of the door. The other soldiers rushed in and started to grab the workers, so I snuck behind the window curtain where I used to hide when we played hide-and-seek. They were all screaming. I was so scared. One of the soldiers knocked over a crib and nearly stepped on the baby. That was when your mother and Maria ran into the room. The centurion grabbed her and they were struggling, so I ran out from behind the curtain and grabbed the baby and ran to the door. The centurion tried to catch me. But, thankfully, your mother grabbed his hand and stepped in front of him, so I could escape with the baby. I ran and hid in the alley across the street. I watched them drag my mother and everyone out and haul them away." Sabina sobbed. "I can't forget it."

Sabina lowered her head and cried. The flood of compassion that rushed into Esteban's heart washed away his self-pity. His concern for Sabina refocused his perspective beyond the pathos of his own world and to share her pain. He reached over and hugged her. A moment later, she returned his embrace.

Chapter 35

A Gladiator is Born

Antonio was hungry, but lunch could wait. Every day for the past six months, he had stood on the porch next to the mess hall door to observe the gladiator training before lunch. Initially, the trainers drove the new recruits to exhaustion, building their strength, stamina, and agility through incessant exercise. Antonio tried to duplicate these efforts by rising before dawn to run up and down the hills surrounding the villa where he was housed. In the evenings, he would continue his exercise routine by repeating the calisthenics he had observed the new trainees perform at the ludus that day. In the meantime, Antonio had become good friends with Adolf, who shared with him the instruction he received from his trainers as they ate their midday meal together. Antonio strove to implement this training in his daily practice.

After a few months, the trainers began to drill the rookies, whom they referred to as *novicius*, on basic gladiator skills such as thrusting and slicing with a wooden sword called a *rudus*, which was twice the weight of a regular sword to build the novicius' arm and upper-body strength. Hour after hour, they would jab and slash a large wooden pole called a *palus* that was secured in the ground in the middle of one of the training stations, practicing their strokes and maneuvers under the critical eyes of the trainers, without risking injury to other trainees.

The ludus was full of different groups of novicius and fighters who were either ready to fight or had fought in the arena, called *Tirones gladiatores* or just *Tiros*. Each group would be assigned to a station in the morning and rotate to a different one in the afternoon. There were several different training posts, but the recent arrivals were limited in the choices that were available to them.

The doctorii had begun to introduce the recent novicius to various training equipment and to new weapons and shields. Today, Antonio watched Adolf attempt to circumvent the hazards of the rotating dummy wheel. Adolf struck a dummy suspended from a large wheel overhead that rotated from the force of his blow, swinging a sandbag around that smacked Adolf's head as he ducked to avoid being hit. Antonio laughed out loud along with Adolf's companions. With that embarrassing collision, the trainer dismissed his trainees for their midday meal.

"Hello, Adolf," Antonio said when Adolf joined him on the porch.

"Hello," Adolf replied.

"Wie geht es?" Antonio said with a friendly chuckle. Adolf turned and glared at Antonio. "Now, remind me, how do you say 'head' in German?"

"Haft die Klappe."

"Don't be so sensitive, you big oaf," Antonio said as he slapped his friend on the back. "Let's get something to eat."

"Was gibt es zum mittagessen?" Adolf asked.

"The usual. Barley soup," Antonio replied.

"When will they ever feed us some meat?" Adolf said with disgust as they entered the mess hall and joined the back of the line of gladiator trainees filing past the cooks serving them bread and soup in large wooden bowls. "I could teach these imbeciles how to cook a tasty venison stew or beef tenderloin," he continued.

"Stop making me homesick," Antonio said as he observed that the tables were already half-full of hungry diners.

"What I really miss is a chunk of sharp cheese," Adolf murmured.

"I told you to stop it. Now, what did they teach you today?"

"Nothing. They gave us some poles and said they will teach us how to use a spear," Adolf scoffed. "I've been using spears since I was a child. There's nothing they can teach me." Antonio recalled the training he had received as a youth in Hispania and wondered how it compared to Adolf's experience. Adolf continued. "They simply told us how to hold the pole and jab. A total waste of time."

Antonio noticed a broom in the corner and a pole next to a couple of buckets against the wall. He could not resist the temptation to have some fun with his comrade. Antonio grabbed the broom and tossed the pole to Adolf. "Let's see how good you are," he said as he took a combative stance. "En garde."

"I don't want to hurt you," Adolf said as people scattered and pushed the tables out of the way to give them a wide berth. "Prepare to suffer!"

Adolf held his surrogate spear in front of him and charged. Antonio held his ground and did not move until, at the last second, he used the handle of the broom to smack Adolf's pole away as Antonio spun around and swatted Adolf on his butt with the head of the broom as he thundered by, to the laughter of the crowd. Rarely did they have live entertainment for their meal, so this contest captured the attention of all in the hall. The diners jumped up so as not to miss any of the action while some started chanting "Accountant, accountant," inspiring others to counter with shouts of "Adolphus, Adolphus."

Adolf, now enraged, turned and faced Antonio. He let out his bloodcurdling war cry and charged. Again, Antonio stood fixed in his position, ready to engage his rushing opponent. This time he did not use his weapon to knock Adolf's spear out of the way but instead dodged the pole while planting the broom firmly on the floor in front of Adolf's feet. Antonio smashed into Adolf's side as he passed, sending him tumbling into the table and chairs nearby. The collision dislodged the iron ball in Antonio's sash, causing it to crash to the floor. Antonio, swinging the broom over his head, lunged toward Adolf, sprawled over the table and chairs, frantically scrambling to regain his footing. The tug of the chain on Antonio's ankle made him lose his balance, and he fell next to Adolf, who seized the opportunity by rolling over on top of Antonio and placing his rod on top of Antonio's neck to the applause of the room. Adolf, by luck, had prevailed.

Adolf and Antonio stood in front of all of the trainees, trainers, staff, and guards that had been assembled in front of the ludus office. General Sulla exited and marched to face them. He fought the impulse to laugh, for he knew he had to execute punishment for this disturbance in order to maintain discipline, but he could not help but be amused by this escapade. He paced back and forth in front of the detainees, slapping his hand with his whip. He stopped, looked at Antonio, and said, "Now, what is the appropriate punishment for this fracas?" His prisoners stood, staring straight ahead, silently unrepentant. Whatever the punishment, the adventure would have been worth the consequence. "We can't have people coming into this facility and disrupting our quiet meals, can we?"

"No, sir," Antonio answered.

Sulla stepped over and looked at Adolf. "I am glad you prevailed. If you could not beat an accountant with a ball and chain, I might have had to send you back to the quarry."

"Yes, sir."

"You each will spend three days and nights in the hole. If you disturb any meal or indoor activity again, you will be flogged. Do you understand?"

"Yes, sir," both Antonio and Adolf replied.

"In the future, Adolphus, train my accountant outside," Sulla said with a grin.

"Yes, sir," he said as Antonio smiled. He would be trained.

* * *

"Be careful, Adolphus, that you don't trip on your own stick," Rufus said as their doctores handed out the poles to the novicius a few days after Adolf had served his time in the hole.

"Yeah, maybe you should put it down before you get hurt," another trainee said.

"Shut up."

"Why? We are just looking out for you. We wouldn't want you to be hurt," a third novicius chimed in.

"I hear there will be physical contact today, so you should go hide over there in the corner," Rufus said, as all the trainees laughed.

"I will smash your skull in, Rufus."

"Oh, I'm so scared of this big dangerous warrior who couldn't even beat a chained accountant," Rufus said with a chuckle.

"I subdued him, but he would destroy you in the arena."

"When Cupid rules on Olympus."

"I wager a day's meals that he will beat you in next month's games," Adolf said.

"If you want to starve, then I won't stop you."

Entertainment was a rare commodity at the ludus, so the prospect of a match between their accountant and a novicius grabbed everyone's attention. A festive fervor swept through the ludus with no one immune from the jovial enthusiasm. Each person had an opinion regarding the match and multiple bets to support it. The cooks served their chosen contestant extra food; experienced Tiros proffered advice; even the leather smith made a girdle for Antonio with a pouch to secure his ball and chain.

By the time the next month's games arrived, the crescendo of excitement had peaked. They even scheduled the bout as the climax of the games because of the level of interest. The sparring contests that normally attracted their attention throughout the day just seemed to drag on as they anxiously waited to watch something new and different. They were used to watching the various types of gladiators spar in these monthly games: *retiarii* net fighters battling *secutores* slashers, a heavily protected *Cataphractarius* against a heavily armed *Gallus* foe, a *Scissores* with his scissor blade pitted against a two-sword gladiator, lasso-and-sword fighters against whip-and-club fighters, the horseback eques against a group of *velites* with lances, and even the *Essedarii* chariot fighters, each calculated to balance the different fighting styles, weapons, and protection to generate the most exciting show, yet they all just seemed to be the regular mundane exhibitions they had seen countless times before, month after month.

Today would be different. Instead of the trained Tiros gladiators, they would watch a novice fight an accountant shackled to a ball and chain, each with real swords instead of the wooden training weapons typically used at their stage of experience. There was a strict rule in these sparring games

Chapter 36

Clandestine Rendezvous

"Go ahead, Sabina. You can see if he left you a message."

"Oh, thank you, Father."

Sabina scurried off as Darius smiled and said to himself, "Young love is so adorable. But naïve. I hope I'm doing the right thing letting her carry on her fantasy with this boy. I'm not sure that I should let this friendship continue now that she is a fourteen-year-old young woman. Gloria would have known what to do. I miss her so!"

Sabina rushed through the crowd in the produce market on her way to Natalie's House. She was anxious to see if Esteban had left her a note in their secret chamber. The night Esteban ran out of the worship service, they had discovered a loose stone on the steps where he was sitting. Esteban knew that she went to the produce market every Thursday, so they developed their private tradition of exchanging notes each week. Sometimes he would leave her a puzzle to figure out. Other times he would write something to make her feel good or just mention something funny that had happened. Occasionally he would let her know where they might meet without his father finding out. Those were rare but cherished occasions—a "chance" meeting in the plaza to buy some trinket, stopping by to help with her chores, and holding hands as they walked among the stone pines by the banks of the Tiber.

As children they had often held hands while they skipped and hobbled along behind their mothers as they walked home, and ever since then, they had often continued that practice. But that walk along the Tiber holding hands was the only time that Sabina recognized that Esteban might have developed romantic feelings for her. But she wasn't sure. Sometimes he seemed to be preparing to say something, and then he either changed the subject or just remained frozen in awkward silence. Did he still view her as just his childhood buddy, or was there more to their relationship?

She was glad that he always showed her respect, unlike the crude comments from many of her male peers, but she wondered if he had even noticed that she had grown into a young woman with a figure. What was wrong with boys? Either they were disgusting or oblivious. Why couldn't they just be normal? She had noticed that Esteban had grown taller and begun to fill out. Why hadn't he noticed her maturing? Some of her friends were already married at this age. She loved how Esteban's broad shoulders evidenced hours of exercise to compensate for his disability. She reflected how she no longer noticed his limp and was taken aback when others mentioned it. As she neared her destination, she acknowledged that the good looks Esteban had inherited from his parents had not escaped her either. Maybe today he would finally reciprocate and indicate a deeper interest in her.

Sabina slowed down when she reached the street where Natalie's House was located. She strolled along nonchalantly, casually looking around to see if anyone was watching her. She stood next to the door, leaned against the building, and pretended that she was looking at something in her bag. Assured that the coast was clear, she quickly leaned down and lifted the stone to reveal a note below. She quickly grabbed it, stuck it in her bag, and continued on her way.

Sulla stepped over and looked at Adolf. "I am glad you prevailed. If you could not beat an accountant with a ball and chain, I might have had to send you back to the quarry."

"Yes, sir."

"You each will spend three days and nights in the hole. If you disturb any meal or indoor activity again, you will be flogged. Do you understand?"

"Yes, sir," both Antonio and Adolf replied.

"In the future, Adolphus, train my accountant outside," Sulla said with a grin.

"Yes, sir," he said as Antonio smiled. He would be trained.

* * *

"Be careful, Adolphus, that you don't trip on your own stick," Rufus said as their doctores handed out the poles to the novicius a few days after Adolf had served his time in the hole.

"Yeah, maybe you should put it down before you get hurt," another trainee said.

"Shut up."

"Why? We are just looking out for you. We wouldn't want you to be hurt," a third novicius chimed in.

"I hear there will be physical contact today, so you should go hide over there in the corner," Rufus said, as all the trainees laughed.

"I will smash your skull in, Rufus."

"Oh, I'm so scared of this big dangerous warrior who couldn't even beat a chained accountant," Rufus said with a chuckle.

"I subdued him, but he would destroy you in the arena."

"When Cupid rules on Olympus."

"I wager a day's meals that he will beat you in next month's games," Adolf said.

"If you want to starve, then I won't stop you."

Entertainment was a rare commodity at the ludus, so the prospect of a match between their accountant and a novicius grabbed everyone's attention. A festive fervor swept through the ludus with no one immune from the jovial enthusiasm. Each person had an opinion regarding the match and multiple bets to support it. The cooks served their chosen contestant extra food; experienced Tiros proffered advice; even the leather smith made a girdle for Antonio with a pouch to secure his ball and chain.

By the time the next month's games arrived, the crescendo of excitement had peaked. They even scheduled the bout as the climax of the games because of the level of interest. The sparring contests that normally attracted their attention throughout the day just seemed to drag on as they anxiously waited to watch something new and different. They were used to watching the various types of gladiators spar in these monthly games: *retiarii* net fighters battling *secutores* slashers, a heavily protected *Cataphractarius* against a heavily armed *Gallus* foe, a *Scissores* with his scissor blade pitted against a two-sword gladiator, lasso-and-sword fighters against whip-and-club fighters, the horseback eques against a group of *velites* with lances, and even the *Essedarii* chariot fighters, each calculated to balance the different fighting styles, weapons, and protection to generate the most exciting show, yet they all just seemed to be the regular mundane exhibitions they had seen countless times before, month after month.

Today would be different. Instead of the trained Tiros gladiators, they would watch a novice fight an accountant shackled to a ball and chain, each with real swords instead of the wooden training weapons typically used at their stage of experience. There was a strict rule in these sparring games that no contestant was allowed to seriously injure his combatant intentionally, but because of Antonio and Rufus's inexperience, there was a much greater chance that someone would be hurt, increasing the allure of the match.

Finally, the fight began. A confident Rufus charged Antonio. The spectators rose in unison, not wanting to miss any of the action. Antonio stood his ground and, at the last moment, stepped aside in order to avoid the impact of Rufus's charge and immediately engaged Rufus as he overshot the target of his assault. Rufus was taken aback by Antonio's speed and agility but soon regained his footing. Rufus had size and brute strength on his side, so he proceeded to use them. He swung his sword with all the force he could muster; it collided with Antonio's round shield with a deafening crash. Rufus continued his assault, pushing Antonio back, but Antonio was too adept to be forced against the arena's wall. Instead, he pivoted slightly with each blow in order to rotate around the center of the arena.

Rufus began to tire, along with the audience. They had not come to simply watch swords hit shields over and over again. Some of the experienced spectators began to yell out advice while others booed. Antonio recognized that Rufus was weakening and beginning to be disturbed by the clamor of the audience. Antonio waited, watching for Rufus to make a mistake.

Suddenly, Rufus struck Antonio's shield from overhead, followed by a volley of similar short strikes, leaving Rufus exposed on his side. Antonio spun around and hit Rufus on his waist with the flat side of his sword in order to avoid serious injury. Rufus wildly swung his sword at Antonio, who simply stepped out of reach and then hit Rufus's helmet with a powerful blow as Rufus overswung. Enraged, Rufus charged Antonio with his shield and attempted to jab him with his gladius. Antonio avoided the thrust of Rufus's sword, but now that they were in intimate quarters, Antonio used the hilt of his sword to strike Rufus's arm, weakening his grip on his sword. Antonio then tripped Rufus, who dropped his sword as he fell to the ground. In an instant, Antonio stood above his vanquished foe, holding the point of his sword to Rufus's neck. The crowd cheered while Rufus lay motionless.

The victorious accountant shook his sword and shield high above his head as he turned to acknowledge the praise of the spectators around him. Suddenly the audience gasped. Antonio glanced down just in time to see the blade of Rufus's sword being swung with full force at his knee. He felt excruciating pain explode from his knee as he collapsed. His vision zeroed in on Rufus, kneeling next to him, attempting to stand, sword in hand. The evil of Rufus's action triggered the wrath Antonio had for Leo. Antonio felt power surge through his body as he stood. Fortunately, Rufus's blade had struck the chain running down Antonio's leg, saving it from being severed. Projecting all his ire for Leo onto this new heinous enemy, Antonio attacked Rufus with all the fury of a lion. Blow after blow, he forced Rufus back, back, back to the wall where he had nowhere else to go. With one swing, Antonio knocked Rufus's sword aside as he spun in toward Rufus and smashed his face in with the hilt of his sword, splattering blood everywhere. Rufus slumped to the earth, unconscious. The crowd roared.

Commodus jumped into the arena and loudly proclaimed that he could train the accountant to beat any of the gladiators at the ludus.

Once around the corner, she opened the note and read: "Please meet me today before sunset at the top of the stairs to the Porticu Liviae Gardens. I have something special I want to show you."

Sabina's heart skipped a beat. "Yes! He does care for me," she thought. She floated home, dreaming of holding hands in the lush royal gardens, her head on his shoulder, watching the sunset. But reality slapped her in the face as soon as she looked in her mirror and saw her long, stringy hair. "Oh no," she thought. "What can I do with my hair?" She looked down at her dirty, worn-out tunic. "What am I going to wear?" It was already late afternoon. How could she get ready in time for this special occasion? Panic rushed over her. She began to cry.

"What is wrong?" her younger brother asked.

"Everything," she sobbed as she rummaged through her sparse wardrobe. Finding nothing to her liking, she threw herself on her bed and wept. It was all hopeless. She didn't own a gorgeous stola like the one she had fancied herself wearing in her dreams. Now, her reality had turned into a nightmare. Her father knocked and opened the door. "Go away," she said.

"What's wrong, Sabina?"

"Nothing."

"Come now, dear. You can talk to me," he reassured her as he approached and sat down next to her. "Please tell me about it."

She looked up at her father, wiped away her tears, and said, "Oh, Papa. I don't know what to do. Esteban invited me to watch the sunset with him, but I don't have anything to wear, and look at my hair."

"Why, you look gorgeous, Sabina."

Sabina threw herself back down and buried her head in

her pillow. "You don't understand," she cried.

How he wished Gloria were still alive. She would know how to deal with this situation. He was torn between discouraging this rendezvous and supporting her. His natural fatherly instinct was to discourage this relationship, but he knew his wife would have a different idea. So he decided to try to imagine how she would handle this crisis.

"Sabina, wait here. I have something that may help."

Sabina looked up as her father left the room. He returned with a large chest and laid it on the floor in front of her. "These were your mother's clothes that she wanted me to save for you. Maybe something will fit and be appropriate," he said as he opened the box.

"Oh, thank you, Papa," she said. "I didn't know you kept these."

"I hadn't realized that you had grown up so much. Now, let's see what we have here."

Sabina lifted the top stola out of the trunk and held it up to her in front of the mirror. Memories of her mother in the dress flooded her mind, bringing tears to her eyes. She lifted one garment after another, hugging each close to her breast. Darius offered his daughter the most glamorous stola in the chest. Sabina laughed and said that it was way too formal for such a casual occasion. She selected the first stola on the top of the chest, which she remembered was her mother's favorite. Her father left the room to give her privacy while she tried it on. It fit her perfectly. She grinned, knowing her mother was still watching over her.

In the mirror she saw her father enter the room with a beautiful broach that had belonged to her mother. She turned and gave him a big hug. "Thank you, Papa. I love you so much." She looked up to heaven and whispered, "Thank you, Mama."

Darius handed Sabina the broach and offered her the brush from her table. "You'd better hurry, dear," he said with a smile.

Sabina was out of breath when she reached the top of the stairs. Esteban was standing there to greet her.

"I am glad you came," he said.

"Thank you for inviting me."

"I saved us a seat on that bench," he said as he escorted her to a concrete bench overlooking the city below and the green hills in the distance. The sky was ablaze with various shades of red and orange, consuming the blue sky in their flames. They sat down, Esteban held her hand, and she rested her head on his shoulder, just as she had dreamed. The bright yellow sun was settling down over the aqueduct with its double-level arch structure. She was surprised to see how the sun seemed to flatten out when it reached the top of the aqueduct as if the water was melting the sun so that it would flow out. Suddenly the sun burst into view through the top of the arch, below the aqueduct channel. They watched as the sun disappeared above the canal and filled the space framed by the arch and hills below. The aqueduct seemed to be a man-made portal to heaven, allowing a dazzling divine beacon to shine down on the temporal world. Slowly the portal closed as the earth swallowed the golden beam, leaving a blood-red afterglow to remind all viewers of their mortal state.

Sabina looked up at Esteban and said, "That was special. Thank you for sharing it."

He gazed into her eyes and smiled.

Sabina felt heat rush through her body, propelled by her rapidly beating heart, awakening feelings that had lain dormant. She closed her eyes to more fully experience the emotions aroused by Esteban's touch as his hands slipped behind her back. Her eager body surrendered to his caress as he held her close. She leaned her head back, her lips slightly open, inviting. The soft touch of his lips triggered a reciprocal response as she held him tight while they enjoyed the ecstasy of their first kiss. Their lips parted. She opened her eyes and gazed into Esteban's, then suddenly they were hugging and passionately kissing again.

Holding each other tightly, they watched as the silhouettes of the city structures, the aqueduct, hills, and trees against the darkening sky infused their union with tender feelings of peace and harmony. Holding her hand, Esteban escorted Sabina to the stairs and stopped. He stood, staring down the steps below for such a long time that Sabina began to wonder what was wrong. She glanced over at Esteban, who did not return her gaze. Finally, he spoke.

"This is the only place where I remember feeling that my father loved me. Just after I turned six years old, I fell down these steps and injured myself. My father came to my rescue. He held me tight and comforted me while he ascended these stairs, and when we got to the top, he defended me against the assault of the local authority. But it did not last long. That was when it happened. Ever since then, he has blamed me for my sister's death. Everything changed right here. My life has never been the same since that day."

Sabina did not know what to say, so she simply held him tight while he continued to stand there stiffly. After a while she whispered, "I'm so sorry." She felt the tension in his body relax.

He continued. "This public garden is my private sanctuary. I often come here when I want to be alone and think. I am glad you are here with me."

The intimacy of this confession eclipsed the passion of their first kiss and sealed their bond. Nothing would ever be the same for either of them again.

Chapter 37

Germania

Antonio felt exposed, standing in the arena with only a lasso and gladius. Experience in the arena proved to be an invaluable instructor. It was how he had learned to use his shield as a weapon as well as a defensive tool. But now he stood facing a whip-and-club gladiator without his familiar secret weapon. He had survived for more than a year fighting in the local arena, and was determined to survive one more fight.

Antonio threw his lasso toward his foe, who simply ducked aside and charged, snapping his whip on Antonio's bare back. Antonio grimaced in pain as he ducked to avoid a blow from his foe's club. Antonio swung his sword at his adversary and missed but was effective in keeping him at bay.

Antonio again threw his lasso with no better result. The gladiator again snapped his whip at Antonio, but this time Antonio discarded his useless rope and grabbed the whip with his strong hands. He needlessly gave it a tug as his rival was already swinging his club above Antonio's head. He quickly swung his sword to deflect the blow and nearly lost it when they collided. The opponents locked their arms, limiting the use of their weapons. They struggled in a battle of strength that Antonio was destined to lose. So he dropped his sword and spun behind his foe, wrapping the whip around his neck and tightening it until his opponent dropped, unconscious.

After the bout, Antonio waited in the ludus office next to Marcellus's desk. Commodus returned from the treasury holding a bag of coins. "You are becoming a rich man, Antonio."

"I hope to buy my freedom soon."

Handing the bag to Antonio, Commodus said, "Well, you've nearly earned it."

All were surprised to see General Sulla enter the room and announce, "Antonio, you and your German friend will be joining me tomorrow morning when we leave to join Emperor Aurelius in Germania."

Antonio's heart sank. The campaign in Germania would take years. His dream of soon buying his freedom was dashed. For over a year he had competed against a host of gladiators at the ludus, each with their own honed skill. Thanks to Commodus's tutelage, Antonio had won his first bouts. Soon, all the Tiros at the ludus had adopted him as their favored son and proffered specific hints on how to compete against the various types of gladiators with their unique strengths and weaknesses. This training was invaluable. With each win, the ludus occupants showered Antonio with small gifts and money, which Antonio had been saving. Each blow in the arena was imbued with power from Antonio's quest for vengeance, which he felt inching closer to reality with each swing. Now, the goal that had seemed to be within his reach had been ripped from his grasp and tossed into the unforeseeable future.

"You will be my personal attendant," Sulla said. "The German tongue you have learned to speak may come in handy. Marcellus, take him to the blacksmith to remove those chains. He won't need them where we are going."

"Yes, sir," Marcellus replied.

Antonio found it impossible to sleep, so he got out of bed in the slave quarters and went for one last walk around General Sulla's villa. It was a beautiful clear night with refreshing crisp air, making it easy to reflect on the events of his life. He realized that he would actually miss his life here and at the ludus. He had enjoyed all the activity and camaraderie with his fellow gladiators. Antonio sat down on a hillside overlooking the valley below, lit by the full moon and bright stars. His thoughts turned to Maria. As he leaned back and looked up at the stars, he recalled when he had first made love to Maria on a night much like this one.

* * *

Antonio's thoughts about Maria had robbed him of sleep, so he ventured out to the garden behind Leo's villa and lay down on the soft grass while he searched the night sky for a sign.

Meanwhile, Maria lay in her bed, fantasizing about the young dark-haired man who had recently appeared in her life, and now he was paying her special attention. How could she sleep? It was impossible.

She rose from her cot and wrapped a robe around herself before she stepped out to stroll in their courtyard. Standing in the cool night air on the edge of the peristyle, she peered out at the garden beyond, lit by a full moon. She closed her eyes and took a deep breath, savoring the pleasant aroma of the orange blossoms. She smiled, opened her eyes, and slowly descended the steps.

Maria, silhouetted in the arched doorway by the light from the lanterns in the peristyle, had not escaped Antonio's view. He watched as Maria glided through the garden like a graceful dancer, head slightly tilted, arms outstretched yet relaxed, her fingers gently brushing the leaves, her hair flowing in the slight breeze. Strolling past a planter, Maria was startled to find Antonio lying on the grass, staring up at her with his hands behind his head.

"I hope I didn't frighten you," he said, rising up on his elbow.

"On the contrary. I'm glad to see you."

"Likewise. Do you care to join me?" he invited as he sat up.

"Certainly," she responded as she settled down next to him.

"Maria, do you have dreams?"

"Everyone dreams, silly."

"You know what I mean," he responded. "Do you dream about your future?"

"Sure. Even a slave longs to fall in love, marry and live in eternal bliss."

"Do you suppose that ever happens? I mean, the eternal bliss part?"

"I don't know, but at least we can dream." She smiled.

"But why does it have to be a fantasy? Look at Leo and Amora. What happened to sour their relationship?"

"Just life, I suppose."

"But why? Can't things ever work out?"

"If they really loved each other," Maria mused.

"But they must have loved each other once."

"I still think they care for each other."

"At times. But there's not much left." Antonio shook his head. "Is this the fate of all relationships?" he wondered aloud.

"No. I think love can grow when we share experiences and sacrifice for each other."

"That is what I love about you, Maria. You are so optimistic and caring. You won't change, will you?"

"Of course, I will. Everyone changes. I just hope it will be for the better."

Antonio chuckled before changing the subject. "Maria, look at those stars. Do you see that constellation over there? See the bright star there and the others on both sides?"

"I see them."

"Well, that's Andromeda. Her arms are outstretched, chained to a rock. You know the story, right?" Antonio inquired.

"A beautiful princess was chained to die on a rocky coast as a sacrifice to a sea monster in order to appease Neptune, who was offended by her mother's vanity."

"Yes. But Perseus, flying by, was struck by her grace and beauty. So, he promised her parents he would kill the monster in exchange for her hand in marriage."

"He killed the beast, and then they were happily married," Maria finished the story.

"Maria, I think of you when I see those stars. I dream of someday buying our freedom."

Antonio looked adoringly at Maria. His heart raced as heat rushed through his body. She gazed into his eyes. He touched her hand beside him. She smiled invitingly. They embraced.

Chapter 38

The Note

"Where have you been?" Leo grilled his son.

"With Timotheus," Esteban answered defensively.

"That is what you said last week, and when I asked his father, he said you were not there."

"We met at the market and then played down by the Tiber."

Leo's eyes narrowed as he glared at Esteban. He feared what he suspected. The last thing he needed was for another family member to get mixed up with those Christian dissidents. Leo decided right then and there that he had to see Rusticus about that cult.

Rusticus, meanwhile, was meeting with Leo's business partners, Quintus, Gaius, Titus, and Crescens.

"I am convinced that we need to remove Leo as the head of our Egyptian Publicani," Quintus said to his partners. "I fear that his excessive drinking and gambling will compromise his judgment."

"Do you have any evidence of this?" Gaius inquired.

"Yes. He lets correspondence from our agents in Alexandria pile up for months before he responds."

"How do you know this?" Rusticus asked.

"His steward expressed concern."

"Was this delay during the winter months when travel is limited?" Gaius asked.

"No. Not always. Besides, I have also heard that his gambling losses are growing, and I am afraid that he may be tempted to utilize our assets to secure his personal debt."

"I do not believe we should rashly jeopardize our business based on rumors. We need to remember that not only did Leo bring us this opportunity, he is the one who has the personal relationships with our local agents," Gaius pointed out.

"I concur," said Titus.

"Regardless, we should be observant to ensure that our investment is safe. We have a lot at risk here," Rusticus continued.

At that moment, Rusticus's steward entered, informing him that Leo was there and hoped to speak with him.

"By all means, show him in," Rusticus replied while glancing around the room at his partners.

Leo noticed his associates around Rusticus's desk when he entered the room, but was undeterred as he marched up to Rusticus.

"Prefect, I must talk with you. There are still hundreds of those crazed zealots infecting Rome!"

"Don't get so excited, Leo. We are doing what we can."

"This cult undermines the emperor's sovereign position!"

"All right, Leo. Show me a Christian, and I will arrest him."

"Leo is right, Rusticus," Quintus interjected. "They do undermine our civil society. They teach that a converted slave is a child of God of equal status with his master, and the emperor is not divine, but a pagan."

Leo continued. "This cult keeps growing, and if we don't stop it, we will face a slave rebellion worse than the one led by Spartacus."

"But how do you find them?" Rusticus asked in frustration. "They are like rats. As soon as you spot them, they scatter and disappear."

"Use your spies and locate the leaders. Chop off the head and the snake dies."

"Yes. We are already working on it."

* * *

Esteban was playing with his monkey underneath the backyard portico by Leo's study when he overheard Rusticus tell Quintus and his father about shocking developments regarding the Christian menace. He moved closer to the window and listened.

"Our spies have located the residence of the Christian bishop and several of their leading men: Marius, Septimus, and a fellow named Darius, whose wife was arrested at Amora's charity and subsequently executed. Most of these rebels live in the *Piscina Publica* region," Rusticus said.

"That is wonderful news," Quintus exclaimed.

"What are your plans?" Leo asked.

"We need a large cohort to prevent those slippery snakes from escaping," Rusticus explained. "So, we will send out seven different companies to strike simultaneously at dawn."

"Excellent," Leo said.

"Who else knows of these plans?" Quintus asked. "Christians seem to have ears everywhere."

"No one yet, besides you, me, my spies, and my trusted assistant. We will hand out their assignments right before they leave in the morning."

"Perfect! Let's hope that this time we will be able to capture these radicals and destroy this movement."

"Don't worry, Quintus. Our spies are monitoring their homes. We will catch them. You can be sure of it," Rusticus added.

Esteban quickly moved away from the window to avoid being noticed as they left. He had to do something to warn

Sabina and her father. He had lost his mother, but he would not let them take Sabina. It was already late in the afternoon, so he had very little time to act. How could he warn them without being detected? The only safe way he could think of was to leave Sabina a note, but she normally only checked their secret cubicle on Thursday, which would be too late. Regardless, he would try every means possible.

Esteban quickly retired to his room and wrote a note warning Sabina. He grabbed his woolen cloak, and started to leave.

"Where are you going?" Prometheus stopped him.

"Can't he ever mind his own business?" Esteban thought. "Oh, I forgot that I promised Timotheus I would...help him with his studies," he said aloud.

"Don't be late. It looks like it will rain."

"Understood," he said. He hated how this slave ordered him around and always seemed to be spying on him. Esteban vowed to himself to put Prometheus in his place when he eventually gained his rightful status.

Esteban rushed down the street toward Sabina's home, all the while trying to figure out how he could scope out the surveillance without being detected. He realized that he needed to be extra cautious not only because his limp set him apart, but also because the cold weather had thinned out the usual crowds. He stopped a few blocks before reaching her home, placed the cloak's hood on his head, and wrapped his cloak snugly around him. He wished he had brought his cane, which he hardly ever used, as it would have been a good prop. He looked around and did not see anything else he could use, so he proceeded slowly down the street and entered the next storefront he encountered.

"May I help you?" the proprietor asked.

Esteban looked around. The store sold nothing but

scarves. "Just looking," Esteban replied. After pretending to examine the merchandise for a while, he turned to the owner and said, "Thank you. Maybe another day," and left.

The next store was on the corner, one block from Sabina's house. Hopefully, there would be something there that would help his disguise. At first, he thought he was out of luck again, as they only sold herbal remedies. Then he spotted long stems of sage, rosemary, and lavender in baskets next to the wall.

"I would like to buy some of these herbs," he said.

"Certainly, young man. Which ones do you want?"

"How about this one and that one?" Esteban said, pointing to the sage and lavender.

The shop owner stepped over to the baskets. "Let me know how much you want," he said as he began to collect Esteban's purchase.

"That is enough. Can you also sell me a bundle of thyme?"

"Of course. Do you have anything to carry them in?"

"No. Can you wrap them in something or sell me a small bag?"

"Certainly. Here you go. That will be two *sestertii*."

"Thank you," Esteban said as he left the shop. He pulled his hood snug to hide his face and began to hobble along, carrying the bag with the herbs sticking out. He wished he had a cane to help him look like an old man. But he had to settle for what he had available. Even though he was stooped over and faced down as he limped along, his eyes darted from one point to another, surveying his surroundings. He didn't notice anything unusual until he crossed Sabina's street, where he spotted two men talking halfway down the road toward Sabina's house. It definitely appeared that her home was under surveillance. He would have no chance to warn her directly unless she were to leave her home for some reason. Esteban continued to walk down the street and around the corner, scanning the locale. Everything else seemed in order, so he decided to go two blocks down the street parallel to Sabina's and then cross over farther away in the other direction to see if the men were still there. This exercise confirmed his fear; her home was definitely being watched.

Esteban threw the herbs into the street and made his way to Natalie's House, waited close by until no one appeared to be watching, quickly snuck his note into their secret receptacle, and moved on. "Please, Sabina, check our box today. Don't wait until tomorrow," he pleaded in his mind. But he knew he could not count on providence. He had to figure out a way to get Sabina to leave her home. At first, he thought of finding some of her friends or even asking a street urchin to pass along a message, but that would not only put the messenger at risk; it would also expose everyone. There had to be a better way. "Oh God, please help me," he prayed as he strained to think of a solution, but nothing came to mind.

It began to drizzle as he walked back toward Sabina's street. On the way he spotted a stick he could use as a cane. "Just my luck. Late as usual. When I need something, it is nowhere to be found, until I don't need it." He sighed as he kicked the stick. Regardless, he picked it up and continued down his path. He noticed that the dark clouds made it appear later than it was. "Prometheus will drill me on why I have been gone so long," he thought. "But I have to find a way to save her. Even if I have to stay out all night."

By the time he reached Sabina's street, the rain was beginning to come down more steadily. He looked towards her house and noticed that the sentries were still there. He moved around the corner, sat down next to the building, and held his head in his hands, disheartened. Occasionally, he peeked around the corner to see if the men were still watching. Each time, his fading optimism diminished even more. While he waited, the rain increased, washing away his hope.

Esteban stared at the herbs he had earlier thrown into the street. By then the rain had turned into a downpour. Desperate, Esteban stood, determined to warn Sabina and her family, even if it meant his own arrest and death. He grabbed the herbs and makeshift cane and advanced slowly in the pounding rain, hoping not to be detected. With each step, his anxiety increased. The guards were nowhere in sight. "The driving rain must have convinced them that it was safe for them to leave at this late hour," Esteban thought. But he realized he was wrong when he spotted them across the street under a doorway. They glanced at Esteban. He continued to limp along, using his cane, the bundle of herbs in his hand. The spies ignored him.

Esteban knocked on Sabina's door. Junius, Sabina's younger brother, answered.

"Esteban!" he said. "Come in. Papa, Sabina, it's Esteban!"

Darius and Sabina rushed to the entryway. "What's wrong, Esteban?" Sabina asked. "Why are you out in this torrent?"

"You have to leave immediately," Esteban exclaimed. "I overheard the prefect tell my father that you all will be arrested at dawn, along with the bishop and some others."

Sabina gasped.

"Who else?" Darius asked, aghast, as he grabbed Esteban's shoulders.

"Marius and Septimus. And a few others that I can't remember. You need to hurry and be careful. Two men have been watching your house all afternoon, and they are still out there."

"Sabina, go help your siblings get ready. Thank you, Esteban. You need to go now," Darius said. As Esteban turned to leave, Darius grabbed his shoulder. "Out the back."

* * *

"All the Christians escaped this morning!" Prefect Rusticus told Leo when he entered his office.

"What? How did that happen?" Leo demanded.

"We thought you could shed some light on the subject," Quintus replied.

"Me? What are you talking about?"

"Leo, we have reason to believe that you informed the Christians of our plans," Rusticus said.

"How can you say that? You know that I want the Christians brought to justice more than anyone."

"Someone warned them, and it wasn't either one of us," Quintus said.

"Well, it wasn't me!" Leo insisted.

"We retrieved this note," Rusticus said as he handed the paper to Leo.

Leo read the note: "Your family must hide immediately, or they will be arrested tomorrow morning." His heart sank as he recognized his son's writing. Rusticus scanned Leo's face and glanced over at Quintus.

"Do you know anything about this note?" Rusticus asked slowly.

"No," Leo replied.

"I hope you are telling the truth," Rusticus paused. "We have no more questions at this time."

In a rage Leo stormed home where he found Esteban sitting on a bench in the atrium. Leo marched straight to him and hit Esteban in the face with his fist, knocking him onto his back.

"You insolent, good-for-nothing cripple! How dare you

mock me with your disobedience?" Leo growled as he kicked Esteban. Leo reached down, grabbed his son, and lifted him up in the air, holding him with both hands in front of his face. "I told you to never associate with Christians, did I not?" He violently shook Esteban. "Answer me, Boy."

"Y- y- yes, Father."

"You disgusting cripple! I should never have let your mother keep you. You are the source of all my problems," Leo yelled as he threw Esteban on the floor. He stomped out of the atrium into the peristyle, mumbling, "You will get us all killed yet." Leo smacked a vase off a pedestal, shattering it on the ground as he passed by. Unfazed, he strode on into the manicured garden, where he stopped, grabbed the back of a bench with both hands, and stared at the fountain, in a daze, his memory fixating on the fateful day at the royal gardens that had changed his life. If it hadn't been for that fateful day, Amora would not have had any interest in that crazy religion that promised life after death. Leo shook his head. This was all Esteban's fault. Leo let go of the back of the bench and marched away, kicking Esteban's cane as he stomped by.

Chapter 39

Rejected

"I am never going back," Esteban said.

"Where will you go?" asked Sabina.

"I don't know. But I know that I can't go back home." He stared into the distance as they sat on the bench where they first kissed. "I hate him."

"What will you do?" Sabina was concerned as she looked at Esteban's swollen black eye and arm in a sling.

"I will figure something out." Esteban stood and stepped to the park's wall in front of them. "I'm fifteen. I can work or maybe even tutor. I don't know yet, but I finally realize that I am on my own and always have been ever since Mother left."

"You can't stay on the street. Maybe Papa will let you stay with us."

Esteban turned and looked back at Sabina. "Do you think he would?"

"We can ask him."

Darius listened intently to his daughter and Esteban standing before him explaining the situation. Once they had finished, he sat still for a while, rubbing his chin. Finally, he spoke.

"You are a good young man, but you have a lot to learn, and I do not want us to become a crutch holding you back. It is appropriate that you seek refuge from harm, but I do not want our home to become a hideout where you avoid dealing with your challenges."

"Understood, sir."

"Do you? I am not just referring to your temporal affairs. You will need to resolve your issues with your father before you will be free to move on with your life.

"I left to escape his control."

"You will always be under his emotional control until you learn how to forgive him. Then you can decide either to build a new relationship with him or to write him out of your life."

"I've already done that."

"Really. You do not realize it, but he will haunt your life until you truly forgive him."

"I don't know if I can do that, sir."

"Forgiveness is not absolving your father of his guilt, but it will allow you to heal."

"I'm not sure I understand what you are saying."

"At some point you will need to identify your pain and embrace it in order to let it go. Until then, you will continue to relive it over and over again in various ways, and thus remain a slave to your father's abuse. It all depends on your willingness to be a man and pursue the difficult course to forgiveness instead of wallowing in your sorrow and striking out in frustration. Can you do that?"

Esteban stared silently at Darius. "I believe so," he finally said.

"Very well. You can stay with us, for a while."

"Thank you, sir."

Esteban grappled with Darius's comments as he and Sabina walked away. Finally, he asked her, "What do you think your father meant when he said that I will remain a slave to my father's abuse until I forgive him?"

"I'm not sure, but it sounds like something they taught us

at church."

"What did they say?"

"First, no one has the right to tell you when to forgive someone who has abused you, but eventually you will need to do it in order to escape the control that the abuser has over your mind so you can move on with your life."

"He doesn't have any control over my mind. I can finally see clearly for the first time in my life," Esteban said. "My father has never cared for me. I hope he squirms in pain and regret after I am gone."

"That is my point, Esteban. Until you forgive, you will still be tethered to your father and his abuse. You will relive it over and over again in your mind, just as Father said. You may move out, but you won't be able to move on."

"I can't move on if I don't move out!"

"You are right, Esteban. You need to escape the abuse, and you have a right to be outraged. But you need to realize that he hurt more than your physical body. He also hurt your soul. He stole the joy and innocence of your youth, and this pain will take time to heal, just like your broken bones."

"I will get over it."

"Now may be too early to talk about it, but at some point, you will need to do it. You will need to share the pain of your father's betrayal with someone else so they can help you carry the burden. I don't mean to rush you, but I am willing to listen."

"I don't see why I need to burden you or anyone else with my pain. I need to be a man and bear it."

"Like your father?"

"What?" Esteban said as he stopped in his tracks.

"Don't you see?" Sabina stopped and looked up into Esteban's eyes. "People are usually in pain when they lash out at others. Can't you see that the pain your father has stuffed inside himself all these years since your sister's death has festered into an abscess that has ruptured and is now infecting you with its poison? Can't you see that your wishing ill upon your father does not heal the wound, but just perpetuates the wrong?"

Esteban stood dumbfounded. These ideas had never occurred to him.

Sabina took his hand and said, "Esteban, when you are ready, I will be here for you."

Chapter 40

The Centurion

General Sulla assembled his officers a few days after they entered Germania and said, "Antonio, repeat what you told me."

"I overheard the villagers talking about a large number of soldiers assembling in the mountain pass to ambush us. I realize that you want to be the first cohort to reach the emperor, but I do not feel it is safe for us to proceed without the full legion."

"What do you think about this new intelligence?" the general asked his council. The legion's *tribunus laticlavius*, *primus pilus*, *praefectus castrorum*, *tribuni angusticlavii*, and the *praefecti* of the auxiliary cavalry did not answer immediately.

"The quest for glory, not fear, is what made Rome great!" blurted out the young, inexperienced tribunus laticlavius.

"How typical," General Sulla thought. "The least qualified is the first to speak." He hated the tradition of appointing arrogant sons of senators to be Rome's legions' second-in-command as a political favor to the ruling class.

"What glory is there in arriving behind other legions?" the tribune continued.

"These back-country yokels are dreaming if they think that an unorganized band of primitive fighters can defeat my cohort of the most experienced eight hundred soldiers in the legion," said the primus pilus, the century of the first cohort.

"How do we even know that this rumor is correct?" asked a tribunus angusticlavia. "We will be the laughingstock of the whole army if they hear that we ran away like scared little girls from some imaginary phantom."

"Our plan to take this shortcut will save us two weeks," another tribunus angusticlavia chimed in. "If we take the whole legion with its supply train, it will bog us down, and we will arrive behind the third Italica and eighth Gemina legions. They got over a week head start on us. I say we press forward to honor and glory."

Another tribunus looked at Antonio and taunted, "Slaves retreat in fear, while Romans rule with confidence." Antonio's blood boiled, but he knew that he must hold his peace. Nothing he said would make any difference, even though they were walking into a death trap. The Germans had assumed that he did not speak their language, so he knew what he heard was reliable, and he understood the risk because Adolf had previously explained German battle tactics to him.

"Be aware, sir, that the enemy will have the advantage of knowing the terrain. You should be prepared just in case this information is credible," said the experienced camp prefect. "I agree, however, that we should not abandon this opportunity based on such vague evidence."

"Very well. The first cohort will proceed as planned, and the rest of the legion with the artillery and wagons will take the traditional route through the valley, except the auxiliary cavalry will accompany us through the mountain pass. Prefect, inform your horsemen that we leave in the morning," General Sulla ordered.

Antonio shook his head, disgusted as he returned to his camp. As he approached, he overheard the senior slave,

Thaddeus, holding a letter, brag to the other slaves, "My brother says that his master is planning something big, very soon."

Thaddeus noticed Antonio approaching. "Tell me, brave gladiator, did the legion officers cower in fear at your report?" Antonio just glared back at him as the slaves laughed. "What's wrong, Antonio? Are you really just a coward who is afraid of a little action?"

"Shut up," Antonio said.

"Oh, he's not a coward," Thaddeus continued. "He's just lazy and doesn't want to climb the mountain trail."

Antonio stopped to address Thaddeus. "We will be lucky to survive this trek. It would be best if you did not make light of the matter."

"So, the lazy coward has turned into a moralist," Thaddeus said. "Or are you really just a German spy like your friend?"

Antonio had too much on his mind to respond to childish taunts, so he ignored the ridicule and walked on.

* * *

The thick underbrush covering the stream below coupled with the dense evergreen forest along the mountainside above them reminded Antonio of the terrain in Adolf's stories of German hit-and-run attacks, putting him on high alert while they marched single file along the narrow mountain trail.

The bulk of the 120-horse cavalry led the way, followed immediately by General Sulla and the first century vanguard unit. The rest of the cohort's soldiers followed close behind, trailed by the slaves and mules carrying the heavy baggage, with the rest of the cavalry and one double-century of 160 soldiers bringing up the rear. All the soldiers were loaded down with their two weeks' worth of supplies, armor, and weapons. Antonio could not even see past the first couple of centuries in front of him. The cohort was strung out for nearly a kilometer through this tight pass. This did not set well with him, so even though he and Adolf were attending to their *contubernium*'s mule, he secured a sheath and gladius to his waist and grabbed a javelin.

No sooner had he picked up the javelin than a volley of arrows shot out of the underbrush below for as far as he could see. Bloodcurdling war cries seemed to extend all along the creek below. The missiles did their intended damage as several soldiers and horsemen fell to the ground. The slaves steadied their mules, and the soldiers secured their shields and turned to face the noise below them.

"No!" Antonio screamed. "Turn around! They will attack from above!"

It was too late. The *frameas* were already in the air. The spears decimated the unprepared Roman line. The Germans, shouting their chilling cry, charged down the mountainside. The thin, depleted Roman line was in disarray. Some of the centurions had already fallen. Their second-in-command and the remaining centurions were trying to form their traditional multi-warrior deep line with little success on the steep hillside while in hand-to-hand combat with the barbarians. Roman battle tactics were useless in this environment.

Antonio's training at the ludus automatically kicked in. He flew like lightning, not being weighed down by the ball and chain that he was accustomed to in the arena. He quickly disposed of his attackers, turned around, and saw Thaddeus on the ground with a German soldier standing over him, preparing to thrust his sword through his chest. Antonio threw his javelin, impaling him from behind. Thaddeus barely turned aside in time to avoid injury from the pila protruding from the German who fell on top of him.

"Where is the cavalry?" Antonio called out to Adolf.

"I don't know," he replied.

The cavalry was their only hope of defeating the enemy. Antonio yelled, "Follow me!"

Adolf followed Antonio as he ran past the mules toward the rear cavalry, dispatching foes on their way. Once close, he noticed that their leader was down, and the rest of the horsemen were fighting their own individual battles without any coordination. Antonio jumped on the first unmounted horse he found and charged down the path, yelling orders to the riders. He remembered every suggestion the Tiros at the ludus had given him while he trained as an equestrian to fight a group of light-armored velites. "To the center...Join together...Watch your left!" Soon the rear cavalry was operating as one unit under Antonio's command. They stormed down the path toward the vanguard unit, thinning out the enemy on their path without breaking stride, giving the infantry a fighting chance.

As Antonio approached the vanguard unit, he could see that the main cavalry was likewise leaderless, leaving General Sulla in jeopardy. Over a dozen Germans had encircled Sulla and the cohort's primus pilus, who were desperately fighting for their lives. Antonio spurred his horse ahead at a full gallop and smashed into the circular wall of German warriors, using his horse as a battering ram, hurling bodies everywhere like shattered debris. The rear cavalry soon caught up and finished dispersing the threat to the general, while Antonio plunged into the disjointed combat bogging down the main cavalry. Again, Antonio quickly barked out commands to capitalize on the horsemen's training, forming a cohesive force. "Form your units...To your units...Fight as one...Charge!"

The cavalry followed Antonio back down the line, gaining control of the battle. Antonio left two dozen riders to help defend each of the six centuries as they rode back down the line. Soon, the Germans retreated, leaving a seriously wounded Roman cohort behind.

Antonio rode back down the trail, ordering the cavalry to maintain their guard while the centurions and *optios* assessed their unit's damage. Once order had been secured along the line, Antonio approached General Sulla and the primus pilus. He dismounted and offered the rein of his horse to General Sulla. "The cohort awaits your command," he said.

* * *

"I understand from General Sulla that you single-handedly snatched my general and his first cohort from certain annihilation at the hands of these barbarians," Emperor Marcus Aurelius said to Antonio.

"I only helped fill the void created when more competent men had fallen," he replied.

"Humble as well. I am not sure this trait befits you, but it does show wisdom. Either way, it is admirable," the emperor said. "I am told that you are a slave condemned for trying to kill your master, yet you saved your current master, my general, and his army. This strange paradox warrants further scrutiny. That is why I asked to interview you personally." Antonio nodded. "Tell me, young man, are you willing to swear allegiance to me and Rome if I grant you your freedom and appoint you to be a centurion to fill a vacancy in your master's legion, as he requests?"

Shocked, Antonio stood silent for a moment, unable to find words to respond. Finally, a faint, "Yes," escaped his lips, followed by a forceful, "Yes, Caesar, I will be your loyal subject."

The Emperor smiled, patted Antonio on the shoulder, and said, "I believe you. I grant you this freedom and commission, conditioned on the Senate's ratification, which is a simple formality, especially for decisions on the field of battle in times of war." Marcus Aurelius extended his hand to shake Antonio's. "Congratulations, centurion."

Chapter 41

Fate

Prometheus walked briskly down the dark street, looked over his shoulder, and slipped into a deserted alley. He proceeded to the designated meeting place around a corner behind a building. Quintus was already waiting for him, accompanied by a young girl. Prometheus listened intently. "Now that Leo has finally been weakened, it is time to strike. Here is the plan."

* * *

"Leo," Prometheus confided, "I overheard some of the slaves whispering today that the chariot race at the Circus Maximus this Saturday is rigged."

Leo stopped in his tracks. "What did they actually say?"

"The long shot from Ephesus will win. He has bribed all the drivers. This type of illicit activity may be the source of your bad fortune, sir. I recommend that you stop gambling on these races."

"How sure are you of this information?"

"I heard it with my own ears, sir."

"And who did you hear it from?" Leo asked.

"Two of the attendants were discussing it at the feed market when a stableman joined in and confirmed it. I do not think they even realized I was there."

"I believe you have been cheated and should not give these thieves any more of your money."

"Then it is only fair that I settle the score by using this information."

"I do not advise it, sir."

"Do you question the veracity of what you heard?"

"Not at all."

"Then I will beat them at their own game. You said the charioteer from Ephesus will win?"

"That's what they said, sir."

"Keep your ear to the ground, and let me know immediately if you hear anything new."

* * *

Later, at the public bath, Gaius approached Leo who was talking with Rusticus and Quintus. "Leo, I am sorry to hear about your son."

"There is no need. He was corrupted by his mother. I feel that my fortune will change now that he and that Christian curse are out of my house."

"You must really believe that. I heard that you made a sizable bet on Saturday's races," Quintus said.

"Yes. Fate will smile on me again. I am sure of it."

* * *

Prometheus opened a small bag of powder and poured it into Leo's amphora of wine before he brought it to him that night. It was not long before Leo stumbled to his room and collapsed on his bed, dropping the goblet from his hand and spilling the wine on the floor.

Once Leo was out cold, Prometheus crept in and carefully removed Leo's ring bearing his seal from his finger. He then snuck into the study, looked around to be sure he was alone, removed two documents from their hiding place and affixed Leo's seal to them. He stealthily slipped the papers under his toga and hid them in his room. Quietly, he reentered Leo's bedroom and slipped the ring back onto his hand before exiting the room.

* * *

Leo and his friends Rusticus, Quintus, and Titus sat in their customary front-row seats at the races. It was no secret that Leo had placed a sizable wager on the new Ephesian charioteer, yet he did not seem to be particularly anxious to his peers. Indeed, he seemed unusually happy, almost giddy. Titus even commented on it.

"You seem particularly optimistic today, Leo."

"Fortune can touch us in unusual ways, and I believe you will witness her smile on me today."

"I hope so, for your sake," said Quintus.

"You fret too much, my friend," Leo retorted as he slapped Quintus's leg. Quintus looked over at Leo disapprovingly. "Relax and enjoy the race. It should be exceptional."

A procession of chariots, each pulled by three horses, entered in the distance and proceeded to circle the track to the cheers of the crowd of thirty thousand. The racetrack was oblong, with two long straightaways connected by relatively tight curves on each end.

"I see Zephyrus," said Rusticus.

"His black stallions are such beautiful creatures," Titus mused.

"It will be interesting to see how they manage the inside post," Rusticus said.

"He will have a hard time beating out Linus next to him," observed Quintus.

"Yeah, Linus usually has a quick start," Titus agreed.

"I don't know. The new champion from Antioch is in a prime position, and he has been very successful here in Rome this past month. I'm putting my money on him," said Rusticus.

"Where's your sense of adventure?" Leo asked. "Does caution suit an old warrior like you?"

"When I don't control the outcome," Rusticus answered. Leo smiled.

"Patrin and his Arabians look good," Quintus observed. "He has done well to earn that center post."

"He has my money," Titus said. "The Arabians have excellent endurance."

"There's Cronus," Rusticus pointed out.

"I don't give him much of a chance," said Titus. "He did poorly in his last race."

"He has no chance," Leo commented.

"Look, Leo. Here comes your bet," said Rusticus. "I can't imagine why you would bet on such a long shot."

"Fate, my friend. Fate."

"If you lose, I can't imagine how you'll bear the loss," Quintus said loud enough for those around him to hear.

"Don't worry, Quintus. Fate is on my side today."

Titus and Rusticus looked curiously at Leo.

"We won't need to wait much longer," Leo said as the chariots began to line up.

The horn blew, the contestants whipped their horses, and the chariots lunged forward. Quintus was right. Linus jumped ahead and cut Zephyrus and his black stallions off at the first turn. Patrin and his Arabians were right behind him. Surprisingly, the Ephesian and Antiochian riders, neck and neck, were next. Cronus launched ahead of Zephyrus soon after the first turn as Zephyrus needed to slow down to make the tight turn after being cut off by Linus. Linus maintained his lead over Patrin down the first long stretch to the second turn while the Ephesian on the outside and the Antiochian on the inside traded third place back and forth all the way through the turn.

"Well, Leo, you may have a chance after all," Quintus conceded.

"He will be out of the running by the next turn," Titus retorted.

Patrin was able to pass Linus down the stretch to snatch first place before the second turn. Again, the Ephesian and the Antiochian battled for third place, right behind Linus, followed by Cronus and Zephyrus a short way back.

"So far, so good," Titus said.

"It's only been one lap, Titus," Rusticus replied. "We still have six to go."

The Antiochian was now boxed in by Linus in front and the Ephesian on the outside, allowing the Ephesian to pass Linus as he slowed down to make the treacherous turn. The Antiochian took it wide and lined up with Linus to fight for third place after the Ephesian advanced to second position.

"What did you say about not making it past the first lap?" Leo chided.

"I am surprised," Titus admitted.

Patrin extended his lead down the far stretch as they finished the second lap. The Antiochian was able to surpass Linus on the turn, not far behind the Ephesian. The first four chariots continued to pull away from Zephyrus, followed by Cronus bringing up the rear.

During the third lap, Patrin maintained, but did not extend, his lead over the Ephesian and the Antiochian, who had caught up with him. Zephyrus closed in on Linus, with Cronus falling farther behind.

"Your rider is putting up a good fight, Leo," Rusticus said. "But the Antiochian will pass him this lap."

"Not a chance," Leo said as he elbowed his friend.

The excitement was now between Zephyrus, with his striking black stallions, and Linus. Every time Zephyrus was about to pass, Linus would move in front to block the way. Finally, Zephyrus decided to go wide to pass on the outside and then quickly cut back inside as Linus's horses also veered wide. The crowd cheered. Zephyrus had gotten his revenge for Linus cutting him off on the first turn. Linus tried to pull back ahead of Zephyrus, and the chariots nearly collided. This would most likely have been a death sentence for one or both of the charioteers as the racing chariots were lightweight and prone to disintegrate in a collision with another chariot or the circus wall, leaving the rider mangled in the reins and debris.

By the fifth lap, it was apparent that it was now a three-chariot race—Patrin slightly ahead on the inside, the Antiochian in the middle, and the Ephesian on the outside, all pulling away from the rest of the contestants, with Cronus lagging way behind. Leo was on his feet, shouting for joy.

"If Leo wins, we will never hear the end of it," Titus lamented.

"I hope he does," Quintus said.

"We've got two laps to go," Rusticus reminded them.

The three chariots in front maintained their respective positions, not having much room to maneuver. The Ephesian would fall back slightly on the wide outside turns, but recover before the next. Half a track behind, Linus was threatening Zephyrus and tried to pass him on the outside. Zephyrus did not give him a millimeter and pressed him wider toward the wall as the turn approached. The crowd rose to watch this life-and-death contest of wills. Linus ceded, but not in time. His chariot caught the wall, flinging the outside wheel high into the air, and the chariot exploded as it hit the ground. Linus held on to the reins to pull himself free from the shattering wreckage, but when he tried to release them, his arm became entangled, dragging him down the track until his crew was able to stop his horses.

The back-and-forth three-way contest for first place had not changed by the start of the seventh and final lap. The Ephesian took a half-chariot lead coming out of the first turn. Leo elbowed Quintus and Rusticus as he screamed for joy. All the spectators were out of their seats as the leading chariots prepared to lap Cronus on the far stretch with the wreckage looming before them. The tension built as the horses, chariots, and riders barreled toward the tightening funnel—Cronus on the inside and the debris on the outside. The Antiochian in the middle appeared to have the best position even though he was in third place, slightly behind Patrin with the Ephesian increasing his lead. There appeared to be an increasing chance that the Ephesian would pass the Antiochian's chariot before reaching the wreckage, securing his win.

Patrin's thundering horses were right behind Cronus on the inside track. Cronus could hear the Arabians' snorting. He glanced over his shoulder and swore he could feel the horses' hot breath on his face. The Ephesian pulled far enough ahead to have room to cut in front of the Antiochian. "Cut in! Cut in!" Leo yelled. Suddenly, Cronus moved from the inside to the middle of the track, blocking both the Antiochian and the Ephesian. The Ephesian had to rein his horses in hard, slowing them to a crawl, to avoid the debris on the track, while Patrin sped ahead to take the lead around the final turn.

Patrin and his Arabians were the first across the finish line, followed by the Antiochian, who had also passed Cronus on the inside. The Ephesian could not speed up enough to even pass Cronus by the time he passed the finish line halfway down the straightaway. The crowd screamed their approval of such a dramatic finish. Leo stood dumbfounded.

"Leo. Leo. Are you all right?" Rusticus asked as Leo stared straight ahead in disbelief, collapsing into his seat, unable to say a word.

"Don't worry, Leo. You will survive," Quintus placed his hand on Leo's shoulder. "I have arranged for you to be able to stay in your home."

Leo turned and looked at Quintus. "What are you talking about?"

"I knew that you could not afford to pay your debt if you lost, so I bought your contract with the bookie."

"I don't understand."

"I knew you could not afford to pay your one-hundred-thousand-denarii bet secured by all of your assets, so I bought your contract. You owe me, not the bookie. I will be much more generous than he would, and I'll let you stay on your estate."

"I am sorry, my friend, but you are mistaken. My bet was only one thousand denarii, not one hundred thousand."

"That is not what your contract says," Quintus pulled the contract out of his bag. "See, it clearly states one hundred thousand, not one thousand."

"Let me see that," Leo ripped the document out of Quintus's hands.

"This is your seal, is it not?" Quintus asked.

"Yes. But this document is a forgery. I did not place this bet. Why would I risk my whole estate?"

"I don't know, Leo, but you haven't been yourself lately. That is why I intervened to save you. Here is the security agreement pledging all your assets," Quintus pulled another document from his pouch. "It bears your seal as well."

"You have been cheated, Quintus. I have never seen this document. Which bookie did you say you purchased this contract from?"

"Your regular bookie. Let's all go see him right now. If I have been cheated, I need to know. Prefect and Titus, can you please join us?"

"Certainly," Rusticus replied. "I will crucify him if he cheated either of you."

The bookie was at his booth outside the Circus Maximus and cordially greeted the group as they approached. Leo didn't bother taking time for normal pleasantrics. Instead, he immediately began to interrogate the bookie. "Arrius, do you have my contract?"

"No, Leo. I sold it to your friend Quintus, here."

"How much did I wager?"

"One hundred thousand denarii."

"You lie!" Leo roared.

"Never, sir." Arrius acted taken aback.

"I only bet one thousand denarii."

"Then why would you sign over your whole estate for just one thousand denarii?"

"I did not!" Leo insisted.

"Of course, you did. Don't you remember?" The bookie stared at Leo a moment, then turned to Quintus and his companions and continued, "Do you have his contract and pledge?"

"Yes, they are right here."

"I am sorry for your loss, Leo, but you must honor your pledge. I couldn't afford the loss if you won. That is why I sold your contract to your friend."

"Well, it all seems quite clear. Are you satisfied?" Quintus asked Rusticus and Titus.

"Yes," they both nodded.

"I did not make this bet and pledge," Leo maintained.

"We are sorry for you, Leo," Rusticus said. "You are

fortunate that you have a friend to show you mercy."

"I have been cheated!" Leo's voice raised louder.

"I fear that your drinking has affected your memory and reason," Titus said.

"Leo, I took great risk to help you," Quintus chided him. "You can stay in your home, but your estate is now mine. Come by my villa tonight, and we can discuss the particulars in private."

"Listen to Quintus," Titus said quietly. "You are very fortunate that you have such a generous friend."

Chapter 42

Apocalypse

In the evening after the race, many of the most prominent patricians of Rome gathered at Quintus's villa. "It is amazing that your husband would go to such risk and expense to save Leo from the streets," Priscilla, Gaius's wife, said to Loretta, standing in the midst of a group of wives.

"Yes, he is a loyal friend."

"And even for a Christian sympathizer," said Julia.

"What? I thought he hated Christians because of Amora's misfortune," exclaimed one of the ladies.

"No. It was all a ruse. He was recently caught passing along intelligence that enabled Christian leaders to escape," another woman chimed in.

"You don't say," said another. "I always wondered about him after Amora supported those deviants."

"I heard that he secreted his son somewhere to protect him."

"That deformed boy?"

"Yes, the whole family is cursed."

Leo entered the room and ran into a cold wall of silence. Everyone stared at Leo, standing near the front of the room, as Quintus approached.

"I am glad you came, my friend," Quintus said. "Let's go into this room where we can talk in private."

Leo did not say a word as he followed Quintus into a large

adjoining room full of couches and chairs in various seating arrangements. "Quintus, I did not make that bet. You have to believe me," Leo said as Quintus escorted him into the center of a room that was unoccupied except for a slave guarding the door at the far end.

"Leo, there is nothing we can do about it now. The bookie verified the documents bearing your seal to the prefect of Rome and the emperor's chief of staff."

"They were forged, I tell you."

"Leo, you need some diversion to get your mind off your troubles."

"Not now, Quintus."

"I have arranged for a surprise to distract you, my friend."

"I am not in any mood for entertainment."

"I guarantee that this young lass will erase all thought of your wager." Leo began to speak but Quintus raised his hand to silence him. "Leo, I need to attend to my guests, but I will return after a while."

"I will be here."

As Quintus was preparing to leave the room, he ordered the slave to bring in the girl. As soon as the slave disappeared through the door, a young girl entered wearing Natalie's yellow stola. The image of Quintus kissing Natalie's hand while he looked into her eyes on the day she disappeared flashed into Leo's mind, igniting his explosion, "You killed her!"

Leo turned and rushed toward the door Quintus was already exiting. "You killed her! You murderer!" he yelled as he burst into the room full of Quintus's guests.

"Guards," Quintus yelled as he ran across the room, away from Leo. "He's gone mad. Guards! Seize him!"

"You killed her!" Leo continued to yell as a half-dozen guards converged to restrain him. "You will die!" Leo scuffled with the guards.

"Take him out of here," Quintus said.

The guards dragged Leo, kicking and screaming, from the room. Quintus collapsed in a chair and fanned his face with his hands. The whole room assembled around him.

"He has lost his mind," Quintus said. "When we entered the room, he started mumbling about his lost daughter. Then he looked at me with these crazy eyes and started yelling that I killed her. Poor Leo. He has gone berserk. The shock of his loss at the races must have been too much for him." Quintus shook his head. "I don't know what I can do to help him."

"Oh, Quintus. You have already done more than anyone else would have done for a friend," Gaius said.

"I just hope he will be able to rest at his home so his mind can heal," Quintus replied.

"How can you even consider allowing him to stay in his old villa after this outburst?" Crescens asked, shocked.

"Dear, you can't let that madman be around us," said Loretta.

"Maybe you're right," Quintus sighed.

"There is no question, Quintus," Rusticus declared. "You need to evict him immediately and keep him as far away from you and your family as possible. I will post sentries to guard your home until this threat has passed."

"I appreciate that. I just can't believe what has become of him," Quintus said as he shook his head. "He used to be so bright. It is a real shame."

"Don't fret about it. You have been more than fair," Titus reassured him.

* * *

Late that night Leo sat alone in the empty corner of a tavern, an amphora of wine and cup in front of him, his elbows on the table, supporting his downcast head in his hands. Two large men entered at the front and scanned the room, seeing Leo, they nodded to each other and took seats next to him. Leo did not even bother to look up. Two women approached, but the men waved them off as one said, "Just wine." The two men drank and talked nonchalantly for a while, establishing their peaceful presence. Then once the manager had glanced their way, one of the men said in a loud voice, "I offer this toast to Senator Quintus." Leo's head shot up at the mention of that name. The man continued, "The most moral and generous member of the Senate." He raised his cup. "To Quintus!"

Leo exploded. He tipped over his table, shattering the amphora on the ground, as he charged the men. They were prepared for the assault and easily deflected it. The manager called for security. Guards rushed to the disturbance, along with the manager, and quickly subdued Leo.

"Throw the drunk out," ordered the manager. "I am sorry for the disturbance, gentlemen," he calmed his clients as the bouncers dragged Leo, struggling, out of the room.

"You can't even toast a senator in this establishment," said one of the large men.

"I am sorry. There is no charge for your drinks."

"I should hope not," his companion said as he straightened his clothes.

The men finished their drinks and left the tavern.

Outside they were soon joined by a third, who motioned towards Leo. Sounds of wagons hauling their loads and workers unloading deliveries in the distance were the only signs of life other than Leo sitting on the curb across the deserted street a half block away.

The third man crossed the dark street and walked casually toward Leo. After waiting a moment, the other two ambled down the opposite side of the street. Leo, drained by his outburst and in a stupor, paid them no attention. Just before reaching Leo, the third man pulled a thick baton out from under his cloak and struck a heavy blow on the back of his head. Leo fell forward onto the ground, unconscious. The two other men quickly joined the original assailant in kicking and beating Leo. No one noticed. The men left, leaving Leo for dead in the gutter.

Chapter 43

The Rescue

"Thank you for teaching me your trade," Esteban said to Darius as they walked down the empty street in the predawn twilight.

"Being a stonemason is hard work, but the key is skill, not brute force," Darius said as he slapped the bag of tools hanging over his shoulder.

Esteban saw a man lying in the gutter ahead. "There's another drunk from that tavern," he said as they approached.

Darius noticed reflections from the pool of blood around the man and exclaimed, "He is injured."

The older man ran to Leo, but Esteban had stopped dead in his tracks. "Father?"

Darius knelt beside Leo, checking his breathing and pulse. "He's still alive." Darius removed his own cloak and looked over at Esteban while folding it. "Don't just stand there!" Shaken out of his daze, Esteban approached as Darius handed him the cloak. "Place this under his head."

Esteban knelt and slipped the cloak under Leo's bleeding head while Darius straightened out his broken body.

"I'm going to get a handcart," Darius said as he stood up and began to run. "I'll be back soon."

Esteban stared at his father as a flood of conflicting emotions washed over him: satisfaction, guilt, pity, sorrow. He reached over and placed his hand on his father's shoulder.

* * *

Everything looked blurry. Leo blinked his eyes again. A pleasant teenage girl leaning over him came into focus as he lay in a small bed built into the wall.

"Dominus, can you hear me?" Sabina said gently as she wiped his forehead with a damp cloth.

"Yes. Where am I?"

"You are in our home."

"What happened?"

A sharp pain shot through his chest and arm as he tried to sit up.

"Don't move. You must rest."

He then registered an excruciating throbbing pain in his head that seemed to flow down through the rest of his body. He moaned.

"You have been seriously hurt. Just rest."

Leo watched the girl stand up and call out, "Papa. He's awake. Please come."

"My father will be here to help. Just lie still."

Leo looked around at his surroundings and saw that he lay in a sparse room with a couple of small beds. Darius entered the room and walked over to his infirm guest. "Who are you?" Leo asked.

"A friend. We have been watching over you this past week while you have been unconscious."

"What happened?"

"We are not sure, but you were beaten quite badly." Directing his attention to his daughter, Darius said, "Sabina, go fetch Esteban."

"My son?"

"Yes. We found you near death in the gutter, so we brought you here. I am glad that you survived. We were not sure that you would make it."

Leo again tried to move but was restrained by the shooting pain. "Just rest, my friend. As far as the doctor could tell, you have a few broken ribs, a broken arm, and a fractured skull. It is best that you lie still to allow them to heal."

"A week, you say?"

"Yes, you have been here a week. We sent a friend to inquire at your villa, but the steward said that it no longer belonged to you and that you were not welcome there."

"Quintus! He set this all up."

"You mustn't get upset," Darius said. He reached for a cup. "Here, please drink this tea. It will help deaden the pain." He held the cup up to Leo's mouth as he gently helped raise his head. Leo took a sip, and then another. "You must be thirsty," Darius said with a smile. "That is a good sign. You need nourishment."

Sabina, holding Esteban's hand, led him into the room and over to Leo.

"Hello, Father."

Darius motioned to Sabina with his head that they should leave.

"You have been staying here?" Leo asked as Darius and Sabina slipped out of the room.

"Yes, Father."

"Are they Christians?"

"Yes, Father."

"And they know what I have done to their cult?"

"They know all about you, Father."

Leo closed his eyes and rested his head back, confused. This did not make any sense. Nothing made sense.

"I will let you rest," Esteban said as he slowly walked toward the door. He stopped and looked back at his father before he exited the room.

Laying in bed, healing, was difficult for Leo, forever a

man of action. The time for reflection was awkward and uncomfortable for him, but many things that had escaped his attention came to the forefront now.

"I hadn't realized how much he has grown," Leo thought as he observed Esteban interacting with their hosts. "He's pleasant and confident. He's not avoiding people, off in some corner by himself, like he always did at home. This congenial environment seems to bring out the best in him. Maybe I was too hard on him," Leo considered. "But I needed to toughen him up to compensate for his disability," he rationalized. He recalled the day the local boys stole his monkey and taunted him. He then recalled telling Amora he wanted Esteban dead soon after he was born. Guilt washed over him to the point that he felt he was going to drown in anguish.

"It wasn't all my fault," he told himself as he searched his memory in an attempt to placate his conscience. "I let Esteban know that I was proud of him," he assured himself as he recalled the evening when he arrived home and saw Natalie and Esteban on the floor playing with a ball.

* * *

Leo smiled at Natalie as he walked in and sat down. Esteban, nearly three years old and still unable to walk due to his disability, traversed the floor to him by scooting around on his bottom and using his good leg, arms and stomach muscles to propel him forward. Leo picked Esteban up and stood him up, facing Amora. "Go to your mother," Leo said as he reached over and picked up some of the papers on the table next to him. Leo wasn't even paying attention when Esteban took three steps before he fell. Amora and Natalie cheered encouragingly. Leo looked up to see Esteban squeal and pump his hands up and down, ecstatic.

Amora lifted him and set him down facing his father. Leo beckoned him forward. The jubilant lad took four wobbling steps before gravity prevailed, to shouts of praise from both his parents. Leo held his excited boy up and again directed him to walk to his mother, now kneeling on the floor before him. He took a half-dozen steps before Amora stretched out her hands for him to grab so he would not fall. The euphoric boy shrieked with joy as Amora hugged him before she sat him down again, facing Leo, who had moved back a short distance. Esteban furrowed his little brow as he stood, looking directly into his father's eyes, determined to please his dad. Leo called out to him and Amora let go. Concentrating with each step, he moved forward, adjusting his stride to compensate for his short, crooked leg. As the toddler got closer to his destination, Leo moved farther back, until the wall impeded his retreat. Esteban pressed forward, one arduous step at a time, until he reached his goal: his father's arms. Leo lifted Esteban triumphantly over his head as he rose to his feet and shouted for joy. "My son!"

However, as much as he tried to appease his conscience, the reality of his abuse was too glaring to ignore. Meanwhile, his son was returning from work.

* * *

Esteban entered the plaza with his bag of tools over his shoulder when he spotted Prometheus and Crescens laughing as they walked towards him. "Just look at that slave wearing Father's fine apparel and hobnobbing with the elite," he seethed.

Esteban had not escaped the view of his nemesis and his companion. Indeed, he soon discovered that he was the source of their levity.

"Well, look who stumbled into our path, Crescens. Isn't he that stupid cripple whose mother was so brainless that she couldn't even stay out of the arena?" Prometheus said as they laughed.

"Do you miss her?" Crescens taunted.

"We can arrange to have you follow her," Prometheus threatened.

Unruffled, Esteban looked them in the eye. He was no longer the retiring child they had known. He was ready to stand his ground, and commenced his own inquisition. "You who are so wise, tell me, what happens to our soul when we die?"

Prometheus and Crescens smirked and looked at each other. "Why, he speaks," Prometheus said.

"At least the kid has some spunk," said Crescens. "Go ahead and educate this poor ignorant youth, Prometheus."

"Sure. I am always willing to educate the young," he said sarcastically. Looking at Esteban, he said, "We die," and laughed. He then offered the textbook answer, "Individual souls are perishable by nature. So, when we die, we are dissolved into element, which then becomes a part of other things in our environment. The universe is one living organism, one soul, one substance."

"But if we are simply part of a greater whole, why do we have a sense of self and of virtue?" Esteban inquired.

"Ah, that is the beauty of the human mind," Prometheus pontificated. "Virtue comes from understanding our role within this universal system of nature," he concluded with the pat answer of the day.

"But if doing what is natural is the essence of virtue, it would not be wise to be good. Yet, we each know when we do something wrong, even when it is expedient, Prometheus," Esteban said as he stared at his father's former steward.

Prometheus was taken aback by the depth of Esteban's question and the sting of guilt. He turned to Crescens for assistance.

"This is nothing more than the duty one feels from the cumulative wisdom of society that we are taught as we mature," Crescens said.

"But this sense of duty proves that we have free will," Esteban observed. "If we are nothing more than an extension of a material universe, then why do we have an independent sense of self and the freedom to make choices and pursue truth and virtue even when it is not in our immediate interest?"

Crescens and Prometheus stood dumbfounded, unable to answer, and frustrated that a young cripple had bested them in this mental exercise.

"Some things cannot be answered," Prometheus finally said.

"You are a stupid thief. My mother taught me more than you will ever know. She is greater than all of Rome, because Rome is just like you, thieves, stealing what others create, and someday Rome will fall when it runs out of people to rob. Good day, gentlemen, I have more important things to do. You both can go rot in hell."

Esteban entered his father's room and glanced over at Leo. Noticing the concern on Leo's face, he asked, "Do you need anything, Father?"

"Please sit down. I want to apologize for not being a good father to you."

Esteban sat, but squirmed in his seat. "It's all right," he mumbled.

"No, it's not. I have neglected you, and it is not right. Esteban, these past three weeks, I have had a lot of time to reflect, and I have a lot of regrets."

They heard the front door open, and Esteban, uncomfortable with the conversation, quickly jumped up. "Darius is home. I should tend to my chores." Darius entered the room and asked, "How are you feeling today?"

"Every day a little better. I can finally breathe without pain."

Esteban left the room without saying a word.

Chapter 44

It's Not My Claim

"Your wife was an amazing lady," Leo's nurse said. "I remember once when she was building Natalie's House."

"Amora's charity?" Leo asked.

"Yes, you know, the home Amora set up for infants in honor of your daughter. Well, one day while I was there, a tradesman came in and asked to be paid. Amora interrogated him, 'Our agreement was that you will be paid the balance when you had completed your work.' And then she asked him if he was finished. He said, 'Yes.' Amora then marched over and opened a closet door, moved some things out of the way under the stairs, pointed, and asked, 'Is that finished?' He said, 'No one will see inside there.' 'But I see it,' Amora said, 'And as long as I do, my coins remain in my bag.'" The woman chuckled. "That man sure was mad as he stomped out, but it wasn't long before he was back with his tools, completing his job. Men often tried to take advantage of her because she was a woman, but nothing got past Amora. She was phenomenal, a great inspiration to me and to a lot of other people."

Leo lay there, dumbfounded, again. He had listened to a long litany of reports about Amora related by numerous Christian women who had come by over the past four weeks to help nurse him back to health. When this nurse finished her story, he heard someone enter the apartment.

"It sounds like Darius is home," the woman said. "I must be getting back. It has been a real honor meeting you, sir."

"Thank you for coming," Leo replied. He sat up while his visitor stood and left the room.

"What a frustrating paradox," Leo thought. "The healthier I become, the worse I feel. All these Christians helping me recover, telling me stories about how marvelous Amora was, and honoring me because of her—it all just makes me feel more guilty. They don't even give me enough wine for me to forget my troubles."

"Good evening, Leo. How are you feeling today?" Darius said as he entered the room.

"Much better."

"Good. I see that you are able to sit up."

"Yes. My bones are still tender, but I am beginning to get around."

"Now don't overdo it, intrepid warrior," Darius said.

How did Darius always seem to be in a good mood, regardless of the circumstances? Leo had been observing him this past month in the intimacy of his own home, so he knew his good humor was genuine. "What is his secret?" Leo wondered. One other thing that troubled him was that there was no sign of a wife, yet he had several children, and no one seemed to be glum missing their mother. His curiosity got the better of him, so he asked, "I do not want to pry, but I notice you do not have a wife assisting you."

Darius paused. After a moment he laid his cloak on a small table, walked over to the chair next to Leo's bed, and sat down. "I knew you would eventually ask," he said. "Leo, it is appropriate that you are here with us. Our wives were very close. Amora actually said that Gloria was her closest friend. Sadly, she was arrested with Amora and was executed shortly before Amora."

The words hit Leo like a ton of bricks, knocking him back down as he moaned, "Oh, what have I done?"

"It is all right, Leo. We miss her deeply, but we know that she is happy and that we will be together as a family again."

"Oh, I am so sorry."

"I know that you played a role in denouncing them, but you did not really know what you were doing."

"How can you let me stay in your home?"

"Leo, we both lost our companions. We share that same misery. How can I not have compassion for you?"

"I killed them. Don't you understand? It is all my fault. I am guilty. I don't understand how you can forgive me."

"Leo, it is not my claim." Darius shook his head.

"What?"

"I already sold it to God. It is not my right to demand justice."

"Then who in the world has this right? She was your wife!" Leo exclaimed.

Darius contemplated the sincerity and seriousness of the question before he answered. "Let me explain. Pretend I loan you one hundred semis. If the bishop pays me for your debt when you can't, and I then come knocking on your door demanding payment, what am I?

"A thief."

"Exactly. That is what we are if we do not forgive others. Thieves."

"What? Why?"

Again, Darius pondered his reply before he spoke. "Leo, do you understand Plato's teaching that humans are eternal beings and that before we were born, we existed as intelligences or spirits in a premortal existence?"

"Of course."

"Well, our great missionary, Paul, explained to Titus that

before God created the world, He promised us eternal life if we are faithful."

"To what?"

"Our premortal promise to God." Leo still looked perplexed. "God knew that in this temporal existence, we would make mistakes and hurt others. So, of course, justice demands that the sinner suffer: an eye for an eye, a tooth for a tooth.

"Certainly. Nothing else would be just."

"Well, because of God's infinite love for us, He promised to send a Savior to pay the price for our sins so that we would not have to personally suffer the demands of justice. This person was Jesus."

"So, you are saying life is like a big circle with Jesus in the center. God will forgive me if I give him my claim to justice when someone wrongs me."

"Yes, and also heal and comfort you."

"But what if I simply want justice? What if I don't care about being forgiven?

"That is the point, Leo," Darius said. "You have already agreed. We all agreed to this exchange in our premortal realm. Consequently, none of us has any right to demand justice. We have already sold our claim. We do not own it, God does."

Leo sat silent for a moment, trying to assess these new ideas and how they applied in his life. Finally, he spoke. "I'm sorry, Darius, but all that matters is that he abused and killed my innocent little girl. I can never forgive Quintus. I can't just pretend that this evil never happened," Leo said.

"Of course, you can't," Darius said. "Leo, forgiveness does not mean we pretend that something bad did not happen or that it really didn't matter. Forgiveness is not sweeping evil under the rug and pretending that it does not exist.

Forgiveness is not allowing abuse or evil to continue. It is not absolving someone from responsibility under the law. No. Forgiveness is based in truth. In order to truly forgive, you need to fully recognize the wrong that was done so that you do not withhold anything when you give it to God and trust Him to execute perfect justice."

"I don't need God to execute justice when I have it in my hands," Leo responded dourly.

"Are you sure it is full and complete justice?"

"Why not? If he dies, justice is satisfied."

"Is it? Does it stop there? Is his miserable life really worth your daughter's lost life, full of hope and joy? Will you forget about Natalie's suffering and live a life of joy once Quintus is dead?"

"No."

"Of course not. We can never execute complete justice. Only God can."

"Yes. He deserves eternal torment."

"But are there others to blame as well? What does justice require of them? What about the slave who didn't watch Esteban close enough or Amora for staying home? Do they deserve death?"

"That's different."

"Are you sure? Are you sure that you do not ascribe some blame to Amora deep within your heart? Maybe she ascribed blame to you. Maybe you even blame yourself. No, we can never completely satisfy justice. We only create more problems when we try to act as a judge."

Leo sat silent, reeling from the sting of truth in Darius's words.

Darius continued. "God sees everything. We only see a part of the picture. We cannot fully understand everything in order to properly judge others. Only God knows the intents of our hearts and our backgrounds, and can make a perfectly just judgment. If we really want justice, then we have to trust God. He knows everything. But what is our criteria for judging? Nothing more than our own limited self-centered view of the world."

"But I still see that what he did was evil and deserves retribution."

"Of course." Darius continued. "As children of the Great Lawgiver, we have the capacity to know what is good and what is evil, but we are in no position to ascribe blame. Forgiveness is giving justice its due, based on the judgment of the only being capable of executing it fully and exactly. Forgiveness consists of turning judgment over to God. It is relying wholly on the wisdom, justice, and mercy of God so that we can be free to move on with our lives without the burden of harboring ill will and bad feelings. These negative emotions destroy our relationships with those who are close to us. No, Leo. Forgiveness is not the enemy of justice. It is its mate. Once you learn to trust God's goodness and justice, you will know that this is true."

Leo was touched by Darius's conviction and sincerity, but found it difficult to let go of his hatred for Quintus and the harm he had caused. "I appreciate your graciousness, Darius," Leo said. "Thank you for sharing your beliefs, but your ideas are hard to accept."

"Most people would agree with you. Someday, though, you may find it helpful to talk with the bishop about your grief, and your feelings of guilt."

* * *

A few weeks later, Leo ventured out and began his attempt to rebuild his life.

"Sorry, Leo, your credit is no longer accepted here," said the cashier at the entrance to the bathhouse. "You will need to return when you can pay."

Leo had never felt so insulted in his life. He marched over to Rusticus's office to demand an audience with his friend. However, when Leo arrived at the office, Rusticus's assistant told him to sit down and wait while he checked with the prefect. Leo fumed while he waited for over an hour. Finally, the assistant said, "Sorry, but Prefect Rusticus is not available."

Leo could hardly believe his lifelong friend had snubbed him. In a rage, he stomped over to see Titus, and again, he was told to wait on a bench against the wall. Soon, Titus's assistant returned and said, "I am sorry, but the emperor's chief of staff is occupied with issues of state."

Leo began to realize that his life as a privileged patrician had ended. He left the building and stumbled along in a stupor among the throng of people on the street. Finally, he reached a public garden and sat down on a bench under a tree. He was lost in a new world that mimicked the one he knew. He sat frozen in fear as he contemplated his situation. How could he navigate in this upside-down parallel universe? Finally, he decided to speak with Gaius, the kindest of his friends, in hopes that he would be merciful. He was not disappointed.

"Tell Caius that I sent you," Gaius said. "He just received a contract for road repair and needs laborers. I can also rent you a small apartment by the North Gate."

"At least I will have means of support and a place to live," Leo thought. "Thank you," he said.

* * *

"Who is that young man Sabina is talking to?" Esteban thought with concern as he approached Natalie's House for their scheduled rendezvous. "What are they laughing about?"

Esteban stood before them. Sabina, surprised, spoke. "Oh,

hello. This is Julio from church. Julio, Esteban."

"Hello," Esteban said coldly.

"Hi. Nice to meet you," Julio replied pleasantly. Turning to Sabina, he said, "I need to go. I will see you Sunday!" and quickly walked away.

"I don't want you seeing him," Esteban said.

"Don't be jealous," she replied.

"Have you been seeing him since we moved out?"

"Don't interrogate me."

"I thought this was our private spot."

"He was just walking by."

"Don't ever see him again."

"You don't own me."

"I forbid it," Esteban ordered.

"You are just like your father."

"How can you say that?"

"You have turned into what you hate."

"If you can't stand me, then go. I don't need you." He regretted the words as soon as they left his mouth, but he was too proud to retract them. Conflicted, he watched as Sabina stormed off. He couldn't stand the scene any longer, so he marched off in the other direction.

Chapter 45

Windows of Heaven

Antonio scanned the surrounding countryside and forests, aglow with over a thousand large bonfires. "I am glad Emperor Aurelius and General Sulla chose this location," he thought. "There must be one million *Quadi* warriors out there." Couriers had just returned that afternoon with news from the main Roman force that Quadi troops were converging on their location, and Roman reinforcements were more than a week away. "Not very good odds," Antonio thought. Their four legions of twenty thousand regular troops and an equal number of auxiliary units were significantly outnumbered. "It is in situations like this that our intense training will pay off," he tried to assure himself. "Yes, the emperor and general were wise in selecting the top of this hill. The surrounding open land will allow us to see the enemy approach from all directions. If we can maintain our lines, there is a chance that we can survive on this high ground tomorrow, but not for a week." He took one long last look at the landscape and mused, "It is amazing that such a tranquil scene will be converted into a bloodbath in a few hours. Yes, this is good ground for a battle, but not good enough."

Antonio turned and started to walk back toward his century's camp. "This will be different from the other skirmishes we have had," he told himself. "This time we are the hunted and not the hunter. Instead of terrorizing our foes with the precision of our formations as we advance to attack, the contest tomorrow will depend on whether our defensive lines hold the onslaught." Pride swelled his heart as he walked past a group of his men sitting around a small campfire. "My men know their duty," he told himself. "They have stared death in the face before. They will hold, but will the other troops?" Concern overtook his pride. "They are all good men. I hate to lose any one of them, but many will not see the sun set tomorrow." He paused. "I must instill confidence in my men," he told himself as he continued to his campsite.

The eight men of his tent were sitting around their fire when Antonio arrived. Adolf was sitting apart on a fallen log, looking at the flames. Tulio was also sitting by himself, writing a letter. "Is it a farewell to his young wife or a petition to his father to care for his family if he does not survive?" Antonio wondered. "Beatus was bragging to Cyrus, itching for a chance to prove his valor." He shook his head, then smiled when he looked at Florin and Philo, trying to distract their minds with a game of knucklebones. The rest of his men were just conversing, reminiscing about past battles, comrades lost, loved ones at home, anything except tomorrow. It would come soon enough.

Antonio sat down next to Adolf.

"Tomorrow will be a tough day," Adolf said.

"Yes, it will. The news from the couriers was not good."

"Look at young Beatus over there," Adolf scoffed. "He's excited for his first battle."

"I hope he survives the initial assault."

"Everyone else knows none of us may survive."

"We are on good ground," Antonio reassured him.

"Humph" was Adolf's only response as they both stared

into the fire.

"Sir," a young messenger said, jolting Antonio from his thoughts. "The primus pilus just returned from a briefing with General Sulla and wants to meet with his centurions."

"Very well. Report that I will be there," Antonio said.

Antonio surveyed his century as he walked to the primus pilus's tent. He heard laughter nearby. "Who in their right mind is making merry at a time like this?" he wondered. As he approached their campfire, he realized that it was the twenty slaves attached to his century. His blood boiled. "How dare they make light of our plight? Many of my men will die tomorrow while these ungrateful slaves rest securely in camp. I will not tolerate this disrespect," he fumed.

Antonio noticed that the slave, Thaddeus, holding a letter, was leading the frivolity.

"What is going on here?" Antonio barked.

"I meant no disrespect, sir. I just received good news in a letter delivered by the couriers today, and I had to share it." Antonio glared at him. "My brother in Rome was just made the master steward of the whole estate of some upstart patrician who married into money but was too stupid to hold on to it. He even believed that Senator Quintus bribed all the charioteers of a race instead of just one. Who would be so stupid to fall for such a simple scam?" Antonio was about to leave a stern warning and move on, but Thaddeus's next words stopped him. "He said that this numbskull was so dense that the senator convinced him to denounce his own wife as a Christian."

"Did you say that the senator was responsible for her death?" Antonio asked.

"Yes. He even took pleasure in the dunce's daughter. How could we not laugh at someone so dimwitted?"

"Give me the letter," Antonio ordered.

"Yes, sir."

Antonio snatched the letter out of Thaddeus's hand. His mind raced as he read the letter and seethed. By the time he had finished, he knew how he would get even with both Leo and Quintus. Now he had to survive to execute his plan.

Antonio clutched the folded letter tightly in his hand as he entered the general's large council tent. Most of the other sixty centurions were already present. He did not need to wait long before the primus pilus stood in front of the assembly.

"The rumors you have heard this afternoon are true. By morning we will be surrounded by nearly one million Quadi warriors. Our relief is over a week away, so it will be up to us to defend ourselves. Each of our four legions will defend one side of the encampment. We have been assigned the eastern front. It is a great honor, but I need not explain that it comes with increased risk. Have your troops fed and battle ready by early-morning light. We expect the Quadi will wait to attack until dawn when the morning sun will be in our eyes, but we cannot afford to be unprepared for an earlier surprise assault. We will bear the brunt of the attack, but we expect that the steel of the other legions will also be tested. The size of the camp means we cannot form a full defensive square around it with typical reserves. So every cohort, century, and contubernium is needed on the line, and my double cohort will be the only reserve for our legion, which I will deploy as needed."

Grumbling broke out among the centurions.

"I realize that limiting the number of reserves to periodically relieve you during a long battle is troubling," the primus pilus continued, "But we need our line to be at least five hundred and forty soldiers long and a full contubernium of eight men deep. Even so, we face great exposure on our flanks, so we have no choice. The auxiliary units of each legion will defend the flank to their right after the initial assault. So after the cavalry and velites have slowed the enemy's initial onslaught, they will retreat to defend the flank between us and the Melitene Legion to the south. Because of the numbers of our foe and our strategic position on this hill, we can take full advantage of our archers. They will continue to support our defenses after their traditional volley during the enemy's initial assault. Do you have any questions?"

"No, sir," the centurions responded in unison.

"You and your troops all know your duty. We must hold our lines at all costs. I have confidence in your valor. We will survive the day. You are dismissed."

Antonio stood on top of the hill next to Adolf in the crisp morning air before daybreak as he surveyed his century, already preparing for the battle.

"They are good men," he said.

"We know our duty," Adolf replied.

"Yes, you do."

"Do you think we have a chance?"

"We have to. I have an appointment with justice in Rome."

A horn blew. The four legions assembled into their positions on top of the hill. One legion faced north, one east, one south, and one west. The horn blew again, and every unit immediately moved like an efficient machine. Each legion's nine cohorts of 480 soldiers marched with precision down the hill in groups 20 men wide by 24 men deep in a checkerboard pattern, followed by the double cohort of 40 by 24 men. Each soldier carried his curved rectangular meter-high shield, javelin, gladius, and a dagger strapped to his waist.

The soldiers stopped halfway down the hill when ordered by the blare of their cohort's horn, intermixed with the sound of the others. Each cohort had its own signals to avoid confusion in the heat of battle. Upon command, each cohort spread out in a well-rehearsed ritual, one third to the left and one third to the right, creating a line 60 soldiers long that connected perfectly with the cohort next to them, creating a 540-man line, 8 soldiers deep, with the reserve line 480 soldiers long and 2 deep behind them. Antonio's century took its position on the southernmost section of the line, with Antonio the point man.

Each legion's 1,000 archers had lined up, 2 deep, behind the cohorts. At the top of the hill, auxiliary units loaded catapults with round stones and scorpions to fire multiple crossbows; 3,000 velites, light infantry with small circular shields, javelins, and short swords, entered each flank, followed by a cavalry of 120 horses and riders.

The sound of crows squawking in the distance drew Antonio's attention to the valley below. The predawn glow lit the surrounding fields and distant forest, from which flocks of crows were fleeing. Antonio scanned the horizon with concern as he watched a million painted Quadi warriors with spears, swords, and shields surround their hill.

"It won't be long now," Antonio thought. "If everyone performs their duty with the same precision that they just demonstrated, we may have a chance." Each depended on the valor of his peers, and each one knew that everyone else was depending on him. Honor would be the key to seeing the setting sun.

Antonio shaded his eyes as the sun breached the horizon and the bloodcurdling war cry of a million Quadi warriors reverberated around him. Enemy troops rushed forward, converging from all directions like swarms of angry bees. Antonio knew that his legion of less than five thousand regular troops and a similar number of less-experienced auxiliary soldiers guarding their flanks were in serious jeopardy of being overrun. He realized that each of the other three legions was facing a similarly terrifying scene.

The catapults snapped, and their projectiles whistled overhead. He watched as the soft stone balls exploded on contact, spraying deadly shrapnel on the advancing foe. But this had little effect because of the sheer number of enemy troops, who were not slowed down as they rushed over their dead compatriots. Hundreds of long arrows shot from the scorpions whizzed overhead. Cries of pain mingled with the war cries of the advancing foe. The catapults snapped again, hurtling clay fire pots overhead that splattered black oil on foe and ground alike. A volley of flaming arrows followed, igniting the oil, which spewed black smoke into the air, darkening the sun's rays. Still, the death inflicted by this inferno did little to slow the enemy advance. A volley of arrows flew again but had limited effect in thinning out the advancing horde. One more volley let fly as the enemy archers began to return fire.

"Prepare for incoming arrows," Antonio yelled. His century consisted of ten columns of eight men lined up along the southernmost segment of the legion's line. Each soldier at the head of a column secured his meter-high curved rectangular shield in front of him, and all the men behind him lifted their shields over their heads, creating a cover that protected the men from harm as the arrows clanged and bounced off their shields.

"Ready," Antonio yelled, and his men arranged their shields in front of them and their pila javelins in their hands. The catapults and archers continued to hurl their missiles at the enemy hosts. Smoke from the burning oil and fields blackened the sky. Antonio watched as their legion's 3,500 velites auxiliary soldiers rushed toward the enemy's advance guard and hurled their javelins, inflicting great damage. But the benefit was short lived as thousands of shouting Quadi soldiers rushed past their slain comrades while the velites retreated to guard the legion's southern flank. The legion's cavalry of 120 horsemen rode down the line, thinning out the advancing units, and quickly joined the velites.

"Javelins and secure shields," Antonio ordered. His eighty soldiers threw their javelins, drew their swords, and locked their shields in preparation for the impending collision with the rushing enemy hosts. Out of necessity, all further orders would be given with his whistle. Soldiers on the front line raised their swords perpendicular with their shields and braced for the impact. The seven soldiers behind each lineman pressed forward. One. Two. Three. Crash! The blow of the collision with the enemy force was felt all the way back to the last man in each column, but the line held.

Each of Antonio's linemen was well trained and had experience in fighting in these close quarters. Their short swords were perfectly suited for these situations. They were lightweight, so they could be maneuvered quickly. The Romans had been trained to use their gladii to stab effectively in the thin space between their shield and the shield of the lineman next to him, and to slice only when it was opportune. Consequently, Antonio's men were consistently inflicting death and injury on their foe with little damage to themselves. The dead bodies in front of the Roman line began to pile up and become a barrier, slowing the advance of the enemy, but the onslaught continued.

A different type of battle raged on Antonio's right flank. The less organized velites light infantry rushed forward with their spears, swords, and shields to engage the enemy before they reached the flank between the two legions. Battle erupted between the forces on the open field. The line blurred as the armies merged and ebbed and flowed as the battle progressed. Initially, the sheer size of the Quadi force overwhelmed the Roman auxiliary force and pressed them back into the wedge between the flanks of the two legions. However, the tighter the arena, the fewer German soldiers had access to the fighting, limiting their advantage.

Romans generally were not good horsemen, so their cavalry consisted of foreigners and was not typically used as an important element of their battle strategy. Today, however, the legion's cavalry played a key role in defending its flanks. With their mobility and enhanced view of the battlefield, the cavalry was able to quickly lend support where it was most needed, inspiring the troops with this vital practical assistance and keeping the defense from collapsing under the pressure of the Quadi onslaught.

The bitter smoke from the burning oil and fields drifted over the battlefield, stinging their eyes and choking Antonio and his men. Antonio blew his whistle, and his linemen retreated, taking their places at the back of their columns. Instantaneously they were replaced by the soldiers behind them as the whole column stepped forward to fill the vacated space. Antonio moved back to the end of his column on the southern end of the legion's line. He surveyed his men while he caught his breath. His eyes were drawn to Adolf, who had advanced to the front of the line in the column next to him. Antonio immediately was concerned as he saw Adolf fight according to his gladiator training instead of the disciplined approach of a defensive Roman line.

"Stay on the line!" he yelled. "You're not a gladiator!"

The noise of battle drowned out his shouts. Antonio began to take courage as he watched Adolf strike down foe after foe with power and vitality unequaled by anyone else on the line. But his ferocity had not escaped the attention of a Quadi captain, who directed a couple of his experienced warriors to engage him. Antonio tried to reach Adolf and warn him, but the Roman line was too tight. Antonio's heart sank as he watched Adolf stab at one of the Quadi soldiers, who expertly deflected his blow, drawing Adolf forward away from the Roman line. Antonio watched with horror as Adolf swung his gladius in an effort to strike down his foe while the other German soldier speared him.

"No!" Antonio screamed.

The man behind Adolf immediately filled his position on the line while the others dragged Adolf back to where Antonio stood. Antonio knelt down beside his friend. "Can you hear me?"

"Yes."

"Just relax," Antonio said as he began to unlatch his lorica segmentata armor.

"Don't...bother," Adolf answered between gasps for air.

"Hold on."

"My friend," Adolf gasped and stared.

"No, no, no!" Antonio screamed as he shook his friend.

Antonio had no time to spare as the Quadi had begun to penetrate his flank. The men in the column bordering the flank were confused. Some saw the danger and turned to face their flank to protect themselves while others maintained discipline and faced the front of the line. The general had placed Antonio at the end of the line to ensure that it would hold, and Antonio would not let it falter on his watch.

"Face the flank! Face the flank!" Antonio yelled as he jumped up. Turning to the reserve auxiliary unit behind him, he ordered, "Advance!"

Antonio grabbed the spear of a fallen soldier and led the reserve unit's charge into the battle, impaling the first Quadi in his path and dispatching a second with his gladius moments later. He used his shield as a weapon to smash the face of the next foe he encountered and stabbed him in the ribs with his sword as he cleared the immediate threat to his troops, and the reserves filled the space behind him. A small cavalry unit of eight riders arrived to buttress their defense. Antonio resumed his position behind his troops and surveyed the situation. Another member of his century had fallen, but his line still appeared secure.

The battle raged on all fronts. Occasionally a Roman soldier would fall from a spear wound or laceration from the Quadi swords while the Roman war machine inflicted death and mayhem on the Quadi throughout the morning, wave after wave. By noon, the primus pilus had deployed half his reserve troops to strengthen the flanks on both ends of the line and another fourth to fill in the holes on the line. By late afternoon, all the reserve units had been deployed when, to their great relief, the Quadi finally withdrew. They had survived the day.

The primus pilus stood in front of his sixty centurions for their evening briefing. "We need to reduce your water to one quarter day's ration," he said.

The battle-exhausted officers looked at each other in disbelief and grumbled.

"We have no choice. We only have enough for two days even at this reduced level." Soft gasps were heard among the group. "Present your casualty reports," he ordered.

"Nineteen out of eighty dead. Thirteen injured, unable to fight," Antonio reported.

Antonio was proud that his men had held the line at its most critical spot. He then learned that his century had fared no better than most of the units in the battle. With this depleted force and no reserve units to relieve their exhaustion, tomorrow's battle would be nearly impossible to survive, even if they had a full ration of water.

The next morning it became clear that the Quadi strategy was to concentrate most of their force on the eastern front, attacking Antonio's line while leaving enough troops on the other fronts to take advantage of any weakness that might be created if they sent units to the eastern line. That was exactly how the day played out. The German forces initiated the battle by only attacking on the eastern front, holding their other forces in reserve, but as soon as the legion defending the northern front sent two cohorts to reinforce the eastern front at midmorning, the Quadi attacked them with a vengeance. But their lines held. At noon the Quadi retreated and did not attack for the rest of the day. The Romans, however, were out of water.

On the third day, the enemy did not attack but employed a siege strategy while surrounding their camp, ready to strike at a moment's notice, forcing the Romans to deploy their troops to the battlefield. The hot August sun beat down on the Roman troops mercilessly. By midday some of the Roman troops began to faint for lack of fluids. In the afternoon the Quadi began to taunt their forces by feigning an attack and withdrawing before any of their forces were injured.

On the fourth day, the Roman situation was desperate, and the Quadi knew it. Roman forces were falling from dehydration and sunstroke more rapidly than in battle. At noon, Antonio watched a Quadi officer on horseback lead a convoy of a dozen packhorses laden with large water containers toward the Roman line. When just out of the archer's range, the officer turned and lined up his caravan in front of the thirsty Roman troops. The officer grabbed his large water bag, took a long swig, poured the rest of its contents on the ground, and laughed. The men leading the packhorses then opened the water containers and walked their horses along in front of the dehydrated troops as the water flowed to the ground, just out of their reach, before the mocking enemy returned to their line, laughing.

Marcus Aurelius and his legates stood on top of the hill watching the Quadi water train retreat.

"We cannot survive another day without water, and they know it," Emperor Marcus Aurelius said.

"They will attack tomorrow at midday or afternoon to finish the job," General Sulla observed.

"Only divine providence can save us." Marcus Aurelius sighed. "Order each of your legions to sacrifice to the great god Mercury tonight and pray for a miracle. It is our only hope."

The next morning provided no relief. Antonio stood with his dying men on the eastern front, facing the glaring sun. The stench of rotting flesh and the acidic smell of ash were suffocating. The men hardly said a word through their cracked and bleeding lips, which provided the only moisture to their dehydrated bodies. The enemy had assembled, poised for battle, which he knew would come before day's end. It would be a massacre. The soldier next to Antonio began to falter. Antonio reached over and grabbed him before he fell, carried him to the back of the line, and laid him down. He was already gone. One more of his men had died in his arms. He knew that none of them would survive the day. He was angry. Was this the gods playing one last trick on him? Baiting him with the hope of revenge, only to snatch it out of his reach while he watched men he was willing to die for suffer and expire in his arms? Where was justice? Where was God?

At that moment someone tapped Antonio on the shoulder. He turned around, and a young messenger said, "The general needs you to bring your troops back up to camp. He needs you to round up traitors."

"Tell the general I will be there momentarily." Antonio's century was now half its former size, but these remaining thirty-nine soldiers were men of valor. He loved them and hated anyone within their camp who would betray them. Antonio and his men marched up the hill to their camp, where they found General Sulla waiting for them, fuming.

"I have received word that a number of slaves throughout the camp refused to participate in the offering to the gods last night. Take your men and round them all up. Once you return, we will give no quarter."

"Yes, sir."

Antonio led his troops through the Roman tent city organized by legion, cohort, and century. Even though it was devoid of fighting men, it remained a hive of activity. Slaves scurried about carrying dead and wounded soldiers, packing and carrying supplies, organizing and cleaning the camp. They approached the head slave for the first cohort.

"Were there any slaves who refused to participate in the sacrifice last night?" Antonio demanded.

"Yes."

"Take us to them."

"Follow me, sir."

Antonio and his men followed him past slaves packing a load of fire pots on a mule and then stopped at a tent being cleaned by a female slave.

"She's one," their guide said.

"Detain her," Antonio ordered.

The slave looked up in bewilderment as two soldiers grabbed and hauled her kicking and struggling back to the group of soldiers.

A little farther and their guide took them to a male slave and his teenage son stacking *sudes* spikes used to form a *cheval-de-frise* barricade. "Both of them," said the guide.

"Grab them," Antonio said.

The young man ran, and soldiers rushed after him. His father stood calmly while he was arrested. Soon the soldiers returned with his son in custody.

Antonio went from one campsite to the next, inquiring about anyone who had refused to participate in the offering to Mercury. He had no trouble locating the traitors as the other slaves were anxious to denounce them. Each legion had nearly fifteen hundred slaves, two per tent, to lead the mules, help set up camp, and tend to a plethora of menial tasks. Antonio found that nearly three hundred of the six thousand slaves had refused to participate in the sacrifice, primarily from the Melitene Legion. A couple of hours later, Antonio and his century returned with his Christian prisoners.

"Here are the traitors," Antonio reported to General Sulla in front of Emperor Aurelius.

"Well done," General Sulla said. Turning to his emperor, he continued. "Caesar, these Christian slaves disobeyed your order and refused to participate in the offering to Mercury. My troops believe that their disrespect is the cause of our plight. I see no solution except executing these rebels to pacify the gods and hope for a miracle." Antonio was in full accord.

Marcus Aurelius nodded and stepped over to face the offenders. "What do you have to say for yourselves?"

One of the detainees stepped forward and said, "Your Honor. We mean no disrespect to you and your gods, but we have taken a vow to only worship the one true God, the Creator of the whole universe. We are your loyal servants and offer you the only weapon we have, our faith and prayers." He fell to his knees and began to pray, with the rest of the Christian prisoners following suit: "Dear God, we praise Thy name and acknowledge Thy wisdom and mercy. Thou knowest our grave condition. If it be Thy will, we pray that Thou wilt deliver us and this army out of the hands of our enemies."

The emperor shook his head and turned back to his general. "Do as you wish," he said as he walked away.

Pointing to an open area nearby with a large tree stump in front of a woodpile, General Sulla said, "Execute them over there."

Antonio grabbed the praying prisoner next to him and dragged him to the front of the stump while his soldiers used their swords and spears to corral the prisoners over to the open area.

"Kneel," Antonio ordered.

The prisoner knelt and placed his head on the stump. His wife screamed and rushed over, yelling, "No! No!" She threw herself down in front of Antonio and begged for mercy. With a nod from Antonio, two soldiers grabbed the woman and hauled her away. The prisoner again placed his head on the stump while his wife wailed. Antonio raised his sword as a raindrop hit his face. Startled, he looked up to see clouds billowing overhead. Another raindrop hit his face. The sky continued to darken. Lightning flashed, accompanied by a loud crack of thunder. Huge raindrops poured down on Antonio, the prisoners, the camp, and the Roman line.

Antonio opened his mouth to capture the lifesaving droplets of divine mercy. He removed his helmet and turned it upside down to catch the rain. As it filled, he looked around and saw the rain pour down on the whole camp. Everywhere, people were looking up with their mouths wide open, welcoming this outpouring of life-sustaining fluid. Many of the soldiers on the line were likewise filling their helmets with the rain while others lifted their large curved shields up to capture more of the rain and funnel it into their mouths. Antonio smiled when he saw one horseman using his round shield as a basin for his horse to drink from. Antonio lifted his helmet and drank freely, water washing down his cheeks and neck. He lowered his helmet and noticed hardened troops on the line dancing and shouting for joy. The rain had not only refreshed their parched bodies but had also filled their souls with optimistic energy.

The scene had not escaped the gaze of the Quadi king. "Angreifen! Angreifen!" he ordered. They still outnumbered the Romans by more than two thousand to one, but he did not want to give them any benefit. Upon hearing the signal, the Quadi warriors sprang from their positions like arrows shot from a taut bow. While the Romans thirsted for water, the Quadi lusted for blood. They rushed toward the Romans, who were scrambling to reform their positions in the midst of the deluge. Horns of the forty Roman cohorts blared out distinct orders, sounding like an orchestra tuning its instruments. The war cries from the Quadi, charging in from every direction, added to the confusion while thunder and lightning from heaven capped the chaotic scene. Antonio surveyed the sight from his vantage point on top of the hill, his view obstructed only by the torrents of water pouring out of the thunderheads above. They would be overrun by the swarming Quadi forces momentarily. "What a dramatic way to die," he thought, with heaven and hell joining forces to bring about his demise.

He looked down at the men of his legion preparing to meet the onslaught when lightning struck the ground right in front of the wave of Quadi warriors. Hail larger than walnuts crashed down on the enemy, halting their advance in an instant. Antonio looked around and witnessed heaven hurtling lightning and hail down on his foes, scattering them in every direction. The sky above the Romans cleared, shining rays of light on their awestruck faces while they watched their enemy retreat in chaos under the barrage of divine intervention. A large double rainbow appeared, crowning the miracle they had just experienced.

* * *

"Sir, I request leave to return to Rome to take care of some personal business," Antonio said.

"That is an unusual request," General Sulla said.

"I realize that, sir. I have not had an opportunity to return to Rome since the Senate ratified the emperor's decision that I be granted citizenship. There are a number of issues that need my attention with this honorable change of status. I have not mentioned anything before because of the demands of the campaign, but now with your great victory, I thought there might be a period of respite, providing a window for me to address these personal issues."

"I understand. You have been a valiant and loyal officer, worthy of such a request. Come. I was just preparing to meet with the emperor. I will present your request and hope that it is granted."

They walked over to the emperor's tent, which was next to the general's.

"Caesar, good day," General Sulla said.

"Enter. I have just concluded my report to the Senate regarding the miraculous circumstances of our victory," Marcus Aurelius said as he tapped the manuscript on his small wooden desk.

"I am sure they will be pleased to read the details of your great triumph."

"We all know it was divine intervention, and I gave credit where it was due. Now, what are the matters that need my attention?"

"Caesar, I anticipate that there will be a short lull in

fighting after this victory while we plan your next conquest. Our loyal centurion here has not had an opportunity to return to Rome since you granted him citizenship, and he has a number of pressing personal matters to attend to. We hope that you will grant him leave to deal with them."

"Excellent," Marcus Aurelius said. "Centurion, you are the perfect person to deliver my report to the Senate. You may have your leave once they receive my letter, and you answer any questions that they may have regarding it."

"I am honored, Caesar."

Chapter 46

She Died for You

Leo tossed and turned in fitful sleep, haunted by the recurring nightmare of Amora in the center of the arena looking directly at him. She mouthed the words "I love you" without making a sound. Amora then placed her hand over her heart and offered it to Leo while she was sucked back into black oblivion with her hand outstretched to him. Leo sat up with a start, sweat dripping down his forehead. But more terrifying than this nightmare was the guilt that haunted him from the reality of his memories. He finally decided to accept Darius's suggestion and meet with the Christian bishop.

"I appreciate you allowing me to meet with you," Leo said to the bishop as they shook hands in his humble home.

"It is my pleasure, tribune."

"Just 'Leo' would be fine."

"As you wish," said the bishop while motioning to the table and chairs in the sparse room. "Darius mentioned that you have been troubled and are looking for counsel."

"Yes," Leo said as he sat down. "As you know, I have lost everything. My whole world has been turned upside down. I am disconnected from everyone. I'm all alone."

The bishop sat down and looked at Leo earnestly. "Sometimes God allows us to fall so that we will finally let Him lift us up. What troubles you the most?"

"I am haunted by guilt for denouncing Amora."

"Do you think that God did not already know that you were going to denounce your wife? Yet He still extends His grace to you and offers you forgiveness."

"I don't see how that is possible. She is dead."

"Amora's death is just a short separation. Christ has conquered death. She still lives and will be clothed in a glorious body when Jesus comes again."

"These fanciful words don't change the reality that she is gone, and I killed her."

"Let me tell you a short story from Hebrew history. One faithful young son named Joseph was sold into Egypt by his jealous brothers. When Joseph wouldn't sleep with his master's wife, she lied and had him imprisoned. But God remembered him and arranged for him to interpret Pharaoh's dream, which saved Egypt from famine. Pharaoh made Joseph his highest-ranking officer. Later, when Joseph's brothers came to Egypt to buy food to survive the famine, Joseph did not seek revenge. Instead he welcomed them and said that their evil deed was part of God's greater plan to save their family. If they had not sold him into Egypt, they all would have perished. Leo, maybe Amora died to save you."

Leo stared at the bishop as tears welled up in his eyes and ran down his face. After a moment, he spoke. "She did. I felt her love in the arena. What can I do?"

"You have already taken the first step by acknowledging the wrong you have done," the bishop replied. "Next, you need to confess your guilt to those you have wronged and ask their forgiveness and then do all that you can to repair the harm you have caused, even if you cannot completely make amends."

"That is only fair, but I cannot bring people back to life."

"No, but God will in the resurrection. If you forgive those who offend you, then you will feel free from your guilt, even if those you have injured do not forgive you."

"That is a challenge. It is very difficult for me to forgive those who have ruined my life."

"We all hold on to our grievances, petty or large, and nurse our hurt feelings until they fester and infect others. But, why do we refuse to let go?" The bishop asked.

"Because justice is not satisfied."

"That is what most people think, but it really is because *we* are guilty, and we do not like looking in the mirror and seeing how ugly our actions are. So, we build a façade of pride to hide our sins, not only from others but primarily from ourselves. But because we are children of God, we each have an acute sense of justice. No matter how deep we try to bury our guilt in the recesses of our mind, we still sense it lurking there, and occasionally it reaches up and grabs our attention. We realize that it is as useless hiding from our guilt as it is sewing clothes out of fig leaves. It simply does not work, so we blame others. We take our guilt, project it onto others, and attack it there in a vain attempt to satisfy the sense of justice that haunts us. We say to justice, 'Ignore my faults. Instead, focus on the injustice over there. Leave me alone.'"

"So, you are saying that to free ourselves from guilt, we need to forgive others?"

"Yes," the bishop continued. "Until then, it will haunt us. But it is hard, so instead we invent enemies to blame so we can redirect our guilt. We create a fantasy world made up of good people and bad people, friends and enemies when, in reality, we are all mixed bags of good and bad. We are all imperfect, broken creatures. No one is in any position to judge anyone else."

"But some evil is so atrocious that it cannot be excused."

"No evil should be excused," the bishop said. "But when we take it upon ourselves to pass judgment on the good and evil in those around us, we usurp God's role and reject Him. We separate ourselves from Him and all the love, peace, and beauty that He offers us."

"This is similar to what Darius explained before."

"He is a good teacher. Leo, do you know what evil is?"

"Yes, the opposite of good."

"That is exactly right. Just like darkness is the absence of light, evil is the absence of good. When we distance ourselves from God—the essence of goodness—we create evil and all the problems, heartache and chaos that follow. When we judge others and ascribe blame, we basically choose to push God aside and walk away from Him."

It had never occurred to Leo that judging other people created evil. Sure, he had seen, and personally experienced, the bitterness associated with being misjudged, but the concept that judging others was a primary source of evil in the world was completely new to him.

"Leo, learning to forgive is one of the most important life lessons we need to learn. It is how we become united with others and with God. Jesus showed us the way. He forgave his crucifiers while their hands still dripped with his life's blood.

"While he was being crucified?"

"Yes. He said, 'Father, forgive them for they know not what they do.'"

"Incredible."

"Yes, and he also offers forgiveness to you and me. Leo, I believe you are ready to ask forgiveness from our congregation."

"I don't see how they can forgive me, but I am willing to tell them I am sorry for the grief I caused them."

"You can do that this Sunday."

* * *

"I want to thank your bishop for allowing me to speak to you today," Leo said as he stood before an assembly of Christians in their catacomb sanctuary. "I want to thank you for the kindness you have extended to me while I recovered, and to my son and my late wife, Amora." He paused and took a deep breath before he continued. "I do not deserve the love and grace that you have offered me." Deep emotion filled his whole being. Tears welled up in his eyes. He could not speak. He felt his body begin to tremble as if it could not contain the rush of passion flowing into it. He grabbed the podium to steady himself. As he stood there, he was nearly overcome with a swirling mix of deep sorrow and ecstasy.

His voice cracked as he spoke. "I am responsible for her death." His frame could no longer restrain the flood of emotion, which erupted into tears flowing down his cheeks. His whole body shook as he sobbed, releasing the pressure built up inside him. Finally, he was able to regain enough of his composure to continue. His voice quivered as he said, "I am so sorry." He took two quick gasps of air. "I am so sorry for all I have done. I am sorry for denouncing Amora." He took another deep breath. "I am sorry for the pain I have caused you. I helped arrange the persecution that has caused you so much sorrow. I did not know. I was mistaken, so mistaken."

He paused and looked over the congregation, all looking at him in rapt attention, many with tears streaming down their cheeks. "I don't know how you can forgive me," he said. "There is no way I can repay you for your loss. I wish I could, but I cannot bring my dear wife and your loved ones back to life. I would give my life to undo what I have done, but it won't help. Please let me know if there is anything that I can do to ease your pain. Please know that I am truly sorry." He turned and began to sit down when he felt an overwhelming sensation of gratitude and joy. He stopped and returned to the lectern. "Thank you for all that you have done." Tears of joy now flowed down his cheeks as he concluded, "I thank your God for the mercy He has shown me." He smiled and said, "Praise be to your God…and my God."

Chapter 47

A New Worldview

"Is that Leo?" Julia asked Loretta as they walked down the thoroughfare.

"It can't be. Doing manual labor?" said Loretta.

"It is," Julia said as they approached a group of laborers repairing the cobblestone road. "I realize he has fallen on hard times, but manual labor." Julia shook her head. "You would think one of his friends would have helped him."

"Not a mad Christian sympathizer. Rational people need to stay away from such craziness for their own safety."

"I'm sorry. I forgot he tried to kill your husband."

"What a disgrace," Loretta said as she glared at him. "And after all that Quintus did for him."

Leo looked up from his work and saw Loretta and Julia staring at him as they approached. He felt embarrassed to be seen in such a position. At first, he pretended to not have seen them and continued his labor, turning his back toward them. Even so he noticed that they were now walking directly over to him. So he stood to face the wives of his old friends. "Good morning, Loretta, Julia." The ladies returned his salutation by spitting in his face and turning their backs on him as they strutted away. Rage rushed through his being. "How dare they treat me this way?" he thought. It took all his willpower to keep from putting these females in their place.

Darius's words, "It's not my claim," echoed in his mind.

He took a deep breath and told himself, "They just don't know the truth." He began to calm down. "Just let it go. It does not matter," he told himself as he loosened his clenched fists and wiped the spit off his face. He knelt and replaced another cobblestone.

* * *

"Senators, a centurion has returned from the front with a report from the Emperor," the steward informed Senator Quintus and Gaius.

"Let him enter," Quintus replied.

"Senator Quintus, Senator Gaius," Antonio said as he handed them Emperor Aurelius's letter. "The emperor has personally directed me to deliver this report to the Senate and answer any questions they may have regarding his conquest in Germania. I trust that you will distribute it to your colleagues and arrange a time for me to address them if they desire to know any further details."

"Thank you, centurion," Quintus said.

"Antonio?" Gaius asked. "By what strange course of events have you risen from the quarries to become a centurion, personally serving the emperor himself?"

"Fate creates its own course, sir," Antonio answered. "The gods arranged for General Sulla Pompeianus to purchase me, and when I saved him during an ambush, I was awarded this position by the emperor."

"Strange course of events indeed," Quintus observed.

Directing his attention to Quintus, Antonio said, "Sir, I have some personal unfinished business regarding Leo that involves you. May I speak with you in private at sunset in the Porticus Liviae gardens near your villa?"

"Private, you say?"

"Yes, sir. It is something personal between Leo and me that I need to take care of, and now that you own his estate, it may affect you. I would not want to do anything that could affect you without consulting you first."

"All right, then."

"Thank you, sir. By the way, do either of you know where I can find Leo?"

"He rented a small apartment by the northern gate," Gaius replied.

"My wife said she saw him this morning repairing the Via Flaminia near the Piazza del Popolo."

"Thank you."

* * *

"Could that be Esteban?" Antonio wondered as he spotted a young man holding a small bag hobble through the Piazza del Popolo. The roadwork was completed by the time Antonio had arrived, and none of the workers were anywhere to be seen. "Fortune has smiled on me again," Antonio thought as he approached the young man and recognized that it was, indeed, the boy he had served four years earlier.

"Esteban," Antonio called out.

Esteban turned to see who had beckoned him. "Antonio!"

"My, look how you have grown." Antonio placed his hands on Esteban's shoulders.

"I thought you were dead."

"Escaping death seems to be my occupation."

"And you have become a centurion!"

"Yes. The gods have smiled on me again. Do you know where I can find your father?"

"Sorry. I thought he would be here, but he has already left. I was bringing him his lunch."

"He didn't say anywhere else he would be today, did he?"

"No, but he said he would be home early, before sunset."

"Very well. Where do you live?"

"Close by. Come, I will show you." Esteban turned and

motioned to Antonio to follow.

"I still cannot believe how much you have grown and how strong you are."

Esteban smiled.

"You look like you will be ready to join the legion in a year or so," Antonio said as he slapped Esteban's back. They both chuckled. "I am sorry that you have had to suffer because of Leo's debacles."

"It is not all that bad," Esteban replied.

"Looking at how grown-up and independent you are, I am actually surprised that you haven't left him, especially considering that he denounced your mother."

The words, "He denounced your mother," struck a dagger through Esteban's heart. He had always known that his father had consented to his mother's execution, but he had never faced the fact that he was instrumental in her death. Those words opened all the wounds of the past—his father's rejection as a child, his neglect and abuse as a young teenager, and the loss of the mother he adored—it all came rushing back into his present consciousness. Anger followed right behind all the resurrected hurt. He resented his father and could not stand to see him.

"Here is where we live. Up on the fourth floor."

"Thank you. I will come by later this afternoon."

Esteban walked to Sabina's house instead of going up to the apartment he shared with his father. He needed to talk to someone who would share his pain.

Sabina was surprised to see Esteban standing in front of her when she opened the door.

"I am sorry for what I said and how I treated you the other day," Esteban said. "So, if you don't want to talk with me, I understand." She looked at him without saying a word. "I do not want to bother you, but I need to talk, and you are the only person who cares."

"What's wrong?" Sabina asked as she motioned for Esteban to enter.

"Antonio has returned and said that my father denounced my mother. I never actually knew this. I suspected it, but I always buried the thought. But now I can't hide from the truth.

"I'm so sorry."

"I thought I had forgiven him, but this is too much. He has never cared for me, and now he expects me to just pretend that it doesn't matter. He has ruined my life. He has ruined all our lives."

Sabina listened while Esteban rehashed all his pain and pent-up anger with his father. By late afternoon, he had unloaded the burden of neglect and abuse that he had carried since childhood. It felt good to finally acknowledge the pain and share it. Now he was finally in a position to listen to what Sabina had to say.

"Esteban, life is unfair to all of us. You have a right to be upset, but it pains me to see you suffer. We have talked before about how forgiveness heals your soul."

"I know, but I just can't do it. It hurts too much."

"I understand. We all grow up in an imperfect world. Some have it worse than others, but everyone is dealing with something," Sabina said.

"I don't see how that excuses it."

"It doesn't. But it creates an emotional vacuum that sucks us in to become self-absorbed. And the pain we focus on creates subconscious fears that control our lives. Fears of rejection and abandonment, of not being valued or appreciated, and of not being able to control our environment. And then, when someone triggers these fears, we react, just like you did with Antonio today. We become slaves to our fears."

"Then how do we escape?"

"Through God's love. The void at the center of our lives was created by a lack of love, Esteban."

"I understand that, but I don't see how God can help me."

"God's infinite love is the only thing great enough to fill this emptiness. If we open our heart to God, He will fill our emotional holes. His love will eliminate these innate fears, and liberate us to love others more freely and deeply. We no longer will have a need to project our guilt onto others, so we can become free to forgive them and enjoy life more fully and realize our true potential."

"It sounds too idealistic. I just don't see how God can fix everything. If He could, then why didn't He just prevent it from happening in the first place?"

"Because we wouldn't grow, Esteban. We need to experience life with all its ups and downs so that we can learn and grow to become more like God and to experience greater love and joy. The same emotional vacuum that pulls us down is what inspires us to seek relief and meaning."

"But how does God fix it? He didn't feel my pain."

"Yes, He did, Esteban. While Jesus hung on the cross and bled from every pore in the Garden of Gethsemane, he took on himself all of our pain and suffering. The agony he felt from his personal injuries during his atonement were only tokens of the infinite anguish he felt from the sorrow we cause each other. He literally bore our grief."

"I'm sorry, but I don't see how that is possible."

"Because Jesus is God, he was able to look down through the ages of history and see all the hurt and injustice we inflict on each other, and because he is all loving, he literally felt our pain. He was able to bear this sorrow only because he is an all-powerful God. What is even more remarkable, his love transcends his compassion for us as victims of wrongdoing and extends to encompass us as the perpetrators of this evil as well."

"I never understood that he literally felt all my sorrows."

"Yes. When Judas betrayed Jesus with a kiss, Jesus also felt the pain when your father betrayed you. When his disciples scattered and left the Savior alone, he also felt your pain when you were abandoned. When witnesses bore false witness against him, he also felt the hurt you felt when friends talked behind your back. When Jesus was struck across the cheek in the presence of the high priest, he also felt the pain of the abuse you suffered from the very person who should have protected you from harm. When the Roman governor stated that he found no fault in Jesus, yet still sentenced him to death, Jesus also felt your pain for the injustice you have suffered. Yes, he has felt all your pain, Esteban, and through his stripes he can heal you."

Esteban sat silent, processing all that Sabina had said. She let him ponder. Finally, he said, "This has been helpful, but I wish I could get over these negative thoughts and feelings."

"Maybe you should discuss them with your father. He seems to be trying to change. Maybe it will help both of you."

"How can I talk with him after all he has done?"

"I don't know, Esteban, but I feel that you need to address this with your father in order to move on."

"You may be right. I just can't see myself doing it."

Sabina smiled and walked over to Esteban. She took his hand and looked him in the eye. "You are a strong person. I have confidence in you." Sabina leaned forward and gave him a kiss.

Chapter 48

Dancing with the Furies

Leo had just taken a bite of the bread and cheese he had grabbed in his small kitchen when he heard the knock on the front door. "Who could that be?" he wondered. He opened the door and turned white. The ghost in front of him was Antonio with a sword on his hip. Leo bolted to the other room with Antonio right behind him, drawing his sword.

Antonio stopped, grimaced, and resheathed his gladius. He took a deep breath. "Execute your plan," he told himself. Having regained control of his wrath, Antonio entered the room to find Leo standing in a corner by a window holding a rod and a curtain at his feet.

"Don't worry, Leo. I mean you no harm," he lied as he walked toward Leo. Leo raised the rod for protection. Antonio stopped and said, "I have discovered that Quintus was responsible. He used you. He hurt both of us."

"What do you mean?"

"Quintus orchestrated this whole thing."

Meanwhile, Esteban returned home and was shocked to see their front door open. He heard voices in the next room, so he entered cautiously, walked over to the open interior door, and listened.

Antonio thrust the letter into Leo's face. "Here is the letter from Prometheus. Read it. Read how they mock you. Read how they gloat over their fraud. Read how they wallow in the rape and murder of your daughter."

Leo grabbed the letter out of Antonio's hand and read it. He turned red with rage as he read. The blood vessels on his neck bulged out. He threw the letter down and clenched his fist as he stared at Antonio.

Antonio unsheathed his sword and held it out to Leo. "Here. Take my sword. Quintus will be alone with me at the Royal Gardens at sunset."

Leo stared at the sword. He knew he had a choice to make that would have eternal consequences.

"Take it. He deserves to die." Leo continued to stare at the sword that seemed to grow in his view and eclipse everything else in the room. "What's wrong? Aren't you a man? Don't you want justice?"

Leo grabbed the sword. "Yes. He deserves to die."

"Here is my belt." Antonio unbuckled his weapon strap with its empty sheath and handed it to Leo. "Take it too," he said, leaving his dagger strapped to his waist for use once Leo had disposed of Quintus. "I must make haste. I need to meet Quintus before you arrive." Antonio rushed out the front door without noticing Esteban hiding nearby. Leo fastened the weapon belt around his waist.

* * *

Antonio met Quintus at the top of the stairs leading to the gardens.

"What is this all about?" Quintus asked.

"Sir, I hate to inform you that your slave Prometheus wrote a letter to a slave assigned to my century in which he details your malfeasance toward my despicable former master."

Quintus looked at Antonio in shock.

"Your secret is safe with me. Now you see why I insisted that we meet in private." Quintus cocked his head, wondering what Antonio was leading up to. "As you should know, I am glad for any misfortune that befalls Leo. But he deserves more. He deserves death. While he lives, you are at risk of exposure, and my vengeance goes unsatisfied. He will be here shortly to kill you, but I will execute him before he has a chance to harm you. Then you can attest that I saved you from this madman. This way you can rest in peace while I execute my revenge without any adverse consequences. I desire nothing further. How you deal with your slave is your business."

"You have put me at risk to further your quest for vengeance." Quintus said disapprovingly.

"There is no risk, sir. Every contingency has been accounted for."

"What if Leo does not come but instead shows that letter to the authorities?"

"Oh, he will come, all right. A man like Leo can't change his character."

"You had better be right, for your sake."

"Don't worry. Look, there he is."

Leo approached, sword in hand. Quintus, standing next to Antonio, began to turn to leave until Antonio grabbed his arm while placing his dagger by Quintus's ribs.

"Oh, I will kill Leo, all right," Antonio said, "but after he kills you." Quintus stood still and looked at Leo, now standing right in front of him, sword raised, staring. The public in the vicinity watched in horror as they backed away.

"What's wrong, Leo?" Antonio asked. "Be done with it."

Quintus laughed. "He's not a man. He is just an effeminate wimp." He spit in Leo's face. When the spittle splattered Leo's face, he instantly recalled his experience in the morning and Darius's comments.

Leo looked at Quintus and saw himself in his nemesis.

Leo groaned and tossed his sword aside, shouting, "It's not my claim!"

Quintus laughed again and said, "You are all so stupid. Did you really think that I would come without protection? Guards!" Twenty guards emerged from their hiding places. "My archers would have cut you down before you finished your stroke. Ha. This is why true patricians are destined to rule, instead of scum like the two of you. Kill the centurion but spare Leo. He has a letter I need to retrieve."

Antonio flung his dagger into the chest of one of the approaching guards and dove for the sword while the other guards charged from every direction. Antonio grabbed the sword as he rolled toward the closest guard and severed his leg before jumping to his feet. The quick manner in which Antonio dispatched two of his foes gave pause to the other guards. They cautiously moved in, tightening the circle around him. All the while Antonio scrutinized his adversaries, looking for any weakness.

Antonio noticed that one of the younger guards appeared particularly nervous. He lunged toward him, causing him to jump back and trip, opening room for Antonio to swing around and slash the guard next to him, breaking free. He jumped onto a nearby bench where he expertly deflected the strokes of the pursuing guards. When the onslaught was too great, he jumped behind the bench and ran toward a tree that was close by in the garden, with the guards right on his tail. The tree split their pursuit, enabling Antonio to isolate and dispose of one more guard before they had him surrounded again. When they got too close for him to maneuver, he spun around, striking several of his foes' swords in the process, before he tumbled to the ground in an attempt to avoid injury and to sever a guard's leg as before. However, this time the guards moved quickly out of the range of his swing, defeating his plan.

He now lay on the ground, hopelessly deflecting countless blows. Suddenly one guard hovering over him disappeared and then the guard next to him. In their place he saw Leo's figure silhouetted against the sky, his arm reaching down to him. Leo nodded to Antonio while he blocked the guards' swings with the sword in his other hand. Antonio smiled and grabbed Leo's hand. Antonio blocked a guard's swing at Leo while Leo lifted him up.

Leo and Antonio stood back-to-back, defending each other. Even though Leo was much older and hadn't seen combat for more than two decades, he still remembered his well-entrenched training, and his body responded accordingly.

Antonio was in his prime and had command of the battlefield. His mind raced while time seemed to move in slow motion. He wondered why Leo was helping him, his enemy. Was it because he hated Quintus more than him? No, he could have killed Quintus and chose not to. Maybe Leo realized that the real enemy was Rome and all that it stood for and that Quintus only personified that evil. Then it occurred to Antonio that he now personified that same evil. He was baffled as to why Leo was helping defend his avowed enemy.

At that moment, Leo noticed Quintus, fifteen feet away, throw a javelin at Antonio's back. Leo lunged forward and intercepted the deadly instrument with his body just before it reached its mark. Antonio glanced over his shoulder just in time to see the javelin plunge into Leo's chest.

As Leo fell to the ground, Quintus's remaining guards scattered as the stationarii guard rushed towards them, followed by Rusticus, carrying Natalie's yellow robe; Gaius, holding Prometheus's letter; and Esteban, hobbling along to keep up with them.

"You are under arrest," Rusticus shouted. Quintus grabbed a sword off the ground and lunged at Antonio, who adroitly moved aside and thrust his sword into Quintus's chest. Quintus collapsed to his knees and looked at Antonio with wide eyes before falling over on his side, dead.

Esteban ran to his father on the ground, mortally wounded, bleeding profusely with his eyes closed.

"I am sorry it took so long, Papa," Esteban cried. "I ran as fast as I could."

Leo opened his eyes and looked up at Esteban. He reached up, grabbed Esteban's tunic by the collar, and pulled him close. Esteban gently grabbed his father's hand. Leo squeezed it. He coughed and spat up blood, then said, "Be faithful." Leo struggled to breathe as more blood ran out of his mouth. He sputtered, "I...am so proud...of you." He gasped for air once more and said, "My son." His grip went limp as his hand slipped out of Esteban's hand and fell on his chest.

Esteban fell down and hugged his father, crying, "No! No! I love you, Papa."

Antonio stared at the bloody sword in his hand. Repulsed, he heaved it away.

Epilogue

The cold, black silence of death enveloped Leo. This nothingness was soon pierced by a pinhole of light in the distance. Drawn to the light, Leo felt himself gliding through the void, rising toward the light, being pulled by the magnetic force of infinite love. As he approached, the warm light grew brighter and brighter, displacing the dark void of death.

Leo raised his hand to shield his eyes from the blinding light yet could not resist the urge to stare into its depths, seeking its source. Slowly, as his eyes adjusted, he began to perceive an image of a face in the distance. As that image came into focus, Leo discerned that it was the face of his Savior, beaming with love. As he neared, Leo was able to make out the rest of his Lord's radiant being standing in the air, his arms outstretched, beckoning Leo to him.

Jesus motioned to his side, and suddenly Natalie, dressed all in white, ran past the Savior to her father and gleefully exclaimed, "I love you, Papi!" Leo reached down, scooped up his daughter, threw her into the air, and grabbed her as she fell like they had done so many times before in mortality. Natalie threw her arms around her father's neck and showered him with kisses. Leo held her tight and closed his eyes to savor this precious moment. Joy, love, peace, and eternal ecstasy filled his being.

Leo opened his eyes and saw Amora standing before him

where Jesus had stood. She smiled, extended her hand, and said, "Welcome home."

Humanity is a river flowing down the course of history set by God.
At times of trial, some souls rise and make a splash
but are soon forgotten by the mass
as it rolls down its predetermined path.
Yet each soul is precious to Him who gives us life,
and who offers peace to all who struggle in this world of strife.

Historical Note

The historical novel *Amora* is based on the true story of the noblewoman who inspired Justin Martyr's petition to the Roman Senate.

This book is intended to add flesh and personality to the skeletal profiles in this story so that modern-day readers can gain a better understanding of the Greco-Roman world and a greater appreciation of the sacrifices made by the early Christian martyrs.

Amora

The following quote from the beginning of Justin Martyr's petition to Emperor Marcus Aurelius and the Roman Senate contains the only known reference to the noblewoman who inspired this story:

> ROMANS, the things which have recently happened in your city under Urbicus [Prefect of Rome], and the things which are likewise being everywhere unreasonably done by the governors, have compelled me to frame this composition for your sakes . . . That the cause of all that has taken place under Urbicus may become quite plain to you, I will relate what has been done.
>
> A certain woman lived with an intemperate husband; she herself, too, having formerly been intemperate. But when she came to the knowledge of the teachings of Christ she became sober-minded,

and endeavored to persuade her husband likewise to be temperate, citing the teaching of Christ, and assuring him that there shall be punishment in eternal fire inflicted upon those who do not live temperately and conformably to right reason. But he, continuing in the same excesses, alienated his wife from him by his actions. For she, considering it wicked to live any longer as a wife with a husband who sought in every way means of indulging in pleasure contrary to the law of nature, and in violation of what is right, wished to be divorced from him. And when she was over-persuaded by her friends, who advised her still to continue with him, in the idea that some time or other her husband might give hope of amendment, she did violence to her own feeling and remained with him. But when her husband had gone into Alexandria, and was reported to be conducting himself worse than ever, she—that she might not, by continuing in matrimonial connection with him, and by sharing his table and his bed, become a partaker also in his wickedness and impieties—gave him what you call a bill of divorce, and was separated from him. But this noble husband of hers—while he ought to have been rejoicing that those actions which formerly she unhesitatingly committed with the servants and hirelings, when she delighted in drunkenness and every vice, she had now given up, and desired that he too should give up the same— when she had gone from him without his desire, brought an accusation against her, affirming that she was a Christian. And she presented a paper to you, the Emperor, requesting that first she be permitted to arrange her affairs, and afterwards to make her defense against the accusation, when her affairs were set in order. And this you granted.

This noblewoman remains nameless, which is not unusual, considering the subservient role women held in Roman society. A female's first name was even derived from the first name of her father, so Julia would be the daughter of Julius and Amora the daughter of Amado. I chose the family name "Anicia" because this was one of the most prominent Roman families, and they were among the first aristocrats to convert to Christianity at the time of Constantine.

Regardless, women could own and inherit property and even divorce their husbands, but they would then generally be subject to their father's rule. We know that this noblewoman was one of the first upper-class individuals of her time to convert to Christianity.

Justin Martyr

Justin Martyr was the first recorded Christian apologist (defender) in the Roman Empire. Much of what we know regarding early Christian practices and beliefs is derived from a review of Justin's writings. He is regarded as the foremost interpreter of the theory of the Logos. This Logos-based doctrine was fundamental to Christian theology until the early fourth century.

Justin was born near Judea to a pagan family near the beginning of the second century, later lived in Ephesus, and then moved to Rome sometime between AD 138 and 161.

Justin initially studied Stoic philosophy, but when the philosopher was unable to explain the nature of God, Justin moved on to listen to a Peripatetic philosopher. However, Justin became disenchanted with this philosopher, who was preoccupied with his fee. Undaunted, Justin then sought to study under a Pythagorean philosopher, who demanded that he first become proficient in music, astronomy, and geometry. Eventually, Justin embraced and taught Platonic philosophy. On becoming a Christian, Justin maintained that Platonism was the philosophy most closely related to the truths of Christianity and opened a Christian philosophy school in Rome. Platonism continues to influence Christian theology to this day.

Two events played major roles in Justin's conversion to Christianity. First, he was startled to see Christian martyrs serenely accepting violent death in the arena and realized that these uneducated individuals had obtained greater power over human nature than any of the philosophers he had studied. He later chanced upon an old man by the seashore, who challenged his Platonic beliefs and spoke of the testimony of the prophets as being more reliable than the philosophers' reasoning. Justin's conversion to Christianity is commonly assumed to have taken place at Ephesus, though it may have occurred anywhere on the road from Judea to Rome.

Justin wrote his first apology (legal petition) sometime between AD 155 and 157 to the Roman emperor Antoninus Pius and his consul, Marcus Aurelius. He wrote and sent his second apology to the Senate after becoming concerned with the arrest of a woman of noble birth who had converted to Christianity.

The Cynic philosopher Crescens denounced Justin to the authorities after unsuccessfully disputing him several times in public. Justin and six companions were tried and beheaded, probably in AD 165, by Junius Rusticus, who was urban prefect of Rome from AD 163 to 167. Justin's trial and martyrdom are preserved in the court record as quoted in the encyclopedia Acts of the Saints. Justin and his companions chose death over amnesty that was offered if they denied their faith.

Marcus Aurelius

Marcus Aurelius was one of the most respected emperors of Rome. His writings regarding Stoic philosophy are highly regarded to this day. Most historians agree that Marcus preferred the simple life of a philosopher, yet he accepted his role as emperor with fortitude because he felt it was his duty.

Marcus became emperor in AD 161 along with his brother, Lucius Verus, but the Senate and public generally regarded Marcus as the supreme ruler. Marcus sent Lucius to lead the military campaign against the Parthians in AD 161. It was won by the Romans, thanks in large measure to the expertise of the junior local general, Avidius Cassius.

In the spring of 162, the Tiber River flooded its banks, destroying much of Rome. The flood drowned many animals and left the city in famine. Marcus gave the crisis his personal attention and most likely provided for the residents out of the Roman granaries and imported grain from Egypt. Marcus also arranged for relief to be sent to the victims of a great earthquake in Cyzicus, near Istanbul. The returning troops from the Parthian War brought back a plague believed to have been either smallpox or measles.

The populace attributed the occurrence of these natural calamities to the anger of the gods of nature against Christians, who disavowed these gods. Often, the Romans even referred to Christians as atheists because no one could see their God. Rumors of cannibalism flowed from the concept of the Eucharist, or Holy Communion, while other rumors of incest arose from the early Christians referring to one another as brothers and sisters and their frequent assertions of love for one another.

Initially, Marcus was quite tolerant of Christians, leaving the matter up to local authorities, but Christian persecution intensified near the end of his reign as he viewed them as an increasing threat to the emperor's power and control.

Crescens

Crescens is an enigma. On one hand, he was a Cynic philosopher, which implies that he rejected all conventional desires for wealth, power, sex, and fame and instead led a simple life free from all possessions, similar to Mahatma Gandhi in our era. On the other hand, a contemporary wrote that Crescens "surpassed all men in his love of boys and was strongly addicted to the love of money." Consequently, greater license was taken to adjust the personality of this character to reflect the attitudes of skeptic philosophers.

Here is how Justin described Crescens:

> I too, therefore, expect to be plotted against and fired to the stake, by some of those I have named, or perhaps by Crescens, that lover of bravado and boasting; for the man is not worthy of the name of philosopher who publicly bears witness against us in matters which he does not understand, saying that the Christians are atheists and impious, and doing so to win favor with the deluded mob, and to please them.

Leo

We do not know much about the aristocratic woman's husband except that he engaged in decadent behavior with his slaves and on a trip to Egypt, prompting his wife to seek a divorce.

Men's promiscuous sexual activity was tolerated and common throughout the empire. Unwanted infants—mainly females—in Rome were abandoned to die from exposure or were raised by the owners of state-sanctioned brothels. Infants were often abandoned at the Columna Lactaria (milk column) in the produce market, where wet nurses congregated to offer their services for a fee.

Junius Rusticus

Marcus Aurelius wrote that Junius Rusticus was his most important tutor. Rusticus was the most distinguished Stoic philosopher of his time. He served as the urban prefect of

Rome between AD 163 and 167. In this role, he presided over the trial of Justin Martyr and his six companions. Rusticus lived from approximately AD 100 to 170.

Titus
Titus Varius Clemens was appointed chief of staff by Marcus Aurelius when he was confirmed emperor by the Senate. Titus was from the frontier province of Pannonia, had served in the war in Mauretania, and had been the procurator of five provinces. Marcus valued Titus's military expertise during this period of conflict.

Maria and Antonio
These characters are composite figures representing the approximately one third of the population of Rome who were slaves. Slavery was an important factor in the Roman economy and the daily life of the upper class. The slaves came from the various conquered regions in the empire, with a large number from Gaul, current-day France.

Quintus and Loretta
Quintus and Loretta are also composite characters, representing the attitudes of the ruling class. The opinions expressed by Quintus and the other Roman aristocrats in the story generally reflect the attitudes and beliefs of many of the Roman upper class of their day.

The Greco-Roman World
Philosophers held positions of high esteem in the Greco-Roman culture and were somewhat comparable to scientists today. Aristotle's teaching that virtue was realized through an active life of moderation complemented Socrates's teaching that virtue was obtained with knowledge and Plato's

quest for harmony. These ideas formed the foundation of the Greco-Roman culture, which highly valued reason.

The Roman Empire consciously adopted Greek culture. The Roman noble class utilized Greek tutors for their children in a concerted effort to more fully ingrain this Hellenistic influence in their lives. However, Romans valued the practical benefits of establishing and maintaining order more than the theoretical ideas of philosophy. This led to the pax Romana, or Roman peace, one of the major contributions that Rome brought to the world. The heavy hand of Roman military rule eliminated bandits and pirates, thus facilitating peaceful travel and commerce. Rome created an extensive system of roads for military and commercial use and other infrastructure improvements that facilitated travel and an increased standard of living. This carrot-and-stick approach of providing temporal improvements along with the rule of law throughout the empire allowed a level of stability and travel between vast areas on a scale unheard of throughout history, which facilitated Christian missionary activity.

The Greco-Roman world was deeply stratified. A very small noble class owned great estates as absentee landlords. Depending on time and location, slaves made up 25 to 60 percent of the population and provided much of the labor to sustain urban life, similar to the way technology does today. Cities were large and crowded. Order was maintained in society through the practice of patronage. The wealthy noble class distributed material benefits to clients they felt were worthy, in return for the honor these clients would bestow upon their patrons. Honor and shame were major motivating factors of daily life. Roman theology mirrored this social structure. The gods granted blessings to humans who, in turn, owed honor to their patron gods.

Philanthropy was one of the greatest obligations of the

Roman elite. It helped form the glue that held their society together by generating gratitude among its vertical ranks. Charity was based on the implicit understanding of reciprocity, with donors receiving recognition and standing in exchange for their gifts. Hence, donors needed to carefully select beneficiaries who would provide the maximum return on their investment. Christianity helped change Roman society's view of charity from a duty of nobility to a universal value of humanity.

Many persons, particularly those in the educated class, lost faith in the pagan religions during the first centuries AD but still participated in their practice as part of their cultural identity. Chance and fate emerged as inescapable forces, even more powerful than the gods. Philosophy shifted to providing therapy instead of expounding theory and, in many ways, filled the role previously handled by religion. Philosophy became the source of instruction for virtuous living, and religious life receded to a realm of superstition and rituals.

Christian Persecution in the Roman Empire

Christianity began under Roman rule that was embedded in an open-minded Hellenistic culture. Romans offered religious tolerance to the geographically and culturally wide-ranging subjects under their rule, expecting in return cursory offerings to the Roman pantheon of gods and an infrequent public acknowledgment of the emperor as "divine." The Christians, like their Jewish counterparts, refused even this modest tolerance of polytheism. Jews appeased the Romans by daily offering sacrifice to Jehovah in favor of the emperor, but Christians were unable to offer any such compromise. Additionally, Christian ideas regarding peace, nonmaterialism, and social equality began to sound dangerous to the ruling class.

The persecution of Christians varied in intensity and by geography, like waves flowing over the Roman Empire. Persecution occurred for the first three centuries AD, until AD 313, when the Emperor Constantine enacted the Edict of Milan, which provided religious freedom throughout the empire. However, the persecution of Christians raised interest among the population as to why they remained so loyal to their beliefs. The more the empire spilled the blood of martyrs, the more Rome sowed the seeds of Christianity. A hallmark of early Christianity was its dedicated resolve to follow the Savior's example and be a faithful witness, even unto death. The word martyr actually means witness, with many early Christians rightfully earning that title.

Scholars estimate that in the year AD 150, there were approximately forty thousand Christians in the entire Roman Empire, which had a population of roughly sixty million. The population of Rome was around one million, so there were probably only a few thousand Christians in the city at the time of this story, even when one factors in a higher concentration of Christians in the major cities. Considering the tight-knit nature of this disfavored community and the high profile of Justin and the noblewoman convert, it is likely that they knew each other.

The Christian Miracle That Saved Marcus Aurelius

The fact that Marcus Aurelius was saved by an apparent miraculous downpour during the Marcomannic Wars is not disputed by historians. The scene is even depicted on the column of Marcus Aurelius that was erected at his command and is extant. About forty years after the incident, the Greek historian Cassius Dio described the event and the miraculous nature of their survival. However, there is debate regarding the role Christians played in the matter.

About fifteen years after this event, the Christian apologist Tertullian described the episode and referred to the following alleged letter from Marcus Aurelius giving credit for the miracle to Christian prayer:

> The Emperor Cæsar Marcus Aurelius Antoninus, Germanicus, Parthicus, Sarmaticus, to the People of Rome, and to the sacred Senate greeting:
> I explained to you my grand design, and what advantages I gained on the confines of Germany, with much labor and suffering, in consequence of the circumstance that I was surrounded by the enemy; I myself being shut up in Carnuntum by seventy-four cohorts, nine miles off. And the enemy being at hand, the scouts pointed out to us, and our general Pompeianus showed us that there was close on us a mass of a mixed multitude of 977,000 men, which indeed we saw; and I was shut up by this vast host, having with me only a battalion composed of the first, tenth, double and marine legions.
> Having then examined my own position, and my host, with respect to the vast mass of barbarians and of the enemy, I quickly betook myself to prayer to the gods of my country. But being disregarded by them, I summoned those who among us go by the name of Christians. And having made inquiry, I discovered a great number and vast host of them, and raged against them, which was by no means becoming; for afterwards I learned their power. Wherefore they began the battle, not by preparing weapons, nor arms, nor bugles; for such preparation is hateful to them, on account of the God they bear about in their conscience. Therefore, it is probable that those whom we supposed to be atheists, have God as their ruling power entrenched in their conscience. For having cast themselves on the ground, they prayed not only for me, but also for the whole army as it stood, that they might be delivered from the present thirst and famine. For during five days we had got no water, because there was none;

for we were in the heart of Germany, and in the enemy's territory. And simultaneously with their casting themselves on the ground, and praying to God (a God of whom I am ignorant), water poured from heaven, upon us most refreshingly cool, but upon the enemies of Rome a withering hail. And immediately we recognized the presence of God following on the prayer—a God unconquerable and indestructible.

Founding upon this, then, let us pardon such as are Christians, lest they pray for and obtain such a weapon against ourselves. And I counsel that no such person be accused on the ground of his being a Christian. But if anyone be found laying to the charge of a Christian that he is a Christian, I desire that it be made manifest that he who is accused as a Christian, and acknowledges that he is one, is accused of nothing else than only this, that he is a Christian; but that he who arraigns him be burned alive. And I further desire, that he who is entrusted with the government of the province shall not compel the Christian, who confesses and certifies such a matter, to retract; neither shall he commit him. And I desire that these things be confirmed by a decree of the Senate. And I command this my edict to be published in the Forum of Trajan, in order that it may be read. The prefect Vitrasius Pollio will see that it be transmitted to all the provinces round about, and that no one who wishes to make use of or to possess it be hindered from obtaining a copy from the document I now publish. (This letter was subsequently attached to Justin Martyrs First Apology in antiquity).

Most historians concur that this extant draft of the letter was altered from the original or is an outright forgery. It is doubtful that Marcus Aurelius ordered preferential treatment of Christians because ten years later, he clamped down on Christian practice in Leon in modern-day France. Regardless, Christians apparently played some role in the affair as they quickly adopted it as their miracle. This gave rise to legends that certainly overstated the participation of Christians in the military as this was discouraged by both Romans and Christians because of the military's close ties to pagan practices. Based on the author's research, the general description of the events in this novel involving this miracle more likely than not reflect an account of what actually occurred.

Premortal Existence

The belief in human premortal spiritual existence was an early Christian doctrine that was held to be heretical in the sixth century.

The concept that each human soul existed in a premortal existence was universally understood and believed by many, Christian and non-Christian alike, during the early Christian era. Plato taught that human beings consisted of a physical body and a soul that was immortal, that our soul existed prior to birth, and that death was the separation of the body and spirit, with good souls ultimately going back to heaven. The universality of this belief is evidenced by the story found in John 9:1–3, in which Jesus's disciples asked him if a man born blind had sinned prior to his birth. Jesus did not question or refute their belief in a premortal existence but simply stated that the man was born blind so that the works of God could be shown through his miraculous healing. Paul was probably referring to this premortal existence when he confirmed to philosophers in Athens that their poets were correct: "We are the offspring of God" (Acts 17:29).

Origen (AD 184–253), the most renowned Christian theologian of the early Patristic Period, taught this doctrine regarding a spiritual premortal existence and quoted Jeremiah 1:5 in support: "Before I formed thee in the belly I knew thee; and before thou camest forth out of the womb I sanctified thee, and I ordained thee a prophet unto the nations." He also quoted Romans 9:11–14 and argued that because God is just, the reason he loved Jacob and hated Esau before their birth had to be based on their actions in a premortal realm.

The belief in a premortal existence was embraced by the various Christian Gnostic sects that rivaled orthodox followers in number. Tertullian (AD 155–240), one of the most ardent opponents of Gnosticism, attacked this doctrine, potentially because it was a fundamental Gnostic belief. He argued that both the human spirit and body are generated from their mortal parents, a concept he founded called traducianism. Jerome (AD 347–420) later argued that only the human body originates from its parents and that one's spirit is created directly by God, Who places it into a physical body at some point between conception and birth. This concept is called creationism, not to be confused with our current usage of this term referring to God's influence in the creation of the universe. In AD 553, the doctrine of human premortal existence was rejected in the Second Council of Constantinople, but no decision was made regarding the competing theories of traducianism and creationism. Today, Lutheran theologians are generally traducianists while other Christians tend to be creationists, except for The Church of Jesus Christ of Latter-day Saints, which believes in a premortal spiritual existence.

The concept that God entered into a covenant with mankind in this premortal realm is supported by Paul's assertion that "God, who cannot lie, promised before the world began," this hope of eternal life (Titus 1:2). Paul directly implies that God extended this promise to humans before the earth was formed. Promises from the Judeo-

Christian God are often expressed as part of a covenant between humans and deity, leading some to believe that eternal life is the reward promised to humans for compliance during mortality with a premortal covenant.

Second-Century Christian Beliefs and Practices

In his first apology, Justin Martyr wrote the earliest description of Christian worship that has survived. He recorded:

> On Sunday all the inhabitants of the city and of the country meet in the same place [usually a home, but in Rome at times of persecution in the catacombs] While time permits, they read the teachings of the Apostles and the writings of the prophets. At the end of the reading, the president delivers a sermon to exhort and invite those present to imitate the examples that have been cited. Then all rise and pray. The prayers ended, bread, wine and water were brought; the president prays to the Almighty Father in the name of His Son and of the Holy Spirit and gives thanks to Him for having deigned to distribute these gifts. The people give their assent, saying Amen, which translated from the Hebrew, means, so be it. Immediately the deacons distribute the consecrated bread, the wine and the water, among those present, and they carry it also to the absent. (Justin, Primera Apologia, 65–66)

The sacramental prayer offered by the bishop in *Amora* comes from the earliest recorded liturgy, and is found in the book, Hippolyrus of Rome, as quoted in Botte's La Tradition Apostalique, page 9.

The early Christian Church's doctrine regarding salvation and redemption centered on human reunification with God. Prior to the fourth century, Christianity stressed conversion and union with God through experiencing of the Holy Spirit working within its followers. After the conversion of Emperor Constantine and the adoption of Christianity as the imperial religion, the emphasis shifted from feeling the Holy Spirit to the importance of orthodoxy in order to maintain order in the Church and the empire. Saint Augustine of Hippo introduced the concept of original sin and greatly intensified the debate regarding works, grace, and free will in the early fifth century. His teachings have greatly influenced the Western Church and its focus on justification and salvation while the Eastern Church has maintained an emphasis on unification with the divine through Christ's atonement without as much attention to the issues of sin and justification that preoccupy the Western Church.

Glossary

Amphora: a Greek or Roman jar that had two handles and a narrow neck and was used for storage and transportation of goods, particularly wine.

Bulla: a locket given to Roman children soon after birth containing an amulet to ward off evil spirits. Girls relinquished their bullas when wed.

Cataphractarius: a heavily armored gladiator armed with a long lance.

Charon obol coin: a coin placed on the mouth of the deceased as payment to the god Charon to ferry the soul across the water that divided the world of the living from the world of the dead.

Cheval-de-frise: a movable anti-cavalry defensive obstacle consisting of a center frame with multiple spikes sticking out.

Clepsydra: a water clock utilizing two pots, in which water flows from one into the other at a measured rate similar to the sand in an hourglass.

Contubernium: the smallest official unit in the Roman army, consisting of eight soldiers and two slaves but typically only referring to the soldiers.

Denarii: Roman silver coins of relatively high value.

Doctores/doctorii: trainers at gladiator schools who typically were retired gladiators.

El libido dominandi: Latin for the lust for power or to dominate. Refers to the Roman passion to conquer the known world.

Essedarii: Chariot gladiators who threw javelins at their foes.

Frameas: ancient German spears with iron heads.

Gallus: Gladiators who were prisoners from a section of western Europe now consisting of parts of Italy, France, and

Switzerland.

instita and limbus: the instita was an ornamental border around the neckline of a Roman stola, and the limbus was a wide colorful border around the bottom of the stola, both of which indicated wealth and status.

Lanista: the owner and/or operator of a gladiator training facility.

Libitinarii: literally were Roman undertakers but often referred to the personnel in the arena representing the gods escorting the dead to the underworld who disposed of the dead.

Lorica segmentata: upper-body armor consisting of multiple metal strips worn by Roman soldiers.

Ludus: literally, games, but generally used to refer to training facilities for gladiators or elementary schools for boys.

Novicius: a novice gladiator in training before he is ready to compete in the arena.

Numidian: from the Numidia kingdom located in Northern Africa consisting of modern-day Algeria and a part of Tunisia.

Optios: the second-in-command of a Roman century.

Pallae: a square woven mantle worn over the stola when the lady went outside.

Palus: a large wooden post used to teach swordsmanship in ancient Rome.

Peristyle: a row of columns surrounding an open space within a building such as a courtyard or garden.

Piscina Publica: Regio XII of the fourteen neighborhoods of Rome, located in the southern section. A Christian exchange bank was located here in the late second century, and it subsequently became the site of Rome's second-largest public bath, known as the Baths of Caracalla.

Pompa funebris: the Roman funeral ritual primarily for the wealthy consisting of an elaborate procession and eloquent eulogy.

Praefecti: Roman prefects, used to refer to the leaders of the Roman auxiliary cavalry.

Praefectus castrorum: the camp prefect of a Roman legion.

Praetorian guard: the Roman emperor's bodyguards.

Primus pilus: the senior centurion of the first and most experienced cohort in a Roman legion.

Publicani: translates to "publican" and refers to the position of or individual Roman tax collector.

Quadi: an ancient Germanic tribe located in the area of modern-day Moravia.

Retiarii: a gladiator who used a net, a trident and a dagger.

Rod of Asclepius: also known as the Staff of Asclepius is from Greek mythology and refers to a serpent entwined on a rod held by the Greek god Asclepius associated with healing and medicine.

Rudus: the wooden sword used to train gladiators and given rarely to gladiators who won their freedom.

Salii priest: priest of the official ancient Roman religion.

Salutatio: the Latin word for "salutation," refers to the greeting of those returning and the morning custom of the paterfamilias (senior male patrician of an aristocratic family) greeting clients and family members asking for favors or giving reports.

Scissores: were gladiators known as cutters apparently using a double blade weapon, but this belief is speculative.

Secutores: a gladiator known as a chaser, who used a gladius (short sword), dagger and heavy shield. He often was matched with a retiarius gladiator.

Semis: Roman coins of relatively minor value.

Sestertii: a Roman coin worth a fourth of a Denarius.

Stationarii guard: the stationary Roman guard assigned to a particular post.

Stola: a loose-fitting garment worn by Roman women that corresponded to the toga worn by men.

Strigils: curved tools used to scrape off perspiration, oil, and dirt used primarily in the Roman baths.

Sudes: literally, "stakes," refers to the approximately five-foot-long wooden stakes pointed on each end with a small area cut out in the center to serve as a handle and/or to interlock with another stake to form an X.

Synthesis: a simple tunic of many colors worn during the Saturnalia celebration denoting unity of class.

Tirones gladiatores/Tiros: trained gladiators who fought in the arena.

Toga pulla: a black toga worn by men at a Roman funeral.

Tribunus angusticlavii: the five junior officers of a Roman legion chosen from the equestrian orders.

Tribunus laticlavius: the legion's technical second-in-command but often a young and inexperienced officer chosen from the senatorial families.

Triclinium: a three-sided knee-high dining table in Roman times or the dining room where it was located.

Tutulus style: a hairstyle in which the hair is worn over the head.

Velites: the auxiliary light infantry of the Roman army.

Vestibulum: the entrance or foyer of a Roman home or villa.

Please Share the Message of This Book

I hope you were inspired by Amora's message of hope and forgiveness. None of us can sink so low that God cannot lift us up. This is possible as we open our hearts to allow God to fill them with his love. His love will empower us to forgive those who offend and injure us so we can move forward and enjoy life more fully. He will free us from our prison of fear, hate, guilt, and despair. We can find peace and joy in this world of strife, right here and right now. God can bless us with the ecstasy of his love if we are simply willing to accept it.

I hope that Amora helped you appreciate the witnesses borne by the early Christian martyrs as they followed the example of the ultimate faithful witness, Christ, and became his voice to touch the hearts of those who observed their sacrifice.

You, too, can be a witness by sharing this message of love, hope, and forgiveness with your family, friends, and neighbors. One of the best ways to get this message out is to rate the book and write a quick review on Amazon. The number of reviews a book receives is one of the most important factors for a book to catch the attention of readers and increase its ranking on Amazon, which in turn exposes the book and its message to many more readers. You can make a difference. Please care enough to take the time to write a quick review. You will bless the lives of many individuals if you do.

Thank you, and may God bless you for your support!
Grant J. Hallstrom

About the Author

Grant Hallstrom founded *HistoryofChristianTheology.com* and is the primary contributor of its content.

Mr. Hallstrom is the author of the book, *Emotional Black Holes*, and several articles regarding the application of theology in one's personal life.

He is also the founder and managing partner of the civil law firm, Hallstrom Klein & Ward LLP, located in Irvine, California. He is married to his sweetheart, Jean, and they have six children and eleven grandchildren.